We were together ~~togethe~~ ...
but you've been with me my whole life.
Thanks for teaching me to love a good story.

For Bert:
Thanks for taking care of the kids so I could go write.
I'd have never finished this without you.

For Jane:
Thanks for pushing me to reach out and grab the dream.

And for everybody else who read the zillion drafts of this
book whether they wanted to or not:
Thanks. I mean it.

Table of Contents

Prologue

November 17, 1983

We have escaped Philadelphia, Victor, the baby and I, but now we know that we can't escape Denortus forever. We will go somewhere remote and try to build quiet lives for ourselves. But we will have to be ever vigilant, for they will find us eventually.

She laid the pen aside, closed her journal and glanced at the baby playing on the floor of the rented room. Her long blond hair swung gracefully as she moved about the space tiding up. Anyone watching her would never know that she lived every minute in terror. Would they find Victor when he was out looking for odd jobs to support them? Where could they go to be safe? And what would the future hold for her darling Jimmy?

She reached down and smoothed her hand across his blond head, watching as he chewed determinedly on a pacifier. She shook her head and sighed. What would become of them?

Twenty-six and a half years later...

Chapter One:

The Siblings Ditch

It was a reception the guests would never forget. Quinn watched Jim walk down the short hallway toward where he and the witch had their backs to the closed double doors.

"Good you're both here," Jim announced brightly. He clapped his hands and rubbed them together five or six times in a way that never boded well for Kayla, Jim's fourteen-year-old sister and the aforementioned witch. Quinn smiled in anticipation of Kayla's discomfort.

"Yes," Kayla dragged out as if to say 'Oh God, what now?!' which Quinn knew she wouldn't say, today of all days. He figured she was dreading the speech she had to give in a couple of minutes and really didn't want anything else to stress over right now.

Jim was Quinn's new brother-in-law. Of course Kayla wasn't a witch in the magical sense of the word, not even in the Wiccan-religion sort of way. Her witchiness was more of a she's-nasty-and-I'd-like-to-spend-as-little-time-with-her-as-possible kind of thing. Kayla and Quinn were the same age, both about to start their freshman year at the regional high school in Granby Maine where they lived. They were operating under a temporary truce at the moment, but it was one that nobody had thought would last this long. Jim looked ready to change the tune of things entirely.

"Where's Lore?" Quinn asked Jim. At six feet five inches tall, Quinn had no difficulty seeing over Jim's head that his older sister (Lorelei, Jim's wife) was nowhere around.

"We've had a bit of a change of plans," Jim said. "She's in the car, on the phone. She'll be here in a minute. Um, so we'll go in for an introduction, maybe a quick spin around the room, then we've gotta go. You guys will have to take care of things here on our behalf. We'll still be back in two weeks, hopefully."

Before Quinn could form a thought suitable for that bombshell, a beautiful woman in a white sundress stepped into the hallway from the other end. Her long chocolaty hair was tied back with a simple white bow but somehow the hairdo managed to hide her slightly pointy ears. They were a sensitive subject for her. She smiled broadly at the group. Quinn's green eyes met her warm brown ones. Though her eyes were crinkling with joy, Quinn thought he saw a hint of worry there too.

"All set?" Lorelei asked Jim, loudly to be heard over the din rising on the other side of the closed doors.

Jim smiled back at her, a smile filled with love, excitement, happiness and a dozen other things Quinn couldn't identify. Jim offered his arm as the doors opened, and together they crossed the threshold into a party in full swing. Quinn stood in the hallway in stunned silence,

4

trying to work out the meaning of Jim's announcement. Kayla looked similarly stunned and a bit dumb with her mouth hanging open. Over the cheer of the crowd, they glanced at their siblings' backs while a mircophone'd voice that was a little too full of southern twang announced, "Please welcome Mr. and Mrs. James and Lorelei Livingston in their first appearance as a married couple!"

DJ Good Ole' Boy, or whatever his name was, played the opening bars of *I'm Yours* by Jason Mraz and true to their word, the newlyweds spent the four minute song dancing and spinning around the room. As the song was ending, Jim and Lorelei waltzed back out the door, past Quinn and Kayla, and down the hall out of sight, pausing to throw a quick wave goodbye at their siblings before they danced right out of their own wedding reception.

With a mean little laugh, Quinn doubted the Best-Sister Toast was Kayla's biggest worry any more.

For a long second, Quinn and Kayla stood frozen in the hall, watching for Jim and Lorelei to return, as if this had been a joke. Of course, it would have been very unlike Jim to pull a prank on them.

It wasn't that Jim didn't have a sense of humor, because he did, but he wasn't a prankster. He was more of a droll-witticism-spouter. But Lorelei had worked so hard planning the wedding reception that Quinn couldn't believe she'd leave the party before it even got started. What could possibly have happened since they got to the ceremony an hour ago that would change their plans so drastically?

Eventually, Quinn became aware of the silence from the reception room. Where there had been music and laughter, and the noise of fifty people talking and getting settled in their chairs, now there was stillness. Kayla popped her head around the doorframe to see what was happening. All one hundred eyes snapped to her face when it appeared, like one of those dinosaurs that supposedly tracked its prey by movement. She smiled nervously, gave a slight chuckle and waved the just-a-moment-finger at the crowd, then reached for the knobs and pulled the doors closed, leaving the wedding guests on one side and Kayla and Quinn on the other.

"OhmyGod! What are we going to do? They'll eat us alive!" she whispered frantically at Quinn.

"Don't overreact. It isn't that bad. We'll go in and explain things." Quinn reached for the doorknob, but stopped when Kayla grabbed his hand.

"What could you possibly say that will pacify that crowd? A few of those people traveled pretty far to be here and now the Bride and Groom have disappeared!" The guests were starting to make noise again, but this rumble seemed different from the happy chatter of five minutes ago. This was more of a miffed grumble from a group who weren't sure if they should be angry or not and were looking for confirmation from each other that they should.

"I'll think of something. I can usually sway people to my side of things. It'll be a piece of cake." With that Quinn opened the door and stepped through. He was momentarily blinded by the camera flash of the photographer who was hovering like paparazzi. After an initial flinch of surprise and some blinking to get his sight back, Quinn pasted his performance smile on his face and calmly but confidently strode over to the DJ who looked as bewildered as everyone else. "Whutsgoin'own?" he asked Quinn quietly.

Quinn looked at him for a minute, trying to translate the fast jumble of sound into words he recognized. Two seconds stretched out as Quinn stared at the DJ, momentarily distracted by his mostly bald head and very bushy eyebrows. Finally, Quinn muttered the phrase back, hoping to understand it that way.

"What's going on?" He smiled in understanding. "Oh, I just need a microphone for a second." Quinn accepted it from the DJ's hand, turned it on, then took a couple steps to the middle of the dance floor.

"Hey everybody. I bet that you are all wondering where Jim and Lorelei went. Well, something came up and they had to leave. Obviously, it was something critically important to cause them to leave their own wedding reception." He chuckled a bit as he paused to look over the crowd. Most people looked confused, but Quinn was concerned about the annoyed and even angry expressions on a few faces.

"They're fine, of course, and they asked me to pass on their deepest apologies to all of you, especially to those of you who came from far away. Please stay and enjoy lunch which will be out in a few minutes. Thank you."

With that, Quinn turned the microphone off, handed it back to the DJ and walked off the dance floor. He saw that Kayla was speaking with the caterer, presumably telling her to get lunch on the tables, pronto. The music was starting up again when the photographer sidled up to Quinn and asked what he should be doing, since the objects of his art had flown the coop. "Just take pictures of everyone enjoying themselves. We'll share that with Lorelei and Jim later, I guess."

Kayla met Quinn at the edge of the dance floor. Both of them were instinctively staying away from the door, not wanting anyone to get the impression that they might be skipping out too. "Ginny, the Banquet Captain, is going to get the lunch out immediately. She recommended that we sit with some of the guests, instead of the head table. She's going to remove it. Discreetly."

They stood quietly for a couple of minutes, watching as the caterer's crew began serving salads and bustling around the room filling glasses for the guests. Slowly, the party noise began again. People chatted, knives and forks pinged on the china dishes, people asked tablemates to pass the butter.

After a few minutes of silence, Quinn felt a nudge on his arm. He glanced down at Kayla, raising an eyebrow in a way that he knew annoyed her. She smirked at him, or maybe it was a true smile and he'd just never seen one before to compare.

"Nice speech. I guess you won them over after all," she said.

With that she patted her head to be sure her long hair hadn't fallen down from its fancy updo and smoothed her skirt as she pranced away from him to sit in an open seat at a table of Jim's friends. Quinn felt his jaw drop open at the unprecedented compliment, before shaking it off and finding a seat as well.

When Quinn finished eating lunch, he excused himself from the table of Lorelei's coworkers to wander through the party, making sure everyone was having fun. He was still thinking about Kayla's comment, beginning to believe he might have imagined it. In the three years since he and Kayla had met and clashed in sixth grade, Quinn could not recall Kayla saying a nice thing to him.

Ever.

Including the three torturous months they'd spent living in the same house before the wedding. Or more exactly, during those three months in which Quinn's unwelcome presence had invaded *her* house, at the request of their siblings.

This complement had really thrown him off track. He wondered what was behind it. He didn't for one minute believe that her words had been sincere. Until six months ago, their battles had been fairly petty, revelling in one-upping each other in the classes they shared, or general hallway rivalry between subjects.

When Kayla ran a losing bid for Junior High Rep on the student council last November, Quinn and his friends had defaced a few (OK – most) of the posters she had hung around the school. He smiled at the thought of the artistically drawn horns, tail and pitchfork that he thought had improved Kayla's obnoxiously perky picture. Her yellow hair and crayon blue eyes made her look like a cartoon character.

It was shortly after she lost the Stupid Council gig when things started to get really nasty. Although, if he was being honest, perhaps it was the devilish makeover that had encouraged Kayla to take the proverbial gloves off.

Apparently, by January, Kayla had decided to get even. Quinn had played Rolf in the school's performance of *The Sound of Music*. Kayla "altered" the sound equipment so that his duet with 'Lisle' had sounded like the Chipmunks, only worse. Then she posted a video of the debacle on YouTube, for which he won a "Moany" award for the worst School Performance of the year. And if that wasn't bad enough, Kayla attached a link to a ton of websites about local people and events so that when someone clicked on those sites, a new window popped up showing Quinn's Chipmunk-i-est off-key warble. He was the local Rick-Roll.

Quinn frowned, remembering the humiliation of trying to get his homework assignment from the Granby Junior High Science department website only to find a banner across his screen proclaiming that he'd been "Quinn-Rolled". Unfortunately, before he could execute a suitably vengeful response to that horror show, both he and Kayla were hauled into the Principal's office along with their legal guardians, his sister and her brother.

Karmically, they may have each gotten what they deserved since that trip to the Principal's office had been Lorelei's introduction to Jim Livingston. Lorelei and Quinn's parents had died in a boating accident when Quinn was seven. Lorelei had been Quinn's guardian for the last seven years.

Apparently Jim and Kayla's father had taken off before Kayla was born and their mother had died six months before Quinn's parents. Quinn suspected the common ground of each being responsible for raising a much younger sibling had prompted Jim and Lorelei to start dating, immediately.

When they all left the principal's office that day, Quinn and Kayla were sent to their respective homes amid much glaring. Jim and Lorelei went out to dinner. Quinn didn't get it, but by late April Jim and Lorelei were engaged. And when the Wexfords' apartment lease was up in May, they moved in to the Livingstons' house.

Quinn thought about going back to the house with Kayla once they managed to wrap up this wedding reception and wondered what kind of explanation Lorelei and Jim might have left for ditching them. Even though Kayla and Quinn were only fourteen, Jim and Lorelei had agreed to let their charges stay home alone while they were on their honeymoon, with the condition that Mrs. Nessman from next door would look in on them periodically.

Jim had said that he and Lorelei usually found Kayla and Quinn to be mature beyond their years, the only exception being the way they treated each other.

Quinn decided to try and hurry the guests along (without being rude), anxious to get home and find out what was going on. Kayla must have decided the same thing since he almost bumped into her at one of the tables. He gave her a sweet smile that he hoped would keep her guessing and turned his attention to wrapping up the party.

****

Kayla had been circulating around the room for the last half hour, playing the role of hostess at a party that was decidedly not her own. It was enough to make her consider what her own wedding might be like some day. Definitely an affair with very few people. Like maybe three: bride, groom and some kind of priestly-type person. If she had forgiven them for this by then, she might, *might* consider including Jim and Lorelei.

11

She saw that Quinn was working the crowd too and thought that her last verbal spar might just have hit the mark. When she had walked away from him before, she noticed a little bead of sweat on his temple. While it was a bit warm in here, (it was July after all!) she didn't think that it was only the heat that caused the sweat. Maybe when he was making his suave little speech to the guests he had been a tiny bit more nervous than he'd let on. That idea made Kayla feel a little bit better.

After all, Quinn was a musician, used to playing music in front of people. He even claimed that he wrote his own songs and played those before...well, maybe not *crowds*, but groups of people. Kayla couldn't imagine opening herself up to that kind of criticism. But if Quinn was even a titch nervous in this predicament, then that justified her nervousness and she immediately felt more confident. Strange that. So of course she'd had to say something to throw off his aim.

Even now, nearly an hour later, he still had that perplexed kind of look on his face. She smiled as she turned back to her crummy job as socialite.

Kayla was surprised at how many of the guests felt comfortable asking her very private, personal questions. She might have expected that of family, but the Livingstons and the Wexfords seemed to have a history of dying young. They didn't have very much family. Probably fewer than ten of the guests were relatives

Jim's boss had asked her if he could expect Jim back at work at the end of two weeks as Jim had planned, "You know, since his plans changed so suddenly," he'd said.

Kayla dodged that one, saying, "You know Jim: Mr. Dependable. I can't imagine him not getting to work when he's supposed to. Can you?" She laughed and made small talk with the toad about how Jim hadn't taken so much as an unexpected day off in three years, before excusing herself and moving on to the next table.

Chaz Turnbrower, a co-worker and high school rival of Jim's had come to the wedding as a guest of one of Lorelei's friends. Jim was thoughtful and uber responsible, a default parent at age eighteen, while Chaz was a weekend thrill seeker with a big mouth. Kayla couldn't think of two people more opposite from each other and, at least in this case, opposites did not attract.

Kayla had actually seen a hint of a frown on Jim's face when he saw Chaz strut into the church. When Kayla stopped at his table to chat with folks, Chaz had the poor taste to actually wink at her, nudge her ribs with his elbow and ask, "Big Bro couldn't wait to get that honeymoon started, eh?"

"Ewww...younger sister here." Kayla shuddered at the mental image of her brother doing married people things. In the shocked silence at the table, she thought quickly of something to say that would change the subject. "I hope everybody had enough to eat. Wasn't the chicken was delicious?"

Thankfully, Lorelei's boss, Holly, picked up on Kayla's effort to change the subject and launched into a discussion about the surprising and delightful decision of the caterer to stray from traditional wedding cake as the dessert and instead serve a delicate blueberry and lemon tart. A few minutes later, Kayla was able to extricate herself from the conversation and move on to the last table.

"Where did they go, girl? That great-nephew of mine won't say a word," was her greeting from the Wexford's tiny Great Aunt Tally, self-appointed matriarch of the table. Kayla had only met her yesterday, but surely GAT (as the Wexfords called her – but not exactly to her face) was a bit less than five feet tall, if you deducted the several inches of bluish gray hair she had piled up on top of her head ala Marge Simpson.

"I really can't say, ma'am," was the best reply Kayla could come up with. Jim had instilled in her the importance of telling the truth to the point where Kayla was terrible at lying and made it a personal policy never to do it. She always got caught. But she had learned that there was usually a verbal way around any situation where she could avoid both the truth and a lie.

"That's what Quinn said." The old woman looked at her with piercing dark eyes that Kayla feared could see way more than Kayla would have liked. "Hmm. I don't think you know where they are and that's why you *can't* say."

"Of course I know where they are ma'am," Kayla hedged, shuffling her feet to stay clear of the walking stick that GAT was bouncing up and down in her agitation "They are on their honeymoon." Kayla hoped that Great Aunt Tally wouldn't push any further. To her surprise, the old woman erupted in a choking, cackling sound that Kayla guessed was a laugh.

"You kids come and see me if you need anything," GAT replied. With that, she smacked her lips as if she had swallowed a mouthful of something distasteful and turned to her coffee cup and dessert, dismissing Kayla. Kayla moved on to other tables with a quiet sigh, hoping the rest of the guests would be content with normal small talk.

****

Two hours later, with her feet aching from the stupid high heel shoes she had worn all afternoon at the wedding, Kayla rushed into the house with Quinn tight on her bruised heels. She expected to find a letter or some other lengthy communication from Jim and Lorelei explaining the reasons behind their crazy, abrupt departure from their own wedding. On the kitchen table, under the edge of the wire fruit basket, (where the family routinely left messages for each other) they found a folded piece of white paper with a large yellow Post-It stuck to it.

"Went to Philly. K-Solve attached ASAP. $ in envelope for food, etc, but plenty of veg in pantry for rainy day. Will call when we can. Love you, J & L" was scrawled across the buttery rectangle in Lorelei's usually flowing script. The page and Post-it hadn't been on the table when they left for the church, so Jim and Lorelei must have come back to the house.

"This doesn't explain anything!" Kayla huffed, waving the note around.

"What does it say?" Quinn asked, his hand waving through the air trying to catch the note. He grabbed at it when she paused to blow a fallen blond lock of hair out of her eye with a sigh and snatched it away with a glare.

"Why on earth would anyone choose to visit Philadelphia over Hawaii? Whatever." He reached for the bank envelope on the table, thumbed through the money, and put it under the silverware organizer in the drawer next to the sink.

"Can I have the white sheet, please?" Kayla demanded before Quinn decided to hold the paper over her head and make her jump for it. He must have decided that would be juvenile since he handed the page back and strode out of the room re-reading the brief yellow note.

Kayla unfolded the paper, wondering what Jim and Lorelei had left her to solve. She loved puzzles. She glanced at the page, read the short letter then collapsed into a kitchen chair.

11/2/2001 – to be delivered in November 2009

Darling son,
If you are reading this letter then I am long gone.
Always know that I love you more than I can say. You're the
Reason I smile, the spring in my step and the flower of my heart.
You know what destiny holds for you.

Though my season is past, I bloom once more with each new
Adventure you undertake. I am sorry only that I cannot
Be there to offer my constant love and support.

To the business at hand: there is something I never told you. Things
Are not as they appear. I leave the rest for you to unearth. Plato said
Gravity cannot be responsible for people falling in love. I beg to differ.

Love always,
Mom

PS: Be careful of wolves in sheep's clothing. Take care of your things.

THE CORDOVAN VAULT

It seemed that Kayla's long dead mother had sent a letter to her brother which he'd received less than a year ago. And Jim wanted her to figure out why.

As Soon As Possible.

Huh.

Chapter Two:

Unearthing Clues

The next morning, Kayla sat at the kitchen table, pen in hand, notepad open, her mother's letter in front of her, ready to unravel its secrets. Yesterday, Kayla stared at the letter for an hour, barely even able to see it. She needed to step away from it for a little while. Reading that letter combined with the change of plans at the wedding, was too much of a shock for her to process.

To say that getting a letter from beyond the grave was unexpected was like saying that getting snow in August was unusual. Even in Maine, it was practically unheard of. But now, after some time to accustom herself to the idea, she was raring to go.

Some of the word choice in the letter seemed odd. Kayla underlined those words, thinking there might be a message there.

11/2/2001 – to be delivered in November 2009

Darling son,
If you are reading this letter then I am long gone.
Always know that I love you more than I can say. You're the
Reason I smile, the spring in my step and the <u>flower</u> of my heart.
You know what destiny holds for you.

J MONKEYS

*Though my season is past, I <u>bloom</u> once more with each new
Adventure you undertake. I am sorry only that I cannot
Be there to offer my constant love and support.*

*To the business at hand: there is something I never told you. Things
Are not as they appear. I leave the rest for you to <u>unearth.</u> Plato said
Gravity cannot be responsible for people falling in love. I beg to differ.*

*Love always,
Mom*

PS: Be careful of wolves in sheep's clothing. Take care of your things.

Flower, bloom and unearth, with references to spring
and season. She sat at the table with her chin propped up
by her fist, staring out the window over the kitchen sink.
What could those words mean? Something hidden under
flowers? What flower?

She walked to the sink to get a drink of water, looking
at the back yard. Midsummer mornings, like this one,
brought sunlight streaming into the room through two large
windows over the sink and another window near the pantry.
The room was painted light yellow with a white and yellow
linoleum floor. The cabinets were made of a light colored
wood that radiated warmth throughout the room, even on
the coldest winter days.

A glint of green hit Kayla in the eye as she stood at the
sink gulping water. Kayla's mom had made the abstract
stained glass piece that topped the windows at the sink in a
graceful arch.

The stained glass window was one of those things that
had been around forever, so long that you didn't even
notice it until it smacked you in the face. It was an odd

piece, with shades of blue around the outside ranging from pale blue to a dark blue-green and back again before changing entirely to a green oblong blob in the center. There were two bits of yellow, one paler than the other and a tiny dot of red shaped sort of like a star.

Jim liked to joke that Mom had been a dabbler in the arts and this was her first and only dabble in that particular art. Kayla didn't really remember, but since there were various types of art around the house, she had to assume Jim was right.

Certainly her perfectionist brother didn't dabble. Jim liked to learn one thing at a time, and do it again and again until he had developed real skill. Kayla rinsed her glass and put it away before walking outside, hoping a little sun and some air might offer a fresh perspective.

The first thing she saw when she walked into the backyard was the giant raised garden bed of lilacs that her mother had planted. Lilacs had been her mother's very favorite flower. Kayla's mom had died when she was six years old and one of the strongest memories Kayla had of her was tied to the smell of lilacs.

Every spring, Mom would cut as many as she could fit into vases. The whole house smelled of lilac for a few weeks each year. Whenever Kayla smelled them (and she did so as frequently as the short-seasoned flowers would allow) she could close her eyes and picture her mom.

Of course! That had to be the flowers mentioned in the letter. The lilacs grew in a hedge in the middle of a small blueberry field. They were kept trimmed so that they were full and bushy, but only about five feet tall. The hedge was encircled by an eighteen-inch-high stone wall, to keep the blueberries from encroaching. Maine blueberries grow along the ground unlike other, bush blueberries and they'd take over if allowed.

A few minutes later, a shout startled a spin out of her.

"What are you doing?" Quinn stood at the edge of the yard, flanked by the lawn mower and weed whacker.

"I'm looking for a marker," she shouted back.

"There's a Sharpie on the kitchen counter." Kayla tilted her head in confusion. "You know, a black marker," he clarified.

Kayla scoffed. "Not that kind of marker." She shook her head and laughed. Idiot. Then again, maybe she could use a little muscle for this project.

Quinn had turned to walk away by the time she decided to offer an explanation, but he turned back as she started to speak. "The page that Jim and Lorelei left for me to solve is a letter that Jim apparently got about nine months ago from my mom."

"Not to be insensitive, but I thought your mom was dead."

"She is. Let me finish – before she died I guess she somehow arranged for it to be delivered in November 2009. Anyway, some of the letter seems kinda cryptic, but there are a bunch of references to flowers. Lilacs were my mom's favorites so I'm looking here for an indication of where to unearth something. That was another word she used. 'Unearth.' That's the marker I'm looking for."

Quinn's eyebrows did that thing where they pulled together in the middle of his face at the same time that they split up, with the right brow shooting up to his hairline. She thought it meant he was taxing his pea brain to figure her out. Of course, this was the second time in two days that Kayla had been almost pleasant, so maybe she was doing a good job of keeping him on his toes.

"OK. So what do you think the marker looks like?" he asked, tentatively.

Kayla looked at Quinn to assess his interest. Generally speaking, they did anything they could to stay out of each other's way. Maybe it was the lingering stress of yesterday's wedding reception. Maybe the heat was getting to her. Whatever the reason, she didn't see any of the expected ridicule in his expression, so she answered the question.

"I don't know, really. I mean, I wasn't expecting a sign that said 'dig here', but there's got to be something to indicate where to start. Kind of an 'X marks the spot'. If you want to help, look around and see if you see anything that looks out of place."

"Sure, why not? It's like digging for buried treasure," Quinn mumbled. "The yard will wait." They crawled around in the blueberries a while in silence.

After they'd each made it all the way around the wall, Kayla sat up. "I don't see anything, do you?"

"No. The only thing that looks weird to me is this one little patch of wall, but it's not anything I'd consider a sign."

"What do you mean?"

"Look here." Quinn pointed to a couple of rocks piled on top of each other. "I helped Jim rebuild that stone wall by the vegetable garden a couple months ago, right? Well, building a stone wall that will stand without mortar, like you find all over New England, is pretty simple.

Backbreaking, but simple. You stack the rocks up so that they are off center from each other. You lay down a row of stones, one, two, three. Then you put the next layer of stones, A and B, on top so that A rests on half of one and half of two, and B is on the other half of two and half of three."

"Yeah, and?"

"Well, the only thing about this wall that looked weird to me is these three rocks right here." Quinn pointed to three rocks on top of each other. "These aren't off center. They're right on top of each other with a small one in the middle. That's weird."

Kayla swatted at a fly and said, "Not much of a sign, but let's give it a try." Quinn jumped up and started walking away. "Don't you want to see if there is anything there?" Kayla called toward his back.

"I'll be back in a minute," was the faint reply carried on the breeze. Kayla shook her head. Musicians, you couldn't count on 'em.

She dug her spade into the ground, which was surprisingly difficult to do. In spite of Jim's care, the topsoil in the lilac bed seemed rather washed out. It was nothing like digging in the sand at the beach. Kayla knelt up hoping for better leverage and tried jamming the little shovel into the earth, but beyond scraping away some old mulch she didn't make much progress.

A shadow passed overhead. "Let me try this." Quinn had come back after all, carrying a much bigger shovel with a pointed tip. Kayla stood up and noticed that he'd brought the wheelbarrow too. He jammed the shovel into the ground and stepped on it, sinking in about six inches.

"Wow, that's effective." Kayla watched as he worked the shovel around, cutting a circle in the dirt where she had brushed off the mulch. After loosening it up, he lifted a big dirt clod and dumped it into the wheelbarrow.

"Any idea what we're looking for?" Quinn asked.

"Not a clue."

"Break up that chunk and see if you find anything. I'll dig." Kayla stepped over to the wheelbarrow, and poked through the dirt, gingerly. "You need to look closer than that," he remarked.

Kayla glanced at him with a sniff and slight eye-roll. "I'm going out later and I don't want to get all grubby."

"Well, you are never going to find anything that way, but it's your project." Quinn's singsong voice carried to the wheelbarrow from the lilacs and blueberries. He had a way of grating on Kayla's nerves with even seemingly benign comments. She shuddered, muttered under her breath and started to break up the barrow contents more vigorously.

Once the dirt was cut into fine particles, Quinn dumped in another shovel full. They dug and sifted until Quinn was standing on the edge of a hole that covered all the space between the marker and the lilac bush, but they found nothing.

Just when she was beginning to think that Quinn might be worthy of the apology that Jim was always harping on her to give him, the moment ended the same way it always did.

"Stupid non-marker," Kayla grouched, frustrated at not finding anything. She kicked the stacked up rocks for good measure. "Ouch!"

J MONKEYS

The toe of her shoe stuck in the stone wall. Unfortunately, her foot was still in her shoe. She lost her balance, and grabbed onto the only thing available for stability, Quinn, leaving a dirty handprint in the middle of his clean white T-shirt.

He grabbed her and said, "Dude! This was a new shirt." He tried brushing off the ground in stain, with no success.

Embarrassed at displaying such a lack of grace, Kayla yanked her foot free of the wall and sniped, "I think the hand print is an improvement over what you usually wear!"

Quinn sighed. "Hurray, the witch is back!" he cheered with fake joy. Kayla squatted down to peer into the hole made by her foot and didn't notice Quinn moving the wheelbarrow. "I better put this back the way I found it," he said.

He dumped everything they had sifted back into the big hole, spraying Kayla with a shower of fine dirt. While she was still coughing, he headed back toward the shed, wheelbarrow rolling along before him and tall shovel in hand.

Kayla shook her head to clear it of dirt, literally. She wiped dirt from her eyes with hands that added more mess than they removed. What was he, like seven years old? He'd actually dumped dirt on her! She coughed a little more and once the dust settled, she looked at the wall where the 'marker' had been. The bottom rock had been wide enough to cover a hole underneath. So the little marker had been an X marking the spot after all. It was completely black inside the hole and Kayla was very leery of sticking her hand in it blind.

THE CORDOVAN VAULT

I should go get a flashlight, but I don't want to track this dirt through the house twice, she thought. *Just stick your hand in, K. How gross could it be?* Before she could think about it further, she plunged her arm into the darkness. Her hand closed around something soft and before she had finished processing the thought, *Oh God, snake!* she had wrapped her hand around the thing and pulled it out.

Thankfully it wasn't a snake, but rather something small that fit in the palm of her hand, rolled in an old piece of cloth and plastic wrap. She opened it, carefully, wondering at the treasure. Gold? Old coins? Diamonds?

She brushed off a small piece of cotton fluff, the kind found in a vitamin bottle, and uncovered a strange old key. The key was two inches long, made for an old-fashioned lock, with a cylinder on the end and a small finger-like thing below it. There were no markings on it, nothing to indicate what it might open. The oddest thing about it was that it appeared to be some sort of maroony-purple metal. The key didn't look painted, but was a definite purple color.

Kayla looked carefully at the fabric wrapper. Nothing there, just a piece of old T-shirt. She stuck her hand back in the hole and felt around more bravely this time, but there was nothing else.

She put the key in her pocket and dusted off some of the dirt covering her shirt, pants, skin and shoes, and walked back toward the house. She was excited to have solved the puzzle, but disappointed that the prize wasn't better. She contented herself with planning revenge on

Quinn for the unexpected dirt bath. She'd make the next battle as dirty, and then she'd walk away the winner.

Chapter Three:
More Than Meets The Eye

Two hours later, Kayla had showered and cleaned up all the dirt she'd tracked in. The Livingston's house was a center hall colonial, meaning it had a hallway that ran down the middle of the house to the big eat-in kitchen across the back. There was a bathroom squeezed between the family room and the kitchen on the east side, and a pantry squeezed between the library and kitchen on the west side.

The stairs inside the front door climbed along the library wall to the square, horseshoe-like balcony above the foyer. Four bedrooms opened off the balcony, one for each of the residents, although Kayla supposed that Lorelei's bedroom (or Jim's for that matter) would become a guest room once they got back from their honeymoon. The wall space between the four doors upstairs was covered with all different kinds of art. Original paintings were scattered along the wall, done mostly by local artists.

About a dozen ceramic disks, kind of like lunch plates that had different animals or scenes carved to stick out, or in relief, dotted the entire horseshoe. Tons of framed photographs were mixed with various childlike art projects, both hers and Jim's, presumably hung by their mother.

Somehow it all worked together, instead of seeming cluttered. It was one of Kayla's favorite parts of the house since it seemed to embody her mother. After cleaning up all the dirt, she noticed that the balcony wall really needed dusting. Another forty minutes and about a thousand sneezes later, she was happy with the result of her work. Looking at all of her mom's art selections, reminded her of the letter. While she was gratified to have found the key, something still nagged at her. After all, what good was a key if you didn't have any idea what it opened?

Kayla went back to look at the letter again, wondering if there might be more to it. The key had been pretty easy to find. She sat at her desk with the letter in front of her and looked at it without reading the words. Kayla had an excellent memory and rarely needed to read something more than once for it to be permanently stored in her brain. Granted, she hadn't known her mother very long, but it seemed like there had to be more to the letter than finding an old purple key.

Another few minutes went by and Kayla was frustrated that she couldn't figure it out. She started to put the letter away, folding the bottom up to the crease in the paper, when it hit her. The first letter of each line was capitalized, regardless of its place in the sentence. The first five letters spelled DIARY. Could this note be telling Jim to find both the key and a diary?

Kayla put the letter away and ran down the stairs to the library. With no other clue in the letter, Kayla hoped that the library was a logical place her mom might have hidden a book. To make the most of the home's floor space, the area under the stairs was incorporated into the library. A glance around the room showed Kayla how many books were in there. Shelves ringed the room from floor to ceiling. Under each of four windows there were shelves up to the sill. Aside from a couple of comfortable chairs in the center of the room, there was nothing but books, probably a couple thousand. Kayla sighed and started looking at the top shelf closest to the door. She'd have to look through everything and see if she could find a diary.

Later when twilight had fallen and dinnertime was nigh, Kayla sat in a big leather club chair, discouraged. She had looked at every shelf and found no diary. She did find something surprising, but it wasn't anything that might help her understand why Jim had left that letter for her to solve.

Apparently, Jim had kept many fridge-worthy pieces of art and gold-starred newsprint pages covered in Kayla's writing, from kindergarten through this past year. He had even kept the research paper she wrote last spring on the ancient civilization of the Mayas. *I thought that was upstairs on my desk*, Kayla mused, before shrugging it off.

She let her mind wander a bit, trying to think of what to do next. A line from the letter floated through her mind. *Things are not what they seem.* Kayla had looked at the titles of all the books and had kind of fingered through some of them, but she hadn't actually taken too many off the shelf. What if some of them weren't real books? The idea of pulling all those books off the shelf was too daunting to consider, but how to narrow it down?

Kayla decided to check the most boring, dusty titles they had. Maybe they were decoys since nobody would read anything that dull.

J MONKEYS

Sheep Husbandry and the Economics of Wool by
Marie Laam and *Phases of the Moon as Seen by the
Ancients* authored by Phineas Dunkan were, shockingly,
real books. A double volume set of *The Complete and
Unabridged Works of William Shakespeare and Geoffrey
Chaucer* was real and about a foot thick.

Further on, she found a large book, bound in leather
with gold edging on the pages. What made it stand out was
the accumulation of dust and the fact that the library had
two copies of this book, *The Republic* by Plato. She had
seen a white paperback version, much smaller than this one
on the opposite side of the room. And the letter had a quote
by Plato, too.

She pulled the big leather tome off the shelf with a
tingle of excitement in her fingers. She opened it up, and
sure enough, after the first few pages, the remainder of the
book was false. A rectangular cavity was carved into the
book, leaving the gold tipped edges of the paper loose so
that it really did look like a book at both first and second
glance.

The cavity was lined with a coverless wooden box,
about the size of a five by seven picture. Inside this tiny
coffin, lay a purple book decorated with an entwined P and
J. Kayla removed it, and laid the fake *Republic* aside. She
opened the book and written on the inside were the words:
Diary of Penelope James, begun April 9, 1977. Her mom's
diary!

She had just flipped to the first page, when a
commotion at the front door prompted her to quickly toss
the diary back into its hiding place and put the fake
Republic back on the shelf.

THE CORDOVAN VAULT

As evening fell, Quinn stood in the kitchen watching the last ten seconds of the oven timer count down. The tangy-sweet smell of pizza filled the room, the last one in the freezer, too. Was it wrong that it seemed to smell even better because it was the last one? Stomping feet and a tinny knock sounded at the front of the house.

Quinn paused to pull his dinner from the oven before walking down the hallway to see who it was. Kayla came rushing out of the library at her usual pace, running. They reached the door at the same time, both surprised to see a pair of uniformed police officers standing on the porch instead of friends of either of them.

A chill crawled down Quinn's spine and around his stomach as he reached for the doorknob. The sight of two police officers outside instantly brought him back to the last time he had seen such a sight, seven years earlier. The anguish of that memory raised the hair on the back of his neck as he noted the serious expressions on the officers' faces. "Can I help you?" he asked, with the fleeting thought that something seemed strange about them.

"We're looking for Quinn Wexford and Kayla Livingston," the female officer stated.

"That's us," Kayla said in a small voice, stepping forward to stand next to Quinn.

"I'm Officer Haywood and this is Officer Dax," she said, gesturing toward her partner. "May we come in?"

"Of course," Quinn said.

"No!" Kayla said at the same time. "I'm sorry if I seem rude, but I'm not comfortable with strangers in the house. Would it be all right if we sat on the porch?" Kayla asked a bit fragilely.

"Certainly," Officer Haywood said. "We've been informed by the Pennsylvania State Police that there has been an accident in Philadelphia." She paused for a second to let this sink in. "I'm sorry to tell you that both James Livingston and Lorelei Wexford-Livingston were killed this afternoon."

Chapter Four:

The New Emancipation Proclamation

"What?" Quinn croaked looking frantically from one officer to the other. Kayla gasped for breath sounding like she had been swimming a long distance under water and was desperate for air.

"James Livingston and Lorelei Wexford-Livingston were killed in a car accident," Officer Haywood repeated. Kayla crossed her arms over her chest as if to shield herself from another blow. Quinn collapsed into a red Adirondack chair on the porch. He fell so fluidly it seemed his bones had disappeared.

Kayla recovered enough breath to wheeze, "How?"

"The investigation is still ongoing and we are not at liberty to give many details at this time, but apparently, the taxi they were in drove off a bridge, landing in the river. It sank quickly and no survivors have been found."

"Oh my God, not again!" Kayla whispered as tears pooled in her eyes. Quinn stopped looking from one officer to the next, searching for the truth, and stared at the deck between his feet.

Haywood rested her hand on Quinn's shoulder. "Is there anyone we can call for you? Do you have any other family in the area?" Quinn shook his head, too lost in thought to think.

"I'll call social services," Dax mumbled to Haywood, turning away to use his cell phone.

Quinn looked at Kayla, his face pale, green eyes like wet sea-glass staring intently into her troubled peacock blues. "Did you do this? Is this a joke to get back at me for the dirt?"

Quinn stared at her, waiting to see her response. He prayed he would be able to spot a lie. He saw her gasp inaudibly, her eyes flaring to huge puddles in her face and she physically shuddered as if in pain. Slowly, Kayla shook her head, her eyes never leaving Quinn's, tears streaming silently down her cheeks. He was sure she wasn't that good an actor.

Dax interrupted the pair, clearing his throat. "I don't have any cell service, can I use your phone?"

Quinn flinched at Dax's intrusive voice, but tore his gaze away from Kayla and nodded to Dax. "It's in the kitchen, I'll take you." He rose out of the chair, took two steps to the door and paused before opening it. "Kayla, we've got to pull ourselves together. I don't know what this is yet, but we're going to need to make some decisions about what to do. Can you do that?" Quinn wiped tears he hadn't realized he'd shed from his cheeks as he spoke, then reached out a hand and gently squeezed her shoulder.

Kayla took a deep breath and shivered, as if she was shaking away her grief for the moment. She closed her eyes and blew out the breath, pausing before taking in another one. She stood taller, pushed her shoulders back, unwrapped her arms and opened her eyes. Quinn imagined that he had just seen Humpty Dumpty pull himself back together – something that seemed impossible to do until you were left with no choice but to do it. Kayla returned Quinn's gaze and simply said, "Yes".

Dax followed Quinn into the kitchen while Kayla and Officer Haywood waited on the porch in silence. A few minutes later, they returned, as silently as they had left. "There's a social worker on her way," Dax announced. "Is there anything else we can do for you?"

"What do we do now?" Kayla asked Officer Heywood, her voice flat with shock and grief.

"Can you think of any reason someone would want to hurt either of them?" Officer Dax asked.

Quinn's gasp sounded like a hiss. "No – I mean Lorelei is so nice to everybody it would be impossible for someone to want to harm her. And Jim is as solid and upstanding a guy as you could ever meet. You think someone did this to them? That doesn't make any sense. They were on their honeymoon. They didn't know anyone there, they got married yesterday!"

"I understand. It's one of several leads the Pennsylvania PD is working on."

They sat in silence for a short time, waiting for the social worker to arrive. Too soon, another car rushed to the curb, this time a small, shiny black car. A short woman in jeans and a knit top hopped out. She strode up the walkway purposefully, studying the folks on the porch as if they were players on a stage.

"I'm Simone LeKarf. I'm a social worker with the state Department of Health and Human Services," she said extending her hand first to Quinn and Kayla, then to the police officers. After greeting everyone, Simone stood with her back to the police officers facing the kids. "I was around the corner with another family," she offered in explanation to their surprised looks. It had only been five minutes since Officer Dax had called her. "So, what's going on?" she whirled around and asked the police officers.

Officer Heywood answered, telling Simone about Lorelei and Jim's deaths in Philadelphia. "These kids are minors. In the absence of family, we called you to...help figure out their next steps."

Simone nodded, pulled out her iPad and tapped the screen a few times. The police officers stepped to the background, allowing the kids to focus on Simone. "What are your full names? Guardians names, birth dates, social security numbers..." She fired off a bunch of identifying questions, barely giving them time to respond before shooting off the next question.

Quinn tried to remember the confusion of his parent's deaths. He had been so young at the time, he never realized until now that he had spent a long time waiting for the other shoe to drop, expecting more bad news. Now here it was and he felt as confused as that little boy who had dragged his prized possessions with him wherever he went, the toy guitar his father had gotten on a trip to Hawaii, and Puffin, the stuffed penguin he had always had. Even now, when the majority of his belongings were strewn about his bedroom, he knew exactly where the little guitar and Puffin were.

He couldn't think about what to do next, couldn't think beyond this moment. He desperately wanted to feel

Lorelei's protective arms around him and hear her voice telling him that it would be all right, that she would take care of him. *God, she was just a little older than me when our parents died. How did she do it?* he thought.

More so than ever before, Quinn appreciated his sister's sacrifices in order to take care of him. She must have felt the same disbelief and fear then that he felt now, but had somehow buried it, coped with the loss and moved on. This realization lead to the thought that Lorelei wouldn't want him sitting around moping about her. She would expect him to pick himself up and move on, as she had done.

Of course, Lorelei had me to care for and I'm all alone now. A movement in the corner of his eye caught his attention and he glanced to the left in time to see Kayla wipe away a tear. Maybe he wasn't as alone as he had thought. Maybe it *was* easier to cope when you had something or someone else to focus on.

The beep of Simone's iPad brought Quinn's thoughts back to the present. "OK, this is interesting." She looked up at the kids. "I guess you are unaware that your guardians' request for your legal emancipation was approved a couple of weeks ago."

Chapter Five:

Deja Vu

Kayla's mouth dropped open and her eyes fluttered for a few seconds as she absorbed Simone's words. Emancipated? What on earth? Quinn's breath rushed out in a noisy gust, neither a huff nor a sigh.

Officer Heywood stepped into the foreground again. "Huh. Well it sounds like you don't need us any longer. If you think of anything, give me a call." She gestured to Officer Dax and they left.

Simone ushered Quinn and Kayla into the house and closed the door on the departing police car. "So. You didn't know about the emancipation," Simone said, settling into an armchair in the family room. "I wasn't involved in the case, but the notes in your file make it clear that your guardians thought very highly of you two, and your capabilities."

"What does it mean to be emancipated?" Quinn asked.

Simone glanced down at her iPad again, tapping a few times. "You are basically allowed to make your own decisions about your future. You have to follow all applicable laws but otherwise you will be treated as adults, even though you are four years away from being adults in truth."

"What kind of laws do you mean?" Kayla asked out of curiosity more than actual interest in the topic. As long as they focused the conversation on this legal issue, then she didn't have to think about Jim being gone.

"Well, you can't get a driver's license until you are sixteen. You can't vote until you are eighteen. You can't purchase alcohol until you are twenty-one. Things like that."

"Oh. Okay then." Kayla didn't know what else to say. She figured Quinn didn't either because the silence started to drag on a bit longer than was comfortable, but before she could think of something, Simone's computer beeped again.

Simone glanced at the message and muttered something under her breath. "I have to go. I've got a domestic violence call with a couple of young kids. Since you are legally free from the control of any guardians, there's no reason why you can't stay here for now. Let's get together tomorrow to discuss the logistics of how you move forward. There are a ton of programs that you will want to know about – programs that provide things like heat, food, health insurance."

They agreed to meet at ten o'clock the next morning and Simone blew out of the house as quickly as she had come in, leaving two shell-shocked kids sitting on the couch in a daze. Their earlier battles with each other were forgotten as they faced the worst crisis of their lives, together.

"What do we do? When my parents died I was only seven years old. I don't know how to handle this stuff," Quinn said, deflating like an untied balloon. He sank back against the couch. There was silence in the room for a few minutes as Kayla and Quinn were lost in thought.

Kayla sat in the silence of the room, Quinn's comment lingering in the air like the haze of a stinky cigar. You couldn't blow it away, you couldn't waft it away, you couldn't even cover it up with air freshener. All you could do was open a window and let it dissipate. *How do you open a window on life?* Kayla wondered, idly. What was a window, anyway? It's a way to look outside. A view. Different windows have different views. *Maybe I need to look at this nightmare from another window, get another view,* Kayla thought with a pause.

Jim spent years telling me that there were more important things to life than tears and fears. "You can be crippled by worry," he always said. "It's much better to take action. If you don't like something about your life, then do something about it." I can't do anything about Jim's...news... right now, but I can do something else and cry later, Kayla thought wiping a tear from her cheek, unable to even think the word "death".

"Why didn't they tell us about the emancipation? Why would they have done that?" Kayla asked Quinn.

"I don't know. Lorelei did seem kinda jumpy lately, but I just figured it was pre-wedding jitters or something," Quinn said.

"I don't know, either. It's a strange thing for them to do, unless they were worried that something might happen to them."

"It's kinda like your mom's letter, the one she wrote before she died. Just in case."

43

Gooseflesh erupted on Kayla's skin at Quinn's words. Suddenly, it was all too much for her. She got up from the couch and pushed away from the conversation. "Whatever. I can't worry about it right now. I'm going to flip through Jim's desk and see if there are any bills or things that need our attention. We can talk with Simone about them tomorrow. What are you going to do?"

"I didn't finish the lawn earlier," Quinn said, gazing out at the cut greenery drying on the sidewalk. "I'll go take care of that. I left a pizza on the kitchen table earlier. You can have it if you want. I'm not hungry." Quinn left the house and a few minutes later she heard the buzzing whine of the weed whacker

Later when the paperwork was organized for their talk with Simone and the lawn was raked, Kayla and Quinn sat eating out of a variety of white boxes and tin tubs of Chinese food. "I can't believe that I'll never see them again," Kayla said into the silence. "I expect them to walk in the door."

"I know, me too," Quinn replied quietly. "I don't want to believe it."

"Me either. I hardly have any family left."

"Yeah, same here," Quinn said, sadly.

Kayla stirred the remnants of a carton of beef and broccoli with her chopsticks, looking for another piece of broccoli hidden among the mushrooms and sauce.

"Was there anything in the desk?" Quinn asked.

"Just the bills and stuff. And some money."

Quinn nodded and reached for a pen and pad next to him on the table. "I started a list of things to talk with

Simone about tomorrow. We should get over to her office first thing in the morning."

Quinn and Kayla tidied up the kitchen and put the left-over cartons of food away. Quinn checked the house to be sure all of the ground-floor windows and the doors were locked up tight. He hadn't done that last night, but it seemed like a good idea since the police thought Jim and Lorelei might have been targeted rather than victims of random crime. They said 'good night' and went to their respective rooms.

Kayla closed her bedroom door and flopped down on the purple bed, in anguish. The need to act that had spurred her on for the last couple of hours had been washed away by the inability to escape from thoughts of Jim. Was he frightened or in pain when he died? Did he or Lorelei suffer?

Jim had been the foundation on which Kayla's entire life had been built. He was the solid thing in her life, when everything else was fluid. Classes, teachers, clothes, interests, habits – they all changed every year. *Jim still had the same hairstyle and wardrobe that he always had,* Kayla thought with a sad smile. *What will I do without him?*

Yesterday morning, she and Jim had made a plan to talk when he got back from his trip, about the strange *thing* that had happened a few times over the last six months. "Phenomenon" was too strong a word, and neither "experience", "situation" nor "problem" fit either.

"So it's happened three times, then?" he'd confirmed while she tied his bow tie.

"Yeah. There was the squirrel sitting on the post, the kid on the bike and the freaky thing in my English class.

But you know, I nearly always remember my dreams and the "real" thing didn't happen right away. Another déjà vu could be brewing."

Jim had nodded, "Well, if it happens while we're on our honeymoon, make a note of it and we can talk it through when we get back." He sighed and said, "We should probably plan to talk about it then, anyway."

Fat lot of good it would do her now. She wiped her cheeks and thought about the creepy déjà vus. The first one had happened about eight months ago, as she walked down the street toward the house. A small gray squirrel had been sitting on top of a fence post, breaking into a late season acorn. He had chirped as she walked by. A breeze blew, rustling the crispy brown leaves on the ground and swaying the tips of the tall pine trees in the distance.

An eerie silence had fallen as Kayla stopped short and looked at the squirrel. She'd been overwhelmed with the sense of having seen this before. Of course, she'd seen squirrels sitting on fence posts before, but this was something more than that. She felt that she had seen this exact moment before. She dismissed it, shook her head and shoulders to clear the silliness and continued walking home without giving the strange moment another thought.

Until it happened again.

The second déjà vu, took place outside again, but this time in a populated area in the center of town. Kayla had been stepping out of the coffee shop with Jim when she felt that same eeriness come over her again. She had stopped short, nearly spilling her hot chocolate down the front of her coat as she looked at the strangely familiar scene.

THE CORDOVAN VAULT

Cars were stopped at one of the two lights in town and the pedestrians were hurrying to cross the street in front of Town Hall. With her head in a fog, Kayla had the random thought that a man riding a bike through the crosswalk would look funny in this wintry scene. Before the thought had completed its passage through her brain, and really it was more than a thought, like an expectation, a man rode a silver bicycle through the intersection and off into the distance.

The shock must have shown on her face because amid the hollering and horns blowing to lend some celebration to the silliness of a man on a bike in Maine in February, Jim tapped her on the shoulder and asked what was wrong. Kayla told him she thought she might have had a dream like that a while back.

The third time it happened, she knew she had dreamt it because she had started a dream journal and this was one of the first dreams she had scribbled in it. The dream journal was nothing fancy, a little spiral notebook, about the size of her hand, which sat on her nightstand with a pencil. Generally, the entries were barely legible since she was still mostly asleep when she was writing them down. But when she freaked out in English class from déjà vu, she was thrilled to have proof that it wasn't all in her head.

It was another simple, everyday happening. Mr. Tkadz (it was a silent "T) liked the classroom set up in a circle or horseshoe to facilitate discussion. Kayla hated to sit with her back to a door. She made a point to get to class early to secure one of the seats on the far side of the room, near the windows, facing the door. Other people in the class must have felt the same way since those seats always filled up first. She had dreamt that she was sitting in class, on the wrong side of the room, with her back right in front of the door. That's why the dream had seemed so strange – she was sitting in the wrong place. In the dream, she leaned forward, looked to her left at someone sitting about three people down the arc and said something about how she really liked the imagery in a poem. She had gone on to talk about the specifics of the poem. When she woke from the dream, it was already fading from her mind, but she scribbled down a couplet she had especially liked and a verbal sketch of the room. She went back to sleep and dreamed something else.

The dream had happened on a Thursday in April. The real thing happened at the end of the school year, about three weeks ago. That morning, she had a test in German class and stayed after to double check her answer on the bonus question with the teacher, Frau Weissen. On her way to English class, she remembered that she'd left her homework in her locker and had to race to the other end of the school to get it.

Of course, all of this took longer than the four minutes they were allotted to travel between classes and she skidded into English class about two minutes after it started. Naturally, all the good seats were taken, so she slid into the closest open desk, right in front of the door.

It wasn't until a couple of minutes later, when she leaned forward, looked to her left at Phil Copperman sitting three people down the arc and said something about how she really liked the imagery of the overblown muffin in his poem "Breaking more than your fast" that the eerie feeling started to build. She mentioned a couplet she especially liked, "take care when you enjoy the muffin top, or over your waistband – your belly will pop" and as she was about to praise his use of multi-leveling language and imagery, she realized that she was repeating exactly what she had said in the dream. It was another déjà vu.

In an instant, she felt her face drain of blood and lost complete track of her thoughts. A couple of seconds stretched out into a lifetime as she looked around the room, her mind a blank to everything except the thought that when Mr. Tkadz had assigned this project last week, everyone had pulled a topic out of his ceramic Idea Kitty to ensure that everyone had a random topic to write about.

That meant that when she had the dream, at least two months earlier, Phil Copperman hadn't written the poem yet, nor had she read it, so how could she have known about the couplet she liked?!

This déjà vu had freaked her out so much that she'd left class on an emergency pee break and called Jim at work to tell him. He'd told her not to worry, that they'd talk about it more at home, but there hadn't been time lately to really talk it through. Too many things had been put off until later, and now 'later' would never come.

The tears that she had been holding back all evening finally spilled over the dam of her will. Kayla cried for herself, for Jim and Lorelei and even for Quinn, soaking the pillows before she fell into a restless sleep.

****

Kayla sat in Jim's car all alone in the dark, at the edge of a cliff. There was no ground outside the car, neither off to the right, nor off to the left. Empty nothing. She started to move, frantically trying to get out of the car, but she couldn't find the release button on the seat-belt. She heard a noise in front of her, and in slow motion, she turned her head to look out the windshield. Quinn was flying toward her, swimming through the air about four feet off the ground. The sun appeared to be rising behind him, obscuring him in silhouette. He reached for her, his fingers tightened into claws. Somehow, the only part of him that she could see clearly in the blinding light was his face, contorted in a snarl that took her breath away as she tried to scream.

Kayla woke suddenly and looked at the clock. It was 2:37 in the morning. Something was wrong, but she couldn't place it as the dream faded from memory. What had woken her? The shrill ring of the telephone startled her and she jumped up to answer it. "Hello?" she asked. There was nothing but static on the other end of the line. "Hello, is there anyone there?"

Kayla glanced at the phone and then hung it up when there was no response. She was wide-awake, but feeling a little befuddled by sleep at the same time. What was wrong? Oh yeah, Jim and Lorelei are dead, she thought. She sighed deeply and went to the bathroom to wash the tear-stains from her face.

When she came out of the bathroom into the darkness of the balcony, she noticed that light could be seen peeping out from beneath Quinn's bedroom door. She walked over and knocked, thinking that maybe he couldn't sleep either. "Yeah," he groaned. Kayla opened the door to his room and carefully picked her way among the debris flung on the floor. "Who was on the phone?" Quinn asked.

"Just static. Did I wake you?"

"No the phone did. Was it static both times?"

"Oh, I don't know, I only answered it this last time. The first call must be what woke me up, too. I saw your light on and remembered that I had wanted to talk to you before everything happened today."

"What did you want to talk about?" Quinn sat up straighter in bed, subtly tucking Puffin under the summer blanket. Just because he wanted to snuggle with his old stuffed animal, didn't mean he wanted anyone to know about it.

Kayla walked further into the room, ignoring the clutter and clothes hanging from every place imaginable, except for the pristine corner filled with a drum-set, a keyboard, a guitar and a cello. She perched on the edge of his desk and looked out at the world below. There was a cool breeze blowing through the open window, making the curtains flutter. Outside, a car drove down the street, momentarily drowning out the symphony of crickets. Kayla took a deep breath and looked at Quinn.

"I wanted to apologize for the whole thing with the sound system last winter. I didn't know until after you and Lorelei moved in that you had invited the coffee shop manager to come see you sing, like an audition. I'm really sorry." Kayla whispered and turned her head so she didn't have to meet Quinn's eyes. The silence hung heavy in the room for long minutes, broken only by the sound of another car driving by.

"You know if you hadn't pulled that prank, Jim and Lorelei would never have met."

J MONKEYS

Kayla swung her eyes to meet Quinn's, horrified. "Are you saying it's my fault they died?"

"No! God, no! I don't know about Jim, but I never saw Lorelei as happy as she is when she's with Jim. She's always too busy to date and was a little sad, I think, when I was growing up. She missed out on a lot of stuff by taking care of me. If I had it all to do over again, I wouldn't stop them from meeting and getting married just to keep them alive. Lorelei wouldn't want that. I was saying it was a blessing in disguise, that prank. A little humiliation was a small price to pay for bringing the two of them together. All right, a lot of humiliation. But let's put the whole thing behind us. You're the only family I have now, so I guess I can't stay mad at you forever. And, I'm sorry too. About the posters and stuff."

Impulsively, Kayla leaned over and gave Quinn a hug. He was surprised but hugged her back. The phone rang before either of them could say anything. "I'll get it this time. It's got to be a crank call at this time of the night." Quinn picked up the phone. "Listen, jerk, it's nearly three o'clock in the morning. STOP CALLING US!"

Before he could slam the phone down, he heard a voice, broken by static, but one that he knew as well as his own saying, "Don't believe – a trap – call Dad – kitchen – rainy". The line went dead with a click.

"Lorelei...Lorelei!" Quinn shouted into the phone, his green eyes locking onto Kayla's shocked blue ones.

Chapter Six:

Vegetables for a Rainy Day

"That was Lorelei?!" Kayla demanded.

"Yeah, no doubt about it!" Quinn hung up the phone and hysterically hit buttons.

"Well, get her back! What did she say? Are they all right? Where's Jim?" Kayla fired off questions, demanding answers but giving him no chance to respond.

"I'm trying. The star six nine caller-return thing isn't working! I don't know if they are all right, but she certainly seemed to be alive! She didn't say anything about Jim. It was hard to hear her over the static and what I did hear didn't make sense. She said 'Don't believe, a trap'. Then there was static and 'call Dad', more static then 'kitchen', static and 'rainy'. My Dad is dead, how can I call him?" Quinn stated, looking up from the phone, confused. "Where are you going?"

Kayla had made it out of Quinn's room, and down the hallway to the stairs before Quinn finished speaking. "To check the caller ID in the kitchen," she yelled over her shoulder.

Quinn followed her down the stairs and got to the kitchen in time to hear her say, "Three calls five minutes apart, each with ID unavailable. Crap! Did you hear what she said about the kitchen?"

"No, just the word 'kitchen'."

"Hold the phone in case she calls back," Kayla said, slapping the phone into Quinn's hand as if he was a surgeon and the phone his scalpel. "'Don't believe it' she said, right? Something is going on here that involves the police in two states so whatever it is, it's pretty big. Safe to say she's clearly gone to some trouble to warn us about something and wants us to do something," Kayla mumbled to herself.

"Can we assume everything we heard has got to be important? I think so; she knew about the phone trouble since she couldn't connect the first two times she called. She would have used the time of the call very carefully. Kitchen…kitchen… what could she be talking about?" Kayla wondered aloud, looking carefully around the room. Fridge, stove, sink, cabinets, drawers. All pretty standard stuff, nothing looked out of the ordinary. Table, chairs, pantry. "Didn't she say rainy, too?" Kayla asked, spinning around to look at Quinn.

"Yeah, 'don't believe, a trap, call Dad, kitchen, rainy'. That's all."

Kayla started walking around the room, touching everything. "Kitchen, rainy, kitchen, rainy."

"They might not be thoughts that go together. There was static in between."

"No, there's something in the back of my brain that says they are connected, but I can't reach it."

Quinn gripped the phone and watched Kayla as she paced, blond hair swaying with each spin to retrace her steps. He wasn't sure where she was going with all of this, but he knew that she was the person to solve this puzzle. She took things apart just to see how they worked. Intangible things and physical things.

The voice changer she had installed in the school's sound system for the play (much to Quinn's dismay) was one example. She had also installed a timer on the ceiling fan in the bathroom at the house so that it would automatically start after the light had been on for seven minutes.

Lorelei had told him that it seemed Kayla didn't like the noise of the fan, but she didn't like the steamy bathroom after her shower either. So, she created a compromise that automatically sucked away the steam while she was in the shower, but gave her a maximum of quiet time. Watching her now, mentally dissecting Lorelei's meaning, he thought getting out of her way could be the best help he had to offer.

Kayla glanced in the pantry as she walked by it with its ever-present giant pile of canned vegetables. "For a rainy day! That's it!" Kayla spun around and stepped into the pantry. "Vegetables for a rainy day. Lorelei wrote it on the post it she left us yesterday." Kayla popped her head out of the pantry to look at Quinn when she spoke.

"Yeah," Quinn said walking over. The pantry was a small walk-in closet with no door, lined with horizontal shelves that wrapped around the entire interior. There was almost enough room in the pantry for two people to stand close together. The shelves were eighteen inches in height from one to the next. There were wire basket-drawers for potatoes and onions and a bunch of staples like flour, rice, sugar and coffee. Quinn stood behind Kayla looking at a stack of canned vegetables that took up three shelves of space. He could easily see over her head. "These cans have been here since Lore and I moved in. Did you and Jim eat a lot of them?"

"No, in fact we *never* eat canned veggies. Jim hates them, says they are too mushy and they taste funny. Look at these labels; these cans have been here for a while." The labels of the cans on the bottom of the stack were slightly discolored from age. Kayla reached around Quinn, grabbed an empty wire basket from the floor behind them and started filling it with the cans. As the wall behind the shelf came into view, they could clearly see a silver metal ring recessed into the wall.

Quinn pulled on the ring and to his amazement, the whole wall pulled away opening a door to a space neither of them had known existed. A flashlight was velcro'd to the back of the secret door.

Kayla grabbed the light and shined it into the space. "It looks like it wraps around the pantry," Kayla said of the L-shaped space.

She stepped into the hidden area, gesturing for Quinn to follow her. The walls were smooth and everything was painted white, the walls the ceiling and even the floor. As they made the turn at the crook of the L, the space opened up from three feet wide to a small square room nearly seven feet by seven feet.

"What the heck is all this?!" Quinn asked gesturing to the built in desk, complete with computer, file drawer and light. Hanging from the opposite wall were two backpacks, big ones like hikers use and two empty hooks.

THE CORDOVAN VAULT

"I have no idea," Kayla replied, turning on the desk lamp and looking around. "We must be in a space carved out of the library. I've never seen any of this stuff and I've lived here my whole life. What is going on? It feels like we've gone down the rabbit hole."

"Maybe this will help." Quinn held up a plastic shiny CD case. "Look, it even says 'Play me' on it. Clever. I guess Jim knew this would make you think of Alice in Wonderland." Quinn popped the CD into the computer and it came on straight away. "Oooh, answers on demand. We don't even have to wait for a boot up."

Kayla and Quinn watched in dumbfounded surprise as a video of Jim and Lorelei came on the screen. "Hi guys," Jim started. "If you are watching this, then we've run into trouble. Let me give you some quick instructions, then grab this CD, the backpacks on the wall behind you and get out of the house. This is not a joke. You absolutely cannot stay in the house longer than fifteen minutes. One of you check the time." Jim's face looked more serious than Quinn had ever seen it. Lorelei sat next to him in the video, nodding.

Quinn glanced at the white clock on the wall. "It's two fifty two," he said to Kayla.

"We are not who you think we are. By 'we', I mean all four of us," Jim continued. "Lorelei and I have been researching our parents' deaths and they were not accidents. The people who killed them are now after us. We expected we would get closer to the truth in Philadelphia but if we contacted you and directed you to this video, then we probably got too close.

"We're going to be staying at a youth hostel called the Last Tain. I know this sounds crazy, but we need you guys to come to Philadelphia and finish what we started. We're in a race to find and protect information from some really bad people. That's why we had to leave the wedding so quickly. They have a head start. Not to sound too dramatic, but lives depend on it. Ours and many others." Quinn glanced at Kayla, surprised to hear Jim speak so boldly.

"Then we need you two to go find our Dad, Victor Livingston. We think he's still alive and living somewhere in the south central US. And Kay, I know you've found Mom's diary; bring it with you. That's enough for now, take the disk and get out of the house in thirteen minutes."

"We love you both. Be careful, look out for each other and use all the advantages you have. Leave your cell phones here so they can't track you by the GPS. We'll catch up with you when we can." Lorelei spoke at last and blew a kiss to the screen before the video shut back down.

Chapter Seven:

Dreams Really Do Come True

Kayla and Quinn sat motionless, in shock. After a few seconds, they glanced at each other, then jumped up and into action. Quinn grabbed the backpacks while Kayla retrieved the CD. "Kitchen," Quinn said as they dashed out of the little hidden office.

"We're leaving, right?" Quinn said once they were back to the sanity of the main house.

"Yeah, I've never seen Jim so serious. How did he know I had the diary? I just found it a few hours ago. I have no idea what is going on or what he's talking about, but I think we'd better go." Kayla grabbed the last few pieces of fruit and new water bottles off the counter and dropped them into a backpack as she spoke.

"OK, we have to be out the door in thirteen minutes. I'll put the cans back to re-hide the door in the pantry. You stuff whatever you think we might need into a backpack and get some clothes. I'll run up to my room to get a change of clothes as soon as the pantry is all set." Quinn pulled the silverware out of the drawer as he spoke. He held up the envelope of money Lorelei had given them and said, "Kay – wherever we're going, we're going to need money. Grab whatever you can. And I think we'd better take Jim's car. Lorelei's new car is a stick shift and I don't know how to drive it, do you?"

"Phewwww. No. I mean I've driven like bumper cars or go carts, and I've backed Jim's car down the driveway a few times, but that's it. Do you know how to drive?"

"Well, I drove Lorelei's old car a bunch of times. Just around an empty parking lot. It's not that hard."

"OK, I nominate you as our designated driver, then." Kayla ran upstairs to change out of her jammies and threw on a pair of shorts, a T-shirt, a sweatshirt and a pair of Keds. She grabbed some random clothes out of her drawers and tossed them into the pack along with her Tevas. In under seven minutes, she had nearly filled her bag, including some toiletries, and the blanket off her bed.

As she came out of the bathroom, a freshly-dusted picture of all four of them caught her eye. Impulsively, she pulled it off the wall, then grabbed a couple of small framed black and white pictures, one of her parents at a barbecue before she was born, and one of Quinn's parents on their boat. She shoved the frames into the backpack with much too little care for things with glass parts, cinched the pack closed, and lugged it down the stairs to the den.

She glanced at her watch and called out, "Quinn six minutes left! Where are you?"

"I'll be right down! Do you have the car keys?" Quinn hollered back from upstairs, presumably in his bedroom doing much the same as Kayla had done.

Kayla opened the roll-top desk and picked up the packet of household finance materials she had made earlier in the evening. There were a couple of empty smaller pouches on the sides of the bag, but nothing that the finance packet would fit in. She rested her stuff against the desk, dropped the packet on top of the desk and ran toward the library. Quinn came running down the stairs so fast, Kayla wasn't sure his feet were actually hitting them. Their near collision was only avoided by Quinn jumping to the right, off the last couple of steps and by Kayla putting on a sudden burst of speed through the library door. "My stuff's in the den. The car keys are on the rack," she said in answer to his earlier question.

"Come on Kayla," Quinn shouted while inspecting the key rack by the front door.

"Ready in a sec," came the muffled reply. Kayla pulled the fake *Republic* off the shelf and pulled out the diary and the purple key that she had shoved there earlier.

"Kayla, we've got to go." Quinn stood in the doorway carrying both backpacks and his guitar case.

"Coming," she said, spinning around. "Is there anything else we need?" Kayla asked, as Quinn reached for doorknob.

"I can't think of anything, but we'll have to take stock of what we have at some point and organize this stuff. It's all shoved in these bags. How are we going to get to Philadelphia? I haven't thought past getting out of the house, have you?" Quinn asked.

"Not really." Kayla paused and blew her hair out of her face. "Well, let's do that, go somewhere to take stock and figure out a plan. Our fifteen minutes is nearly up."

They pulled the door open and stepped onto the porch in time to see a car's tail lights going around the corner and out of sight. "You know, that's the third or fourth car I've seen go by the house since the phone woke me up. It's three o'clock in the morning. Isn't that kind of a lot of traffic for the middle of the night in Granby, Maine?" Kayla asked with a glance at Quinn.

"Yes it is, considering the bowling alley is the only thing in town open after 9:00pm and they close at midnight. Let's get out of here." The day's events, capped with the shocking phone call from his sister and the bizarre message on the DVD had finally worked together to completely creep Quinn out. Kayla must have felt the same way because he saw her shake off a chill and as he carried all of the luggage to the car. Kayla opened the garage door while he was locking the front door to the house. She hopped in the passenger side and buckled her seat belt while Quinn concentrated on the unfamiliar task of driving.

"Where should we go? he asked, after a few minutes of silence.

"Why don't we pull into the rest stop near Hawleyville? It's after the next exit on the highway. It's well lit and no one will think it's odd for people to be there in the middle of the night."

****

Quinn drove along, his thoughts bubbling up like water in a Jacuzzi, all in a jumble. He was barely able to process them as each question rippled to the surface with a hundred others.

What is going on? Where should we go? Do we have what we need? Did that car have anything to do with us? Did I pack clean underwear? Is Lorelei okay? What about Jim? Why didn't they tell us whatever they want us to know earlier? How much gas do we have? What happened to my parents? What time does the sun come up? Should we call Simone or Officer Heywood? Quinn's mind continued swirling until Kayla interrupted the whirlpool with a poke to the shoulder.

"You're going to miss the exit."

Quinn shook off the whirling thoughts and turned into the rest stop. He parked under a streetlight and popped the trunk as Kayla got out. "Let's dump everything into the trunk and then sort it," he said. As they sifted through the mound of clothes and supplies, they began to sort them by category: clothes, food, other.

The clothes were of little consequence so they rolled them up to conserve space and packed them into the backpacks. In the food category, they had two bags of granola bars and beef jerky that Lorelei or Jim must have put in the backpacks at some point, a sleeve of crackers, a jar of peanut butter, a few jars of tuna (but no can opener), three peaches and a couple of bruised-but-edible bananas. They also had six bottles of Gatorade, again complements of Jim and Lorelei, and the three water bottles Kayla had gotten from the kitchen.

"With the way you eat, we'll be lucky if this lasts us a day." Kayla nudged Quinn in the ribs with her elbow. They carefully packed the food into the side pouches, splitting it evenly between the two bags. A few bottles didn't fit in the smaller pouches. They settled them into the main pouch of Quinn's bag. "So what's left?" Kayla asked.

"Well, we have the two towels you grabbed, and your blanket. We have this bag of shower supplies. Good thinking by the way, I didn't get anything like that." Quinn rolled up the towels and blanket, placing them in the bottom compartment of the two packs. That left Puffin, a compass, Kayla's now empty purse, Quinn's digital camera, Kayla's mom's journal and the picture frames. Quinn picked up the pictures and chuckled as he looked at the one of his Mom and Dad.

"What's so funny?" Kayla asked with a small smile, the way people do when they don't know what's funny, but they don't really want to be left out of the joke.

"I'm assuming you packed these photos in a sentimental moment?" Quinn asked.

"Yeah, I was walking by and they sort of grabbed me."

"I did the same thing." Quinn pulled two extra sets of keys out of his pocket and shook them by the rings. "Jim's keys and Lorelei's were hanging together on the same hook and somehow, I couldn't leave them there." He dropped the keys into his bag.

Kayla picked up Puffin, gave him a gentle shake and said, "Kinda like this guy? Oh! And I have this." She showed him the purple key and relayed the story of finding it after the dirt bath.

Quinn turned the key over in his hand, then shrugged and rescued Puffin from Kayla's grasp. Puffin joined the contents of Quinn's pouch, carefully and securely packed. Kayla laughed, adding the key to her key chain and then looked around at the remaining items to be packed away. "Hey, did you bring that blue plastic envelope thing that I had on the desktop? It was right near the backpack."

"No, sorry. I didn't see anything like that. What was in it?"

"Ughh," Kayla said with a groan. "It was all the household finance stuff I organized earlier. And the money

I found earlier. How much money was in that envelope from Lorelei?"

"Oh, right," Quinn said pulling the envelope from his back pocket. He counted the cash, saying, "There's three hundred dollars in here. That should last a while, but how much did you find in the desk?"

"I found another thousand dollars in the hide-a-drawer. We'll have to go back for the whole folder."

"We're going to Philly after that, right? How're we going to get there? Should we drive?"

"Do you want to drive?" Kayla asked.

"Not really. Wouldn't we have to go through New York City? All those other cars and stuff," Quinn shuddered. Just getting them this far from home had been nerve wracking. He didn't want to imagine merging with cab drivers while trying to read signs and stuff. "And I don't know how to get there, do you?"

"Can we follow signs? Like for the major cities: Boston, New York City, Philly."

"Yeah, that seems like a good way to get lost. If I had my cell phone, I could get directions. I feel kinda naked with out it."

"Me too. All right." Kayla rubbed her temple for a second, as if she needed a moment to refocus. "Let's go back to the house and get the extra money, then head south toward Boston and stop somewhere for a map."

"Let's do it." Quinn said as he stored the last few items in his pack.

"I know Jim said to be out of the house fast, but a couple of minutes shouldn't matter. Who knows how long this will take? Thirteen hundred dollars will go a lot farther than three hundred."

Quinn agreed. Once they got to their street, Quinn turned the headlights off so they could pull up without being seen. "I don't know who might be watching," he said, "but it doesn't hurt to be careful. Let's wait here a minute and see if anything looks suspicious. Good thing the car is too old to have day-time running lights."

The Livingston's nearest neighbors were technically on either side of their house, Mrs. Nessman and the Bracos. But Granby was a rural town and while the Bracos were the closest, they were about an eighth of a mile away. Quinn and Kayla could see their own house from the Braco's driveway, through a break in the blue hydrangeas that bordered the Livingston property. Quinn pulled into the Braco's driveway and he and Kayla sat in the darkened car in silence for a few minutes.

"I don't see anything do you?" Kayla asked.

"No, I'm sure it's fine. We're being paranoid. Do you want to wait here? I'll run in and get the packet. It's blue, plastic and sitting on the desk, right?"

Kayla nodded, "OK, I'll beep if I see anything."

Quinn got out of the car and quietly closed the door behind him. As Kayla watched him walk away, she noticed that a low ground fog had settled around the car, obscuring the view.

It looked like the car was floating on a cloud. A chill sprinted up her spine and over her shoulders to race down her arms. She was sitting in Jim's car all alone at night with no ground visible outside the car, like in the dream she had earlier. She scrambled to get her seat-belt off, but couldn't find the release button in the dark. Her mind raced ahead, trying to remember the déjà vu, for surely that's what it was.

She heard a noise outside and as if in slow motion, she turned her head around to see out the windshield. Quinn was halfway to the road when a black sedan sped out from behind the Livingston's house and across the lawn, clipping a hydrangea in its haste. Quinn waved to Kayla to crouch down in the car as he hid behind a tall tree along the street.

As the black car raced down the street and around the corner without so much as a pause at the stop sign, Quinn took a few steps toward the car. He could make out Kayla's lips screaming his name. She was frantically gesturing for him to stop while she struggled to get out of the car. He saw a burst of orange reflected in the windshield half an instant before an unseen force lifted him and threw him through the air before dropping him face down on the ground and shoving him across the gravel driveway. The explosion blasted sound and fire into the air.

Chapter Eight:

The Infamous They

Kayla jumped out of the car amid a hailstorm of house pieces screaming, "Quinn!" worried that the ten seconds it had taken for her to understand what was happening was too long. She had yelled for him to stay behind the shelter of the giant oak tree, but he hadn't heard and had stepped closer to the car before their house exploded across the street. The force of the explosion tossed him through the air, making it look like he was flying.

Kayla tried to make her way over to where Quinn had fallen, but was temporarily blinded by a brilliant burst of fire. She put up an arm to shield her eyes and felt her way along the car to the front.

Finally, her eyes adjusted enough that she could make out Quinn's body lying on the ground. She bent over him, trying to block him from the embers still floating on the wind. With shaking hands, she flipped him over and felt his throat for a pulse. For a long heartbreaking second she couldn't feel anything. Then, after repositioning her fingers, she felt a steady beat. "Thank God!" she sobbed. She patted him down to be sure no embers were smoldering in his clothes and gently shook him. "Quinn, Quinn! Wake up! We've got to get out of here."

Quinn came around after a few shakes and together they were able to get him into the car. While it seemed to Kayla that the time it took to rouse Quinn was very long, in fact less than a minute had really passed. At fourteen, she'd certainly been watching others drive for years and knew the mechanics of how to operate a car, but she had never actually driven on the street before.

But Quinn was in no shape to drive; he was still dazed from the explosion. Once Quinn was secure, Kayla started the car nervously, hit the brake a little roughly, put the car in gear and drove away as quickly as she could without raising the suspicions of their few neighbors, now starting to emerge from their homes in their pajamas to view the destruction.

Once they reached the highway, Kayla started to shake. She could barely keep the steering wheel straight and had to put on the cruise control because her legs were too weak to hold down the gas pedal. "They tried to kill us! Why would someone want to kill *us*? Are you all right?" Kayla glanced at Quinn. He sat stretched out in the passenger seat, long denim-clad legs in front of him. He definitely looked the worse for his adventure.

His short brown hair was sticking out in all directions, but not in its normal way. His gray Barenaked Ladies concert t-shirt was torn at the shoulder and seemed to have holes burned into it. Kayla saw that his face was skinned on the cheek and the rest of him was covered with mud.

Twenty-four hours ago she hated Quinn. Now she was terrified that she was going to lose him too. When she thought about how he had tried to be supportive when Officer Heywood broke the news of Jim and Lorelei's deaths, she felt a deep sense of shame at all she had done to him over the last year. She had publicly humiliated him again and again with his altered duet. She had ruined his audition to perform in the coffee shop and earn some extra money. She had been cold and down right mean to him when he had moved into the house. She had even gone so far as to "accidentally" ruin some of his concert T-shirts by adding the black shirts to a load of wash heavily spiked with bleach.

And why had she done these things? Because Quinn forgot to give her phone messages, and he always used the last paper towel but never replaced them. Because Quinn played five different musical instruments with ease but when she was nine her dance instructor had told Jim to stop wasting his money, that Kayla's talents must be elsewhere because they did not lay in tap or ballet. And because even when wearing a "new-kid" label, Quinn was more popular than she was.

Kayla physically flinched away from the thought, unaccustomed to that level of raw self-awareness. Was that really the heart of the trouble? Had she spent the last few years torturing this kid out of jealousy? No, that couldn't be. She was a better person than that, a good person.

The car skidded along a curve in the highway, whipping her attention back to the road. She slowed down to only three miles-an-hour over the speed limit and flexed her fingers to loosen her death grip on the steering wheel. She glanced over at Quinn; he seemed to be dozing. Her mind began to wander anew, alternating between snide thoughts about her attitude toward Quinn and a quiet thankfulness that her mom wasn't around to see how she'd turned out. She feared that Mom would have been very disappointed in her this last year. Worse yet, she was more than a little disappointed in herself. Regardless of whose faulty personality caused the friction between them, now Quinn was injured because he was going back to get something she had forgotten.

"No more," she said quietly. "From now on, we are a team."

Quinn glanced up at her, clearly still dazed from the explosion. "I didn't hear you; what did you say?" he asked.

Although Quinn had taken the lead in getting them out of the house, Kayla felt that it was her turn to take charge. Quinn needed a few minutes to pull himself together. "Don't worry about it. There's probably a wad of napkins in the glove compartment. Why don't you use them and one of the bottles of water to clean up? That cut looks nasty, even in the dark." Kayla thought for a few minutes while Quinn was busy wincing in the mirror. "I think we should ditch the car and take the train to Philly."

"Why?" Quinn asked, carefully picking pieces of leaf out of his cheek.

"Well, they are after us too, now. Every cop show on TV has people being tracked by finding the car. I think we should try to shake 'em off our tail."

"OK, slow down there miss Law and Order! Who do you think is after us?"

"They. Them. Whoever it is that ran Jim and Lorelei's taxi off the road. They must have planned the explosion at our house too. They were probably in that black car."

"So you think that whoever captured Lorelei and Jim, if that's what happened, also blew up the house?" Quinn asked skeptically.

"Well, yeah. I mean, the house didn't blow up by itself."

"It might have. It did in that book by Steven King."

"Right…Well that was a fictional haunted house with an ancient boiler and the crazy guy didn't let off the pressure like he was supposed to. I don't believe in ghosts and our boiler was pretty new. Why did Jim want us out of the house so quickly? He was adamant that we be out in fifteen minutes. He must have expected danger. And who was in that black car? I don't think it was being driven by ghosts!"

Kayla's two-minute-old resolve to be kinder and more supportive of Quinn was being put to the test and she didn't think she was passing. The white knuckled grip on the steering wheel was back, indicating that her stress level was awfully high.

She took a deep breath and took her hands off the wheel one at a time to wiggle her fingers and loosen them up. "All I'm saying is that I think it's safe to assume that someone might be after us and we have an opportunity to throw them off the trail. What do you say?"

"I guess you are right; I just don't want to believe it. Let's ditch the car, catch a commuter train to Boston from Nashua, New Hampshire and then take an Amtrak train from Boston. I guess we'll have to make due with the $300, too. In the action movies I've seen, it wasn't the car so much as it was the credit/debit card that tripped people up. If 'They' think we were in the house, we probably shouldn't let them know we are alive by a quick trip to the ATM."

"Ewwww. OK. If you are feeling up to it, why don't you have a look around the car to see if there is anything we should take with us."

"I can do that," Quinn said, opening the glove compartment again. He pulled out everything that was in it and flipped through the pile. Gingerly, he pulled out a few pieces of unopened mail, a bunch of Dunkin' Donuts napkins, a nail file, a pack of matches, some change and a flashlight. He held up two CDs. "I was wondering what happened to these," he said with a knowing look. "I believe Cher and Smash Mouth will be coming with us!"

"You have the strangest taste in music," Kayla said, with the grace to look a little guilty at having never returned the CDs.

"Hey, you borrowed them." Quinn laughed. He continued looking around the car and came up with a pretty big pile of stuff to keep, including a total of forty-three dollars and fifty-seven cents, the list of addresses of the people invited to Lorelei and Jim's wedding, two memory cards from a digital camera and a magnet.

He opened the pieces of mail he'd found in the glove box, and was surprised to find something that really shouldn't be kept in the car. "Look what I found," he said, waving the fancy piece of paper around. "It's the title to the car. Do you want to sell it? We might be able to make back some of the money we lost in the explosion."

"We can't sell Jim's car! He'll kill me." Kayla glanced over at Quinn, who was looking at her with a give-her-a-minute-and-she'll-catch-on expression on his face.

"What? Oh." *Jim might not be around to be angry about the car.* "I guess you're right. The important thing now is to find Jim and Lorelei. Lorelei did say to use all of the advantages we have and more money is an advantage."

"If we're going to ditch it anyway, we might as well get some money for it right? It's not like we'll get the car back later," Quinn reasoned. He stored the latest additions to their inventory in the bags and crawled back into his seat, fastening his seatbelt once again. "It's about three hours to Nashua, right?"

"Yeah, I guess. Why?"

"Do you mind if I take a quick nap? I'm exhausted, but I'm sure you are too. We could switch places if you want and you could nap first."

"No that's okay, you go ahead. My mind is spinning. I don't think I could sleep. You're injured; you should nap. Are you sure you don't want to go to a hospital?" Quinn had refused to see a doctor as soon as they had gotten in the car.

"No, I'm fine, a few scratches, nothing serious. Wake me up in an hour and we can switch places."

"OK."

"Hey, Kayla," Quinn paused, as if not quite sure how to proceed. "Thanks for being concerned."

"Hmm. We'll figure all of this out, I know it. Go to sleep and don't worry for a few minutes." Kayla said, uncomfortable with such a vulnerable Quinn.

****

At precisely nine o'clock, Quinn pulled the car into a somewhat disreputable looking used car lot outside of

Nashua. After a conversation that took entirely too long by Kayla's estimation, and a shocking lack of request for identification, they were able to sell the car for seven hundred seventy-five dollars in cash and cab fare into town. They got into the taxi and headed to the train station.

"Two tickets to Washington, DC, please," Kayla said to the ticket agent.

"DC? But I thought we were…" Quinn interjected.

Kayla cut him off with a squeeze of his hand before he could finish the thought. "Yes, Washington, DC. One way."

"A train leaves from Boston's South Station at ten seventeen. The last local train leaves for Boston in twenty minutes from track three. That'll be two hundred and thirty-seven dollars," said the gray-haired, spectacled matron behind the Plexiglas fronted ticket booth, in a voice that communicated ever so clearly that she had spent a lifetime behind that glass.

Quinn paid for the tickets and the pair walked off to track three to wait, each carrying a backpack across their shoulders with Quinn holding his guitar case carefully enough to avoid bumping the few other people in the station. They sat in awkward silence for a few minutes, each facing forward, before tripping over each other in an effort to fill the uncomfortable space with conversation.

"What do you make of all this?" Quinn asked.

"So what do you think is going on?" Kayla asked at the same time. "Sorry, you go first." Kayla glanced at Quinn as they again talked over each other.

"Sorry, you were saying?" Quinn chuckled and paused, waiting for Kayla to re-start her thought. Another glance her way showed that she was waiting for him to continue. He laughed again. "Why is this all weird now?" he asked, gesturing between them.

"I don't know, but it definitely is, right?" Kayla agreed with a small laugh, grateful that the tension had been broken.

Quinn was quiet for a moment and said, "You know, this is the first peaceful minute we've had together since the police showed up on our porch. Before they arrived, we couldn't spend twenty minutes together without fighting. Since we heard about the accident, we've been on the same team, dealing with grief, strange phone calls, hidden rooms, rushing around – to say nothing about the house blowing up! Now that we have nothing to do for a few minutes, I'm not sure we know how to interact."

Kayla stared at the lines on the tile floor for a minute, then shifted her focus to watch a small gray mouse run across the track. "I think you're right. Have you always been so smart?" she asked with a look up at him.

"Well, I don't know about that," he said shaking his head dismissively.

"No, you probably have been and it's one of the things about you that annoys me. You're really insightful." Kayla looked up to see their train coming in from a distance. She stood to shrug her bag back onto her shoulders and said, "You know, even though we've gone to the same school for three years and lived in the same house for three months, I don't think we know each other very well at all. I mean, I really don't know anything about you except that you're tall, you like music and pizza, and you lost your parents when you were young too."

"Yeah, I think that's fair. I don't know much about you either. Why don't we try to put aside everything we think we know about each other and work together?" He held out his hand in a let's-start-over kind of gesture.

"From now on, we are a team," Kayla said as she offered her hand and they shook on it.

"Déjà vu," Quinn said with a slight shudder.

"What?!" Kayla asked, spinning around to look at him. "Oh, right," she said almost immediately, seeing his silly expression. "I said it in the car earlier. You were still in shock from the explosion."

"Oh. OK," Quinn said, a bit perplexed as he boarded the train behind her. He bobbed his head at her in a manly sort of upward nod saying, "Hey, why did you buy tickets to Washington, DC if we're going to Philadelphia?"

"Oh, that. I thought we could take another opportunity to confuse anyone who might be following us. This way, only you and I know our real destination."

"I still don't think anybody's following us but I suppose there is nothing wrong with being careful, although it probably cost more," Quinn answered.

"Oh, yeah. I didn't think of that," Kayla admitted, mentally noting that she'd have to pay closer attention to how they spent their money than she had typically done in the past.

They selected seats, stowed their bags and settled down for this first leg of their five-hour trip, each absorbed with trying to figure out what was going on. Both of them were completely unaware that the bespectacled ticket matron had made a phone call to top off her retirement fund and give her enough money to finally leave her Plexiglas prison behind.

"They boarded a train for Boston out of Nashua and will be going on to Washington, DC," she said once the call connected.

"Excellent," was the reply. She made arrangements to collect her fee, unaware that she was actually trading her plastic prison for a pine box six feet under.

****

After an uneventful change of trains in Boston, Kayla found herself speeding through Rhode Island and Connecticut. There were not far from New York City now, which was the last stop before they reached Philly. The muffled drone of the train chugging along gave her a sense of security that had been missing for the last eighteen hours.

It was like riding in a cocoon where there was nothing to worry about but staying awake through the repeated *clack, clack, clack* of the train rushing over the tracks. Quinn had given in and fallen asleep shortly after the train started moving. Kayla wanted to sleep. She had been awake since two thirty in the morning, but was too keyed up to rest.

She stared out the window, watching the world slide past for a while, wondering why someone had gone to the trouble to convince them that Jim and Lorelei were dead and wondering what it was that Jim and Lorelei knew but hadn't told either her or Quinn. What had Jim meant when he said, "We are not who you think we are". Who were they, then? As she always did whenever she had questions that she didn't know where to get the answer to, she wished that her mom was around. Her mom – the diary! With a silent *Thanks Mom!* sent heavenward, Kayla leapt from her seat, tripping over Quinn's ridiculously long legs to rummage through her backpack and find the small purple diary. She sat back down, brushed her hand gently across the cover to feel the letters P and J intertwined together on the cover. The diary had been pretty well hidden. Had her mom written the secret of who they were inside it?

Chapter Nine:

Shot by a Finger

Kayla read through her mom's diary. It began on her mom's fifteenth birthday, April 9, 1977. It was filled with the typical things a fifteen-year old girl might write. Kayla felt closer to her mom than she could remember feeling, because Kayla was nearly the same age now as her mom had been when she wrote the diary.

She had written about how felt about classes in school, trouble with her sister, and dreams about a boy she liked. There were fewer than twenty pages with writing on them and they detailed unsurprising stories until she mentioned a fight with her parents about a boy, Victor Livingston.

It seemed there was a bit of a Romeo and Juliet feud going on between Penelope's father and Victor's father. Penny wrote that her mother said that Mr. Livingston was a member of a cult called Lur Babsel. Penny's Dad was part of a group called Denortus and those two groups had been fighting forever. It was so bad, that Penny's mom had insisted that Penny stop seeing Victor in July of 1979.

Clearly that didn't happen, Kayla thought with a snort, *since my last name is Livingston.* She read the last entry.

November 17, 1983

J MONKEYS

*We have escaped Philadelphia, Victor, the baby and I,
but now we know that we can't escape Denortus forever.
We will try to go somewhere remote and build quiet lives
for ourselves and little Jimmy. We will have to be ever
vigilant, for they will find us eventually.*

Kayla looked at the date of the last entry, surprised to
see that the story seemed to break up. What had happened
between July of 1979 and November 1983? *Other than the
arrival of little Jimmy, of course.* Kayla smiled at the idea
of her big brother being referred to as "little Jimmy".

A closer look at the binding of the journal showed that
a lot of pages had been cut out of the book both before and
after the last entry in November 1983. Before she had a
chance to ponder the meaning of either the pages being
removed or the significance of the two groups Mom had
written about, Quinn nudged her in the ribs, gently, but
with enough force to get her attention.

"What's up? I've got to tell you about my Mom's
diary. I'm not sure if it's relevant to us, but,"

Quinn cut her off mid sentence. "Kayla, we can talk
about that later. We're here. Grab your stuff and let's get
off." Quinn carried his pack and guitar case toward the
door, while Kayla snatched up her bag, half-full water
bottle and the diary. She rushed to catch up only to have to
wait in line to get off the train.

"What's with those two guys in the black jackets? The
little guy there and the big guy at the other end of the
bench?" Kayla asked Quinn, tapping him in the back with
her water bottle after a few minutes of shuffling down the
aisle when space permitted. She pointed out the window at
the two men standing about ten feet from each other, but

equally distant from the train. They didn't have any luggage, and didn't seem to be making any efforts to get on the train.

All that she could see was that the tall guy was quite a bit taller than his friend. Even standing so far apart, it was evident that the top of the little guy's head didn't even reach the tall guy's shoulders. They were dressed alike, right down to the dark sunglasses. Tall Guy's hair was a bit darker and a bit shorter than Little Guy's, but otherwise, there wasn't much to distinguish them from each other.

"Yeah. So?" Quinn muttered.

"It looks like they are looking for someone – they keep looking at their sleeve then at the people getting off the train."

"Yeah. You know what's weird about them?" Quinn asked, taking a closer look. "The jackets. See how everyone else on the platform is wearing short sleeves? All the business people have their suit jackets folded on their luggage. It's got to be at least 100 degrees out there. There's no shade and the train must be piping out some heat, right? But those two guys are wearing all black and have those jackets zipped up. Do you think they are hiding something in their coats?" Quinn asked leaning over Kayla to peer out the window a little more closely, bumping her head with his guitar case.

"What do you mean, like a gun? Do you think they are looking for us?" Kayla whipped her head around to look at Quinn, nearly whacking her head on the case again.

"I don't know…Oh – look! They stopped that really tall kid with hair like mine, then let him go when they got a closer look at him. Yeah, I think they *are* looking for us."

J MONKEYS

"What should we do?" Kayla asked frantically slinking down behind Quinn.

"I don't know. Wait! They're getting on the train. Grab your bag, let's go!" Quinn and Kayla pushed their way past the two businessmen ahead of them and exited in a flash, jumping down to the platform.

They ducked behind a couple of soda machines and waited the minute until the train conductor yelled, "All aboard!" The train started slowly moving again and was gaining some speed as it pulled away, when Kayla saw the two guys on the train looking at Quinn through a window. Tall Guy pointed at Quinn, while Little Guy put a cell phone to his ear. Tall Guy made a gun out of his finger and thumb, pointing it at Quinn and pulled the pretend trigger as the train rolled out of sight.

"OhmyGod!" Kayla exclaimed. "They *were* after us. Did you see that? He pretended to shoot you. Let's get out of here!"

Chapter Ten:

A Pineapple Welcome

Quinn glanced at Kayla, noticing how her face drained of color first, then flushed beet red as she got more flustered. Her eyes looked like giant goofy glasses that had the eyes painted on the outside. He reached out a hand to her shoulder to calm her down, although he was a bit freaked out himself.

"Little Guy was on the phone as they pulled away. I think they would expect us to take the next train out of town. Let's stay here and carry on with our plan, but let's lay low." Quinn spoke calmly, but with some urgency and couldn't stop seeing Tall Guy and his pretend gun playing over and over in his mind. The thing that really sent a chill down Quinn's spine was that as he pulled the "trigger," he had winked at Quinn – as if to let him know that it wasn't over yet. "Let's at least get out of the train station, though. And fast, they know we're here now."

Quinn rushed from the platform into the main lobby of the 30th Street train station and headed over to the information booth, dragging Kayla behind him by the hand. "We're looking for a youth hostel?" Quinn asked the woman behind the counter, as he skidded to a stop by lightly crashing into the booth. He hoped that she would tell them how to find the Last Tain and a couple of others so that he didn't have to tell her which one he was looking for. It would be better not to leave too easy of a trail to follow.

The red-haired old woman held her hands up in a whoa-there-what's-your-hurry sort of way, then took several seconds to locate and don the reading glasses dangling from a chain around her neck. "Most of the hostels are full because of the rally, but you could try the Bank St. Hostel. Take the blue SEPTA line out to 2nd Street. The Hostel's on the corner of Bank and 3rd. The Cherry St. hostel is over that way, too. And of course, the Last Tain is over off Elfryth's Alley."

She drew on a map of the city as big as a placemat, somewhat obscuring the print beneath her doodles, circling the blue line, the 2nd Street stop and the location of the hostels. With a quick thanks, they took the "place-map" and walked away, anxious to get out of the building immediately.

They bought subway cards and got on the blue subway line as quickly as they could, trying to blend in with a crowd of tourists. "It smells like Boston," Kayla mumbled. Quinn sniffed, catching a whiff of that perfume unique to cities, a combination of sewage, stagnant water and trash, with a hint of urine. They stood, holding onto a pole, while the train rocked left and right on its tracks, hurling toward the next station. "So, what's a youth hostel?" Kayla asked, as soon as they were back on the street and able to hear once again.

THE CORDOVAN VAULT

"They're cheap, no frills places for young people to stay when they travel. They're really common in Europe and the major cities in the US have them, too."

"Oh. Can you believe that I've never been out of New England before? Well, Jim did take me to Disney World in Florida when I was ten, but we flew straight to Orlando from Boston."

"Really? You know, Lorelei and I moved around a lot before we settled in Granby." Quinn and Kayla continued their journey, walking the few blocks north, amazed at the variety of shops they walked past. There was a store called Suits that sold, oddly enough, suits. There was an art gallery, a small grocery store – more like a big convenience store really – a souvenir shop, store after store with no houses in sight.

"Where does everyone live? I don't see any houses or condos or anything," Kayla asked as they walked along.

Quinn looked at her with a raised eyebrow. He'd never thought of himself as particularly worldly before, but he didn't think he'd ever been so wet-behind-the-ears as to think that everybody lived in a house. "Um, I'm pretty sure that a lot of the space above the stores is apartment space."

Kayla mumbled something that sounded like "oh" as they continued walking.

"Here's Elfryth's Alley."

They turned the corner onto Elfryth's Alley and were amazed at the difference in the view. It was like stepping back in time. The street was narrow and made of old cobblestones, smooth, round rocks like those found in a stream or river. Centuries of grass tried to grow between the stones, but the constant trampling of car and foot traffic kept it down.

Both sides of the street were lined with a row of brick houses all stuck together like condominiums. A few small trees grew in the front of the houses, flat against the buildings themselves. Many of the houses were covered in ivy, the green making a pretty contrast to the red brick buildings. None of the houses had screen doors, but rather were fronted by old looking wooden doors in a variety of colors. The sounds of traffic and city life found at either end of the Alley were muffled by the structure of the alleyway itself.

"Wow, this is beautiful!" Kayla exclaimed. "Look at this little courtyard. Quinn, are you coming?" Quinn was standing near the entrance of the alley reading a sign.

"Yeah." Quinn jogged down to Kayla, careful on the uneven street. He carried the weight of his backpack and guitar case lightly, but noticed that Kayla kept tugging at her pack as if it was getting really heavy and beginning to chafe at her neck.

He spun her around to face him and tugged at the chest strap of her pack. "If you tighten this strap, it'll feel lighter. I was reading that sign. It says that Elfryth's Alley is the oldest continually inhabited street in the city. It was part of the original Swedish settlement of this area in the 1630's. That's pretty neat."

Quinn looked at the courtyard in amazement. An archway of vines grew in a gap between two buildings, making a short covered walkway that opened up into an historic courtyard with the old community well pump in it. No sound could be heard and except for the sight of modern patio furniture, Quinn felt like he had stepped into the past.

They continued down toward Front Street and came upon a tiny sign and an alleyway so narrow that they couldn't walk next to each other. The sign read "Skyler Path".

"After you," Kayla said.

"No, no. Ladies first." Quinn gestured for Kayla to go first. Unlike the prior path with the quaint tree-covered walkway, this little street had no visible lights or modern furniture. The buildings along Elfryth's Alley on the right and left of the path entrance were wider on the second floor than on the ground floor so that they touched, creating a roof of sorts over the entrance to Skyler Path.

Beyond the building-roof, stood a huge old tree. The branches reached past the top of the three-story buildings, and the trunk was wider around than Quinn and Kayla standing back to back. The combination of the building structure and the ancient tree made the alley dark enough that it was like walking into blackness.

"And they say chivalry is dead...no, I think you should lead." Kayla scuttled behind him.

With a huff and a sideways glare, he started down the darkened path. The gloomy shade soon ended and they could see a small patch of blue sky where the alley opened into a nearly empty courtyard. The only thing in it was a seven-foot high wall, overrun with ivy. In the center of the wall there was a wrought iron gate, with a giant black iron pineapple in the center of the two doors.

Behind the gate, twenty feet away, they could see a narrow, double door entrance to a building, also painted black. A chain hung along the front of the gate with a faded, hand-painted sign that read "ring for hospitality" dangling below the pineapple. "I guess this is it," Kayla said. She pulled the chain and heard a sound like an actual bell jingling inside the building.

It seemed that a minute had gone by and Kayla was reaching for the chain to ring again, when they heard, "Hold your horses! I'm acomin'.

The door was pulled open and a shriveled, old man came into view. He was stooped with age, his shoulders bent inward, and nearly bald with a few hairs attempting to cover an otherwise shiny and smooth landscape. His clothes were neat, but decades out of fashion and time had dulled the original color of his shirt and pants to a dusky gray. All in all, he resembled an old turtle, hunched over, crusty and slow. "Whaddaya want, girly?" he asked, shouting across the courtyard from the stoop.

"Um, is this the Last Tain?" Kayla called back, hesitantly.

"Ayaap. Whaddaya want?" the old man growled at them.

"We're looking for a place to stay. Do you have any rooms available?"

"Jus' one. Are youse marrit? Don' look marrit. Ya brother and sister?" He stumbled off the porch, down a couple steps and shuffled toward them to look at Quinn intently, his dark eyes peering from under a serious brow.

"No, sir," Quinn said, sensing that the old man would immediately see through a lie but might be willing to help them if he knew the whole story. "We're not really related, but my sister is married to her brother. They're missing,

but we think they were staying here. Jim and Lorelei
Livingston? And we need a place to stay," he said as an
afterthought, thinking that the old man might be more
willing to talk with them if they were paying customers.

"Quinn! Don't you think you should be a bit more
discreet?" Kayla did her best to speak like a ventriloquist,
without moving her lips and mumbling under her breath,
hoping that age had limited the man's hearing.

"Ha! I may be old, girly, but I'm trustworthy enough,"
the old man laughed as Quinn moved his hand to subtly
wave Kayla's comment off. "Ya'll give me your word that
ya won' be doin' anythin ya shouldn't?"

"Yes, sir," Quinn answered promptly, not really sure
what he was talking about.

"Ya'll shake on it? Ya know a man ain't worth the dirt
to bury 'im if he don' keep his word. Integrity, ya know.
Cain't do nuthin' without it."

Quinn reached his hand out to the man, nodding. Not
to be left out, Kayla stuck her hand out as well. The old
man laughed again and shook both their hands as he opened
the pineapple gate and lead them through the courtyard
across the threshold and into a common room. The
building was old and quaint from the outside, but dirty and
rundown on the inside. The common room had twelve
tables in it, each with two to four chairs around it and most
were littered with dirty dishes.

"This is a bed and breakfas' type hostel, so I serve
breakfas' in here from six thirty to eight in the morning,"
he gestured to the cluttered, dingy room. "I lock the doors
at nine thirty at night. If you're not inside by then, you'll
be out for the night. I'm an old man and cain't be flittin'

around late, lettin' people in an all. It'll be thirty dollars a night for the room. Do my rules seem all right to ya? If not, youse can find another place to stay." The old man stood behind a battered bar, complete with a huge pitted old mirror behind it, waiting for a response. He stated his rules matter-of-factly and so quickly it was clear that he'd recited them over and over through the years. Obviously, he didn't care if they chose to go elsewhere.

"That'll be fine, sir," Kayla said, mirroring the respectful tone that had served Quinn so well a few minutes earlier.

"I have a couple of questions," Quinn interjected. "First, what's your name?"

"Barris Keltsea."

"Nice to meet you Mr. Keltsea, I'm Quinn Wexford and this is Kayla Livingston." Quinn gestured to Kayla.

"Wexford an' Livingston, eh?" Mr. Keltsea looked closely at the pair, noting Quinn's emerald green eyes, with their calm, steady gaze and Kayla's clear blue ones flitting about the room, taking in everything she saw and filing it away. "Ayap. Your kin checked in a coupla days back. Ain't seen hide nor hair of 'em since. Wha' was your other question, boy?"

"Would you like a hand with these breakfast dishes? We'd be happy to help out if you could show us where to stow our bags." Quinn looked at Kayla questioningly and interpreted her shrug and slight nod as willingness to pitch in.

Mr. Keltsea took a step back and looked them up and down. Kayla stood a little straighter and tossed her hair over her shoulder. "Willing to work are ya? I'll tell ya what, hows about youse help me out with the breakfas' every mornin' and the tidyin' up after? Add in a couple of hours a day helpin' me clean out the basement and I'll let you stay for the week for free."

"That would be great!" Quinn said, happy not to have to drain money from their small fund.

"Wonnerful! I'm sellin' the place; cain't keep it up like I could when the missus was alive. My daughter is comin' from Seattle next week to help me settle up. Be a he'p if youse could get that basement packed up. Ain't been down there in some years; stairs is too steep. Wish I could hire some men to do it all for me, but cain't afford it. Willin' to barter though."

Mr. Keltsea asked them to sign the guest register. Kayla scanned the names on the page while Quinn signed, quickly finding Jim's cramped writing a few lines above Quinn's pen. Jim and Lorelei had been in room eight.

Mr. Keltsea assigned them a room, and rustled around in a drawer behind the counter looking for the key. "Room twelve is at the top of the stairs. Bathroom's at the end of the hall. Youse can drop your bags off and come on down to clear up. Kitchen's through there." He pointed a thumb over his shoulder at a pair of doors behind the bar and shuffled around the bar to a door off the common room.

"Nice job on the free room, Quinn," Kayla said when they were alone at the top of the stairs. Quinn nodded in acknowledgment of the complement as he fought to get the key in the lock on their room door. The hallway was dimly lit, but the need for a thorough cleaning was obvious. The floor was a dark wood that may have once been shiny, but not in recent memory. There were dark paintings hanging here and there along the corridor, and more then a few places where a lighter shade of dinge showed the original "white" of the wall before a long-hung painting was removed, adding to the air of decay. Quinn finally got the door open and the change in air pressure in the hallway sent gauzy cobwebs floating in each corner.

"Dibs on the top bunk," Quinn said. He propped his bag in the corner closest to the door with a thud and gently laid the guitar case on the bed. The room was sparsely furnished. Twin sized bunk beds were stacked against the right wall. There was a small desk-like side table against the left wall and in the corner next to it there was a mirrored stand with a large bowl fitted into a round cut out. A large pitcher designed to match the bowl sat on a shelf below.

Since room twelve was on the corner of the house, they had two windows, one by the old-time "sink" with the pitcher and one at the end of the beds, close to the door. A couple more old paintings hung on the walls, similar at first glance, to those in the hallway. They were dark with age, so that even when you looked closely, you couldn't tell what they might have originally looked like.

"That's fine by me," Kayla said, replying to Quinn's bed choice announcement and surveying the tiny room. "You did notice that there's no ladder, right? Though, I guess it's not as much of a problem when you're eleven feet tall." She stood her pack next to Quinn's.

"Hardly. Come on, let's do dishes!" Quinn stepped out of the room and started back down the stairs.

"Why so anxious to clean? Have you seen your bedroom at home? That explosion probably helped it."

THE CORDOVAN VAULT

It was true that, generally, Quinn was quite a slob. He liked to do yard work, but that was more like painting with living things. The yard was a canvas and he could make it look however he wanted. His bedroom was a just place to store stuff. Why put it away when you'd have to take it out again later?

"The faster we get that common room cleared up, the faster we can start trying to find Lorelei and Jim. Mr. K might be in the mood to lend us a key to their room after we do something for him."

Back downstairs, they looked around the common room and decided to divide and conquer. Kayla took a stack of dishes to the kitchen and started washing. Quinn carried the rest of the dishes into the kitchen with a few trips, then found a relatively fresh hand towel and some squirty stuff to clean the tables.

Once the tables and chairs were clean, and a few of them had been really grimy, he flipped the chairs onto the tabletops and searched for a broom. Sweeping really only made the floor moderately better. Quinn went back to kitchen to find a mop and bucket.

The kitchen was a good-sized square room, lined with restaurant type appliances. There were two swinging doors behind the end of the bar in the common room – one swung into the kitchen, the other swung out. Inside the kitchen, there was a long stainless steel counter on the right with a grill and oven. The wall opposite the doors had a giant sink with more stainless steele counter space on either side.

An enormous pile of dirty dishes sat to the left of the sink. There was a much smaller pile of clean dishes to the right, drying.

The left wall had four doorways. One was a walk-in refrigerator, one was a walk-in freezer, the third led to a butler's pantry for storing the dishware and cleaning supplies. A plethora of plastic pineapples cascaded down on Quinn's head when he was rummaging around for mopping equipment. Thank God they weren't heavy.

The fourth door led to a dry and canned goods pantry. Kayla was standing in the middle of the kitchen, looking at a TV mounted to the wall next to the 'out' door.

"What's this? I'm slaving away and you're watching TV?" Typical, Quinn thought.

She glanced at Quinn and smiled guiltily. "I found the remote and flipped on the news." Kayla gestured toward the TV, sending a handful of suds onto the floor. "Don't slip," she said, as she turned back to the sink.

"What's the news?" Quinn asked, filling his bucket with water.

"There was mention of a gang of art thieves on the loose. Something about break-ins in a less than stellar part of town. And the heat wave continues, apparently adding fervor to the environmentalists who are considered a bunch of hot-heads already."

"What environmentalists?"

"I wasn't really paying too much attention, but there's some rally in town. I guess people have come from all over the country to protest global warming, or something. They are over at Independence Park."

"Oh. I'm going to mop the common room floor, then tidy up the bar area. How are you doing in here?"

"I've cleaned the counters and started washing dishes. I need about another half an hour."

"Okay, I'll be back." Quinn walked through the out door with the bucket and mop.

****

Forty minutes later, Mr. Keltsea came back to check on the kids' progress. "I guess yous'll be worth the free room and board after all. The common room and kitchen are cleaner than they been in years.

"Thanks. What's with all the pineapples?" Kayla asked, gesturing toward the butler's pantry.

"Ever'body knows pineapples're the symbol of hospitality. The king o' Hawaii gave a pineapple ta one of them English explorers as a welcome. All throughout the colonial times, the pineapple was a symbol of welcome. At a party, you had a pineapple on the table. When the hostess wanted everyone to leave, she took the pineapple away to let people know the party was over."

"OK, but why do you have so many?" she persisted.

"The misses liked to use 'em as centerpieces or some such nonsense. Said her family had always used 'em. That's why they're on the fence gate." Mr. K changed the subject to the topic he had wanted to discuss. "Ya said yer kin was missing. How do ya know that? They got here the day before yesterday. Could be they're in their room right now. I got an extra key some'er." He shuffled around in a couple of drawers, pushing aside papers and old registers and things. After a minute, he found a key to room eight. "It's a few doors down the hall from youse."

Quinn took the key from Mr. Keltsea and turned to run up the stairs, as if expecting to find Jim and Lorelei sitting on their own bunk beds. Kayla caught up to him on the landing and together they dashed down the hall past three ugly old paintings to room eight. Quinn opened the door with a little too much force. It banged against something in the room and snapped closed. He opened it again, a bit more carefully and stepped into the room with a gasp.

Kayla pushed her way around him, since he was blocking the whole door where he stood looking at the room. Instead of bunk beds, this room had a double bed in the center of the right wall with small night tables on either side of it. The desk and 'sink' were on either side of the door to the room. They also had a window and some tired artwork.

What caused Quinn's surprise, wasn't the furniture, however. It was the state of the room. There were clothes and things strewn every which way. The drawers to the nightstands were open, the sheets on the bed were rumpled and pillows had been tossed on the floor.

"Newlyweds," Mr. Keltsea said with disdain from the open doorway, shaking his head at the condition of the room.

Quinn gave a small jump of surprise, he hadn't heard Mr. Keltsea arrive. "There's no way Lorelei left the room looking like this," Quinn said. "Did the police come through here?"

"Nope, I didn't know anything about anything until youse mentioned it."

"So who's been in here?

"No one. The missus always cleaned every room each day, but I haven't kept up on it." Clearly, he felt the need to be defensive. "She'd never of allowed a room to look like this one, newlywed or no! Shameful."

"Someone has been through this room. Lorelei would never leave a room looking like this," Quinn said again, in defense of his sister. "From the time our parents died, until the minute she left on this vacation, Lorelei's been fastidious about taking care of our things. I'm a slob, not Lorelei. No way."

"I tell ya, I've two keys to each room plus my master set," he gestured to the ring of keys on his belt. "You've got one key and that fella and his missus have the other."

"You're right Mr. K," Kayla said as she walked him out the room door. "I'm sure they didn't think about putting stuff away when they left. Typical young married couple on their honeymoon. We'll clean it all up." She closed the door behind him, then waved Quinn quiet when he started to speak. After a couple of minutes, they heard Mr. Keltsea shuffle down the hallway.

"What was that nonsense? There is no way my sister would..."

"Of course not," Kayla interrupted. "I just wanted to get rid of him. Think for a minute. Jim's crazy organized. He couldn't stand this room for as long as it would take to get like this! Someone had to have come through and tossed it."

"But who? Why? And how?"

"All good questions." Kayla started to pick up and fold clothes absentmindedly "The only idea I have relates to 'how'. I guess either Mr. K knows more than he's saying or whoever tossed the room got the key from Jim and Lorelei. Unless, of course, they picked the lock." Kayla snatched up a pair of underwear from the floor. She folded it and tucked it under clothes she'd already folded.

Quinn sat heavily in the chair at the desk. Seeing the room this way made it clear to him that something bad was happening, something dangerous, even deadly. Somehow, the destruction of their house wasn't as devastating as seeing this room with Lorelei and Jim's things strewn about. The gouges on his cheek from the explosion made his face ache. He watched as Kayla scurried around the little room picking up clothes, brushes, and pieces of paper. He saw her tuck another pair of Lore's undies under a shirt and decided at that moment that he needed to make a fresh start with Kayla.

Quinn had played a good tune earlier about forgiving the past, but that was in the terror of emergency. Who knew how long that would last? But he did know that anyone who cared enough about his sister to try to preserve her dignity by hiding fancy, I'm-on-my-honeymoon-skivvies from him deserved his respect. He got up to help and silently vowed that they'd figure out what was going on, together.

When they had cleared the room of Livingston belongings, made the bed and tidied up, Quinn asked, "What do you think we should do?"

"Let's put their luggage in our room and go for a walk. If Mr. K was involved in this, maybe we shouldn't be here when we form our plans."

"Good idea. Plus, I'm hungry."

Kayla laughed. "Me too. Let's get something to eat and make some plans."

****

Later that evening, Quinn lay curled up on his top bunk replaying the last thirty-six hours in his mind. He was more tired than he could ever remember being, but couldn't turn his mind off enough to get to sleep. Over a Philly cheese-steak sandwich that was as good as expected, here in the home of the cheese-steak, he and Kayla had talked about what they could do to find Lorelei and Jim. After the scare of thinking that they were dead, he was so thrilled to know that Lorelei was alive that it was hard to concentrate on figuring out what she wanted him to do.

Instead, he lay in his bunk, staring at the wall, where he could make out the outline of the mirror in the scant light that came through the small holes in the old window shade. He thought about the plans they had made for tomorrow.

After their breakfast duties, which started at 5:30 am, they would spend a couple of hours in Mr. K's basement and be done by eleven o'clock. The next step was to comb through Lorelei and Jim's stuff and look for some clue about where they might be. Kayla thought that if they went to the places the lovebirds had been and saw the things they had seen, something might seem out of the ordinary. Kayla wanted to re-read her mom's diary. The stuff about those two groups was odd, but given the house exploding and the two guys at the train station, Quinn was ready to believe anything.

A light snore from below reminded him that he needed to sleep. They had been running on adrenaline since early that morning and they needed to be up early tomorrow. Quinn rolled onto his left side, trying to get comfortable amid his bruises and scrapes, and brought the blanket up to his chin. His last thought before drifting off was to hope that wherever she was, Lorelei had a warm blanket too.

Chapter Eleven:
The Philly Ice-Age

Promptly at five thirty in the morning, Kayla and Quinn yawned their way into the kitchen. Mr. Keltsea was bustling around the newly cleaned room, as much as a man of his advanced years could bustle. Breakfast was simple fare: pastries from the bakery around the corner, a fruit platter, and juice. Coffee and tea stations had to be stocked and prepared, too. He handed them each a long white apron and Quinn volunteered to fetch the pastries. Kayla was finishing an apron-string bow when Mr. K plunked a vat of fresh fruit down on the counter in front of her.

Before the hour was over, everything had been prepared to his satisfaction. "Tomorrow, youse'r on your own. I'm gonna sleep late for the first time in more'n fifty-seven years."

"Is that how long you've been here?" Kayla asked. "Did you build the Last Tain?"

"Naw, I married the missus fifty-seven years ago last November. The Tain's been in her family since before the war."

"World War II?" Quinn asked, making another pot of coffee.

Mr. Keltsea blinked at Quinn and shook his head. "The War for Independence. I wouldn't be so broke up about selling if'n we was only here since WWII." He rubbed the bar like it was a favorite dog. "Benjamin Franklin, hisself, sat at this very bar, you know. Bes' we kin figure, the Tain was built some time around 1690. Always been in the family, pass'd down. But now, none of the family wants it. Doesn't make enough money for all the work that youse gotta put into it. Well, youse come get me at 9:00 and I'll tell ya what I want done down in the basement. I'll be in my sittin' room." He slowly made his way back to his rooms, muttering, "World War II. Kids cain't tell the difference between something that's sixty years old and something that's more'n three hundred! Humph."

Quinn shrugged at Kayla, seemingly unconcerned with Mr. K's disappointment in their lack of perception. He went to open the doors for the guests as Kayla brought out the last tray of pastries.

Breakfast was uneventful. There were more people staying at the Last Tain than there seemed, however. About twenty people came to eat. Most of them were younger than thirty years old and the main topic of discussion was the rally. The most important of all of this week's speakers was to be heard today. Kayla scarcely paid any attention to the conversation going on around her. She and Quinn were trying to keep up with the dishes and things so that they would be almost finished by the time breakfast was over. They were anxious to discharge their duties and get to the real meat of the day – starting to look for Jim and Lorelei.

THE CORDOVAN VAULT

When breakfast was over, Mr. Keltsea sent them down to the basement with the instructions to "get it cleaned up". Surprisingly, the basement was only accessible from the outside through a tiny hatchway and steep stone steps, more like a ladder than a flight of stairs. Quinn was the first one down. "Oh. My. God." he stated as he flipped on the light.

Kayla joined him in shock at the bottom of the stairs. "So much for the disgrace of Jim and Lorelei's room."

They seemed to be standing in the only open space. Beyond them was a sea of stuff. There was no other word for it. Just stuff, everywhere. Stuff piled on top of more stuff. "This is…I don't even know how to describe this. I've never seen a mess like this. It's like a piled up version of tornado aftermath," Kayla whispered in horrified awe.

"I don't think this family ever threw anything away. All three hundred and twenty years of crap is still in this basement." Quinn looked around, wondering how to begin the monumental task of organizing the avalanche of junk.

They started by clearing a walkway down the center. As it was, there was no place to move, let alone sort things. By stacking boxes as high as Quinn could reach, they were able to open up enough space to begin. The basement was about thirty feet long and about half as wide. The ceiling was low; Quinn reached it easily. They stacked chairs on top of old sofas, with ottomans on top of the upside down chairs.

A few spare mattresses were tossed on top of that. Two old bookcases were dug out, and lined up back to back to be used as sorting space. They moved old bicycles next to each other, with a really old cabinet-style TV wedging the bikes against the wall. Then there were the trunks and luggage. There were at least a hundred suitcases in styles going back a lot of years. There were backpacks, rolling luggage, soft-sided, hard-sided, and light weight bags so heavy Kayla couldn't lift them. The trunks were just as bad, although there were not quite so many, maybe only fifty. They were made of wood and leather ranging in size from twice the size of a shoebox to the size of a coffee table.

They opened some of the older cases, unsurprised to see that they had apparently been abandoned. "Maybe we should ask Mr. K what he wants to do with the stuff in these before we open them all," Kayla remarked.

After two hours of heavy lifting, they had managed to carve the beginnings of order from chaos, at least in one small area. They climbed the ladder-stairs, happy to be back in the fresh air outside the building. Kayla stretched her back, unused to that type of labor.

They rested for a short while in the old courtyard. It was really quite pretty. There were four raised garden beds scattered among the cobbles. The garden bed fence designs depicted scenes on each side, like boats arriving on land and someone being greeted by native people with pineapples. Another showed the Liberty Bell and presumably other things of local historic significance. One whole garden bed looked to have a mix of deities from various cultures. Quinn and Kayla identified Egyptian, Greek/Roman, Norse, Celtic, Native American, and Buddhist.

The final bed depicted nature, flora and fauna in the four seasons. The designs were very ornate and incredibly detailed for something that was left out in the weather. The garden beds themselves were in desperate need of pruning and weeding, but it seemed that each had flowering bushes and herbs filling the bed in a way achieved only by decades of growth. The overall effect was pretty, in a wild way. The perfume, a combination of flowers and herbs, was somewhere between lovely and overpowering, depending on the breeze.

Once they had relaxed and recharged for a few minutes, Quinn and Kayla set out to begin solving the mystery that Jim and Lorelei had left them. Sure, it was a race to find and protect information, according to Jim, but what information? Protect it from whom? Where should they look for it? These were questions that Kayla wished Jim had left answers to on that DVD. If time was so critical, then why didn't he leave them more concrete information to go on? It was frustrating.

They searched Jim and Lorelei's belongings and found a guidebook to Philadelphia. One of them, and Kayla was ready to bet it was Jim, had highlighted some of the sights. Many of them had notes written in the margin. It seemed that someone wrote their impression of each sight after they had visited it. Some were written by Jim and others by Lorelei. Without anything else to go on, Quinn and Kayla decided to go see the things that Jim and Lorelei had seen, and planned to see.

According to the guidebook, the Rodin Museum of Art had the best collection of Rodin sculpture found outside of France. They decided to start there because the note in the book was odd – there was a big yellow checkmark across all the writing and one word was highlighted – plaster.

J MONKEYS

They took the Phlash Visitor bus, which was a neat blue trolley that cost only a dollar and drove all over town. After paying the museum's entrance fee, they passed through a metal detector to get in. A woman sifted through Kayla's purse and Quinn had to empty his pockets into a plastic bucket. When they asked about the security, the woman mentioned something about shutting the barn door after the horses were gone, then asked them to move along so she could admit the folks behind them.

Rodin was mainly a sculptor. They wandered around for an hour and Kayla thought the most interesting display was a wall, about ten feet long, that was polka-dotted with round plaster discs. Each disc depicted a different image in relief. Some were animals, some were flowers or trees, some were people in various costume. Some discs had simple scenes like a ship on the sea or people climbing a mountain.

The plaque at the beginning of the exhibit noted that Rodin had sculpted hundreds of these discs. They were the most easily purchased of his work. Because there were so many in existence, they weren't terribly valuable, but were interesting because these discs seem to have been some of his practice work for more famous pieces.

Quinn sat on a bench opposite the polka-dot wall, shifting and fidgeting. He sighed and glanced at his watch. "Are you ready to go yet?" Kayla glanced over at Quinn to be sure he hadn't been replaced by a whining little girl. "You've been looking at those stupid discs for fifteen minutes."

Kayla shook her head and walked over to sit next to him. "These don't look familiar to you? We had a few things like this hanging on the gallery wall," Kayla said, referring to the second floor balcony in the Livingston house, outside of the bedrooms.

"I vaguely remember them. They were between your room and Jim's, right? Were those done by Rodin?" Quinn asked.

"I don't know. I barely remember what was on them. They were always there, so I never really looked at them, you know? The note here says that Rodin's discs were readily available for purchase, so maybe ours were his."

"Too bad. They were probably destroyed in the explosion. I still don't understand why we have to study these. Can't we move on? I'm bored."

"I swear, you're like a spoiled child. OK, baby. Let's go. Do you need to use the potty before we head out?" Kayla's sing-songy tone and goo-goo gaa-gaa noises earned her a disgusted look. As they headed out of the museum, they were subjected to a search similar to the one they had to go in.

"What's this all about?" Quinn asked a different guard at the door.

"We had a break in last week. We can't take any chances; sorry for the inconvenience, sir," she replied automatically as she processed him out.

Once outside the museum, Quinn stretched and sucked in a deep lungful of air. It was a beautiful day, not too hot, which was a rarity for July in a city practically on the Mason-Dixon line. The sky was nearly Windows' blue with a couple of Simpsons' clouds. With the green trees and the red brick buildings, Philadelphia looked like a painting by a gifted child. Only the au'd city and the noise challenged the senses. To take advantage of nature's gift, they decided to walk the twenty blocks back to the Last Tain.

On the way, they stopped at Independence Mall and wandered among the throng of people milling about the environmental rally. There were small kiosks and tables with information on global warming, the effects of ranching on the global environment and the dire consequences of continuing life with an unchecked carbon footprint. There were petitions to be signed, intended to sway legislators for this and against that. A woman was handing out samples of an environmentally friendly soap and talking about the dangers of chemicals found in modern, commercial soaps.

Happily for hungry teenagers on a tight budget, a bunch of kiosks were handing out samples of organic snacks. The kids were able to collect up a nice selection of organic watermelon, tomatoes and cucumbers, cheese made from cows fed only organically grown grass, a bunch of biodegradable sacks of smoked almonds and even a few slices of delicious ham cured in the traditional colonial style from a pig fed only natural and organic slop.

With their dinner wrapped in environmentally friendly waxed paper, they were able to continue down rows of vendors advertising and offering samples of products that would help decrease the average family's dependence on non-renewable energy. Perhaps the most interesting sight of all was a debate happening all the way down the end of the green. There, two experts were discussing (or rather arguing as heatedly as they could) their points of view.

THE CORDOVAN VAULT

One guy was ranting, very articulately, about how the human race is heading toward the sixth age of extinction, this time due to global climate change instead of an asteroid or biblical flood.

For every point that he made, the other guy had a seemingly logical argument about how global warming was all hype. What Kayla found particularly interesting, was that the guy arguing that the planet was headed toward apocalypse, was saying that global warming could actually bring about a new ice age.

The rise in temperature of even a couple of degrees would be enough to speed up the melting of the polar ice cap so that the influx of cold fresh water would disrupt the Gulf Stream cycle of warm water from the Caribbean flowing toward England and cold water flowing back down. The disruption might be enough to throw Philadelphia, the Northeastern US and Europe into an ice age.

As they wandered back toward the Last Tain, Quinn said, "It seems to me that all this arguing over who's causing climate change is silly. Does it really matter if this is part of a natural cycle or caused by humans? If we, humans I mean, have the power to make even a slight change for the better, doesn't it seem logical that we would do so regardless of the cause?"

Kayla nodded in agreement. "Especially if we can't survive in a world with a dramatically different climate. If that guy was even half right and we're headed to the next "age of extinction" then I think we should try to avoid that. I mean, I don't know about you, but I'd prefer not to be extinct, ya know?"

"Yeah – that sounds bad," Quinn agreed with a laugh, his tone as sarcastic as Kayla's had been. A chill prickled down his neck and spine, snapping off the rest of his laugh. He glanced over his shoulder to see what might have caused it, but he saw nothing unusual in the crowd of people they were leaving behind and dismissed it from his mind. Back at the Tain, they dined on organic, biodegradably packaged snacks and headed to their respective bunks early.

Chapter Twelve:

Best Laid Plans

The breakfast alarm rang early and the next day started out much the same as the last. Quinn ran to the bakery and Kayla flipped on the kitchen TV to hear the morning's news while she prepped breakfast. Quinn arrived with the pastries in time to hear the end of a report about a mugging of a young couple in the subway near the rally and the weather report. A hurricane was making it's way up the coast and expected to hit North Carolina in a few days. If it didn't swerve out to sea, it could bring a couple of inches of rain to the metro Philly area.

After breakfast, when the last cup was washed and the common room floor was drying, Kayla and Quinn sought out Mr. Keltsea. They needed some direction in order to make any more progress with the basement and they were anxious to get that chore out of the way.

"Now that we've got some basic organization started down there, what do you want us to do with all that stuff?" Quinn asked.

Mr. Keltsea scratched his head. "Don' know. Cain't afford to have it hauled away. What all is down there?"

"Furniture, about six generations of abandoned luggage and a wall of boxes that we haven't opened yet."

Kayla stretched her arms and shoulders as if readying herself for the effort to come.

"I never did like it down there, so dark and damp. Haven't been down them steps in years. It was whispered that the family hid treasure som'ere in the house. I never believed in that, but do you think any of the stuff might be worth somethin'? I gotta clear up the taxes on this place before I can sell it and I don' know how I'm gonna afford it." Mr. Keltsea leaned heavily on the back of a chair in his sitting room.

"I'm sure some of it's valuable," Quinn answered. "We've barely scratched the surface, but the furniture has got to be worth something, at least. I see stuff like that on Antiques Roadshow from time to time."

Kayla turned her head to look up at Quinn with big blinking blue eyes and a curled lip. "You watch Antiques Roadshow?" she asked.

Quinn shrugged. "It's neat to see what people think is valuable and what they think is junk. I like guessing their expectations. You can tell when people are genuinely, happily surprised or if they are putting on a show for the camera."

Mr. Keltsea seemed to consider Quinn's words. "Go through it all. All the luggage, the boxes, ever'thin'. See if youse find anything that seems valuable, and maybe we can sell it for a few bucks." He motioned for them to follow him through the sitting room, back into the common room. At the end of the dining area, in the corner opposite the bar was a door tucked into an alcove. The old man pulled the ring of keys from his belt and shifted past the first seven until he found the one he wanted.

He opened the door to what Quinn had assumed was a closet, and waved them through. Quinn looked around in surprise at the big empty room about the size of a basketball court. Three sides of the room had windows, a bit grimy from disuse and hung with dusty curtains that might have been sheer, before he was born. There were extra tables folded up and leaning against the far wall.

"The misses al'ays called this the ballroom. I've kept it closed since she passed; no need of it. Why don' youse bring some of the stuff up here to organize it all. Must be hard to move thin's around down there." He gave Quinn a spare key to the door and cautioned him to lock it up when they were through.

With those instructions, Quinn and Kayla headed back outside to access the basement. They brought up the two empty bookcases and stood them against a wall in the ballroom. Then each carried a few pieces of luggage up from the basement. After a handful of trips, Kayla stayed to start unpacking while Quinn continued to make trips up from the basement. After forty-five minutes or so, he staggered into the room with a giant old wooden trunk on his back, gently dropped it the floor and collapsed beside it.

He caught his breath for a few minutes and realized that Kayla had made quite a lot of progress while he played Sherpa. She had three tables set up: one that was being used as a workspace, and two that had stacks of clothes on them. She was nesting empty luggage inside other pieces of empty luggage, but had a couple of large suitcases open on the floor under the tables. They were holding shoes. Lots of shoes.

Kayla glanced over at Quinn, tossed him a water bottle and opened the next suitcase. This piece was a modern-looking black garment bag and Kayla pulled out three ladies suits: one black pantsuit, a gray skirt and jacket, and a long black skirt. There were three blouses and a pair of black dress shoes with high, stocky heels. A small bag of jewelry was found in one shoe. She added the clothes to one of the piles she had started on the open tables.

"It seems that the Last Tain wasn't always a place for just young people to stay. I've found a bunch of professional clothing. You know, last year we did a charity drive where we collected business-wear from folks and donated it a group in Boston who recycled it to people trying to break out of a cycle of poverty. I wonder if they have anything similar here in Philly. This stuff looks gently used and in classic styles that don't go out of fashion."

Quinn agreed that it seemed worth looking into. He heaved himself off the floor and set up a couple more tables to open luggage. They organized half of the one hundred and eleven pieces of luggage that had been brought up so far, in order of seeming newness with the newest first.

They had three tables covered with suits and other clothes to be donated to the newly professional, fourteen plastic bags of casual clothes to be donated to the needy, six bags of underwear, socks and other unmentionables to be thrown away and a small pile of jewelry. The jewelry consisted mostly of necklaces, earrings and hairclips, with two sets of shirt studs and cufflinks.

Little of it looked particularly valuable, however, there were several rings that appeared to be gold, a few pair of stud earrings that looked like they might have small gemstones in them and one ring that might be gold with a large ruby.

They had been working for at least two hours and decided to wrap it up. Quinn carried the garbage outside while Kayla prepared some space for the next day. She opened another table near the remaining stack of luggage. They decided to leave the jewelry in a couple of shoe boxes on one of the tables, sorted by type. Necklaces in one box, earrings in another, with anything else that looked valuable in yet another box.

Mr. Keltsea must have heard them closing up the ballroom because he materialized in the common room as Quinn poured two glasses of water at the bar saying, "Whew, I can't believe we've made such a small dent in that luggage."

"What'd youse find?" he asked, settling onto the empty bar stool next to the chair Kayla slouched in, propping her head up with her hand, her elbow resting on the bar.

"So far, not too much. We emptied about sixty of the newer pieces of luggage. We found a bunch of clothes that we thought you could donate to various charities and a bunch of stuff we threw away. There was a little bit of jewelry which we put aside." Kayla finished her water and explained about the charities. "I was thinking that the older suitcases and the trunks likely have vintage clothes in them. People pay a lot of money for vintage stuff. What do you think about having a major tag sale once we get it all organized?"

"I dunno," Mr. Keltsea said, shaking his head and rubbing the back of his neck. "That'd be an awful lot of work. Do youse think it would be worth it?"

"It's hard to guess without having seen what's in the rest of the bags and the boxes, but I think it might be. We should be able to get through the rest of the luggage in another day and through the trunks in one or two more. When is your daughter coming?" Quinn asked.

"I 'spect 'er next week. Prob'ly Tuesdy or Wensdy."

"I'm not sure we could get it all set up in a week, but maybe we could start and your daughter could take over," Quinn offered.

"All righty." Mr. Keltsea turned away and started to shuffle back to his sitting room. Quinn stopped him with another question.

"Sir, I had another idea that I wanted to propose to you, too. I overheard some of the folks at breakfast talking about how there wasn't much in the way of affordable night-life around this area. What do you think about hosting a coffee house in the common room one evening?"

"Too much trouble an' not enough profit," Mr. Keltsea grumbled. "An' I lost my liquor license years ago."

"No, no, not alcohol. Coffee. You already have the cups and stuff that we use at breakfast. When I went to the bakery this morning, I saw that there was a restaurant equipment rental shop on the corner. We could make fancy cappuccinos, lattes and things. I know where you can find a musician who'll work for tips, me!" Quinn spoke quickly, as if he knew Mr. Keltsea would agree if he heard the idea fast enough.

"And I could make and sell the refreshments. I would also work for tips." Kayla liked Quinn's idea. They couldn't spend their evenings looking for Jim and Lorelei, so this way, they had a chance to earn a bit more money. "If you're closing the place in less than two weeks, this could give you a chance to recoup what you've already spent stocking your pantry."

"I *have* got a lot of coffee and tea put back." Mr. Keltsea murmured, rubbing his hand across his chin. He eyed the youngsters critically. They looked earnest, but he was skeptical. "I'm too tiret to be up all hours of the night cookin' an' cleanin'."

"Just leave it all to us," Quinn said, knowing he'd almost gotten the opportunity he'd been working for the last year.

"Well, boy, that covers the trouble. What about the profit?"

Quinn thought quickly, "Anyone who comes to a coffee house is likely to buy a coffee and by eight o'clock at night, most of them might buy a pastry too. Figure that's maybe six dollars a person. If we can get a hundred and fifty people in here between seven and eleven o'clock, that's maybe $1000, pure profit to you."

"How youse gonna get a hunnert and fitty people ta come down here?"

"We'll advertise it at the rally," Kayla answered, channeling Quinn's excitement.

Mr. Keltsea thought about it muttering unintelligibly to himself, before slapping his hand on his knee with a chortling laugh. "All righty. Tomorry's Thursday, so how about ya try this coffee house 'ting on Friday. If youse can clear $750 on Friday, youse can run it on Sunday, too."

A short time later, Quinn and Kayla were back in their room, laying on their respective beds, pooped. "Did we really commit to organizing that whole basement in less than six days?" Kayla asked.

"Yup," Quinn replied from above.

"Did we also commit to planning, organizing and running two four-hour coffee houses later this week?"

"Yup."

"And we've made zero progress toward finding Jim and Lorelei."

"Yup."

"Nor do we have any idea who's trying to kill us or why."

"Yup."

"Is any of this concerning to you?"

"Yup."

"Is that all you can say?"

"Yup."

"I walked right into that didn't I?"

Quinn heard Kayla's bed creak. He rolled onto his right side and hung his head over the side to peak down. She had moved her head and shoulders so that she could see beyond the underside of his bed and was gazing up at him, her right eyebrow arched in question. "I'm feeling a little overwhelmed right now," he said. "'Yup' is all I can manage."

Kayla nodded and shifted back onto her bunk. "Me too."

THE CORDOVAN VAULT

"Listen, it's one thirty. Let's take a break for an hour. Don't worry about any of this stuff. Do something fun and when we re-group in an hour, we'll get some fresh air and I bet we both will have some fresh ideas." Quinn plugged his ear buds into his ears and sifted through his play lists, looking for something fun to listen to. Kayla flipped onto her stomach and picked up the logic puzzle magazine from the floor where she'd left it last night and clicked her mechanical pencil in preparation for a puzzle that didn't have potential life and death consequences.

Later that afternoon, Kayla and Quinn sat on the grass in the park at Christ Church. Kayla had her notepad and mechanical pencil handy, her small day-trip sized backpack detached from the large one and at her side. Quinn watched her fuss with her key ring, trying to get it into a tiny little pocket in the front of the day-pack. He rubbed his hands together and wiggled his fingers, "What are you doing?"

"I always put the keys in the same pocket so that I know where they are. I hate looking around for keys, don't you?"

"Okay, well, that seems a little obsessive-compulsive given everything that's going on," he said dismissively. "Let's tackle each of those other …uh, issues…you mentioned earlier and come up with a plan for each. Most important issue first. Hit me." Kayla looked up at Quinn to see him searching the sky and suspected he was waiting for divine intervention. She threw a loose dirt clod at him, hitting him square in the chest. "I didn't mean literally," he said, brushing dirt off his shirt, half annoyed and half laughing.

Kayla smiled. "Most important first? That's kind of a toss up between How-Do-We-Find-Jim-and-Lorelei and Who's-Trying-To-Kill-Us. Which one you want first?"

"Good point." Quinn bobbed his head back and forth for a few seconds. "Let's go with Who's-Trying-to-Kill-Us. What do we know about that?"

"Our house blew up at three o'clock in the morning the day before yesterday. We saw a dark car speeding away from the house before the explosion and then there were the two guys on the train platform. They obviously knew that we were coming and they were looking for us on the train, so they knew *how* we were arriving. And that guy shot you with his finger when we escaped them."

"Do we have any ideas who they are or why they want to kill us?"

Kayla made notes in her book. "The only thing I can come up with is that both my mom, and Jim and Lorelei said things weren't as they appeared. My mom's diary mentions those two factions or groups, which were opposed to each other, Denortus and Lur Babsel. But it seems like a stretch to think that people are trying to kill us over my grandparents' membership in some clubs."

"Did the guys on the train seem vaguely familiar to you?" Quinn paused for an instant before he noticed Kayla's nod. "Me, too. I don't know why though. Well, I think it's safe to assume that whoever wants to kill us, it's the same people who caused Lorelei and Jim to go missing. Those two things have to be related; it's too much of a coincidence otherwise. Maybe if we work on finding them, they can tell us who's trying to kill us and why. So, let's not bother to try and figure out who the guys on the train were, right now. Let's just avoid them. Next. What clues do we have toward finding Lorelei and Jim?"

"Hold on a second. You know, before we left Maine, we decided not to use our debit cards so that 'They' didn't know we were still alive." Quinn nodded, not sure where she was going with this. "Well, since the incident on the train, they obviously know we are alive and that we are here. We don't have very much money left. Let's go to some ATMs on the other side of town and empty our accounts. Then we'll have more cash to continue our search."

"Good thinking...we should do that right away, well, as soon as we're done here. So what about clues for finding Lorelei and Jim?"

"Very few. Jim and Lorelei's whole change of plan, leaving the wedding reception right when it started and honeymooning at the Last Tain instead of some nice hotel in Hawaii, seems odd. They were sightseeing, but in a somewhat tactical fashion. They kept notes in their guidebook on what they had seen. Who does that? That's crazy organized, even for Jim.

And they had only been here for one day, but the book had a lot of notes, in different color pens. How could they have seen all of that stuff in one day? Also, did you notice that they only seemed to go to art museums? They're in Philadelphia and there's nothing to indicate that they went to see the Liberty Bell, for pete's sake. Can't they take away your citizenship for something like that?"

"That does seem strange. Lorelei doesn't really like art. She doesn't dislike it, but I've really never known her to spend a lot of time staring at old pictures."

"Jim either! So what were they doing?"

"OK, that's all very weird. So what do we do? How do we find them?" Quinn absently picked a wide leafed blade of grass and made a kazoo with it between his thumbs.

"Let's go see a few more of the places they went. Maybe we can find a pattern in the type of exhibits or something. And those police officers who came to our house said that their taxi had gone off a bridge. Maybe we should look into that. Somebody would have been driving, right? And where did this all happen?"

"Yeah, good idea! Let's definitely look into that."

They continued on like this until they had action plans for each of the "issues." The other two commitments were easier to create plans for, as there were obvious and concrete actions they needed to take. They decided to inventory the pantry when they got back to the Last Tain and from there, they would make a list of snacks and desserts they could prepare for the coffee house.

Kayla had seen an old stamp in one of Mr. Keltsea's drawers with the Last Tain and its address on it. They would take the stamp and ink pad over to the rally and stamp people's hands and any papers already attached to light poles and things. They didn't want to create an actual flyer because they didn't want to spend the money, but also because they didn't think handing out hundreds of pieces of junk paper to environmentalists would endear them to the people they hoped to attract. It seemed wasteful, so word of mouth would have to do. They also decided to ask a couple of the folks staying at the Tain if they wanted to help spread the word.

As far as the basement went, they agreed to increase their time down there to three hours a day and work as quickly as they could. Hopefully, they could continue to organize as they went along to increase efficiency. If they didn't have it done by the time Mr. Keltsea's daughter arrived, they'd have to put the job in her hands.

Quinn was still overwhelmed by the amount of work in front of them. Of course, in his spare time, he needed to write a couple of sets to play at the coffee house, but that was really the least of his worries. He sensed that Kayla felt better having a plan, even if it wasn't a great plan. She seemed to be most confident when she knew what step to take next. They went out for a cheap dinner and headed to bed early, still trying to catch up on the sleep they'd missed the other night.

****

By Thursday night, they were well underway. Quinn lay on his bunk listening to Kayla snore. She was so tired, she had fallen asleep less than a minute after laying down. It had been a day full of physically exhausting work, but Quinn's head was still racing through chores and wouldn't let him rest. After breakfast that morning, they had finished organizing the contents of the remaining luggage in under three hours, using a few of the larger suitcases to sort the clothes.

They had a quick lunch of freebies from the rally then visited the Moore College Gallery to look at more art, following Lorelei and Jim's footsteps. Moore College was a well-respected art school for women. It was founded over 150 years ago and had created a number of galleries to showcase student art, faculty art and alumni art, as well as space to display international exhibits. One gallery, called the Philadelphia Wall, was space for the students to display thematic exhibits from their classes.

The exhibit currently on display depicted art forgeries: some infamous, and some nearly overlooked. One area displayed a number of famous paintings reproduced by students hung alongside lithographs of the originals. Quinn was impressed. There were a few that were so similar to the original that he couldn't tell them apart. But still, no pattern in Lorelei and Jim's sight-seeing had emerged.

Kayla had suggested that they go see the Liberty Bell in order to maintain their citizenship. The exhibit was neat. Before reaching the bell, small billboards explained the bell's history along the long low building. Quinn found it funny that the bell had to be recast three times because of cracks and a bad tone, and even so, the people of Philadelphia were so "distressed" by the constant ringing of the bell that they petitioned the Assembly to ring it less often. How quiet must life have been then, compared to today, that the occasional ringing of a bell was too noisy? Sure there would have been horse drawn wagons and people in the streets, but no cars, no airplanes, no buses, no subways or trains.

Of course the population of Philadelphia in 1790 was tiny compared to today. According to a billboard at the Liberty Bell Center, the country's first census showed that Philly had 28,000 people in it compared to the 1.4 million who lived in the city today. And the Philly metro area has nearly six million people in it today. Population change alone would make things dramatically louder today than in Ben Franklin's day.

After dinner at a diner, they had retreated to the kitchen at the Tain. A lengthy tour through the pantry, 'fridge and freezer helped Quinn and Kayla put together a list of possible snacks and desserts. They baked a couple of cakes in the giant oven before going to their room for bed. Quinn was exhausted too, but as he lay there playing the day over in his mind, he was frustrated that they were no closer to achieving any of their goals.

The call from Lorelei had come almost four days ago, and he was getting really worried that they hadn't been able to do anything for her. They had stopped at a local police station and asked about the accident Officers Dax and Heywood had spoken of. The Philadelphia police had no report of a taxi or any other type of vehicle going off a bridge into the river in the last month. If it hadn't been for the call from Lorelei, and of course the house blowing up, he might think that Dax and Heywood's visit was somebody's bad idea of a prank.

These thoughts circled around in his mind like some disturbing merry-go-round, or maybe a frustration-go-round, that wouldn't stop and let him off. So while Kayla snored away, peacefully dreaming, he was stuck. He flipped over, knowing that he'd shake the whole bunk bed, savagely hopping it might disturb her slumber, and tried to beat some fluff back into his flat pillow. Quinn closed his eyes, willing himself to sleep. As he was doing it, he thought it a foolish thing to do, but it must have worked because when he next woke, it was to see early morning light out their window

Chapter Thirteen:

Money, Money Money

Friday morning dawned clear and bright. Kayla dressed quietly at five o'clock, feeling like she had only just fallen asleep. She assumed Quinn was in the bathroom at the end of the hall getting ready. *How quickly we fell into this morning routine*, Kayla thought. So different from home. Before Jim and Lorelei's wedding and especially when school was in session, Kayla and Quinn couldn't get out of each other's way enough to catch the same bus. Some days it was a leggo-my-Eggo fight over toast, on others it was a war over the last umbrella in the stand.

One morning five months ago, Kayla actually had gone to the basement and turned off the hot water while Quinn was in the shower in order to "conserve" energy. She winced at the memory. Still, today, united they stood with a zillion things to accomplish before the day was through. Kayla shook off the thoughts and finished tying her shoes as Quinn knocked at the door to be sure she was dressed before coming in.

They had decided the night before, that divide and conquer was the only way to pull off everything today. In addition to handling breakfast for the guests at the Tain, spending three hours in the basement organizing, and spending most of the afternoon at museums, they needed to wander around the rally, inviting people to tonight's coffee house. Kayla managed breakfast on her own, while Quinn started preparing for the coffee house.

Including today, there were only three days left of the environmentalists' rally and while it was important to focus on solving their own problems, Kayla and Quinn agreed that without earning additional money, they would never be able to continue their search. They could only stay at the Tain until Mr. Keltsea and his daughter closed it down, likely at the end of next week.

After that, they would need to stay somewhere else, and they'd most likely need to pay for it. Even having emptied their back accounts at ATMs, they had less than $2000 to live on. Decent hotel rooms cost more than a hundred dollars a night, so that money would go fast once the Last Tain closed. They were too young to get regular jobs, so they needed to earn money when they could. Mr. Keltsea needed money too, so if they could pull off the coffee house tonight, it would be really good for everyone.

Quinn made cookie dough for several kinds of cookies during the breakfast service and put it all in the 'fridge. They'd bake the actual cookies this afternoon. Once everything was cleaned up (they beat their previous best breakfast clean-up time of 9:45 by eleven minutes), they headed down to the basement. They carried the last of the trunks up to the ballroom before Quinn attacked the wall of boxes.

With all of the luggage out of the basement, some space was starting to open up. Quinn could see that along the perimeter of the room, there were things that looked much older than what they had uncovered so far. Kayla thought that she had spied a spinning wheel, though she wasn't positive that's what it was. It did look like the thing in the picture she remembered from Sleeping Beauty, however.

In the ballroom, Kayla worked through the trunks as efficiently as she could, although she had to work somewhat slower than with the luggage due to the age and fragility of the trunks' contents. The third trunk she opened had women's clothes in it and she was able to guess the age by the style of clothes. Men's clothes hadn't changed much over the years. A dark suit worn a hundred years ago looked much like a dark suit today.

Women's clothes were a different matter all together; they changed dramatically every ten years or so. The first trunk with women's clothes that she opened contained dresses unlike anything she had seen before outside of pictures. One dress was a dark blue color, in a shimmery smooth fabric, like satin. It looked like clothes worn in the 1950's show, Leave it to Beaver, that she used to watch on TVLand.

Kayla created a clothes hanging area by bracing a pole along the top of two bookshelves, held in place by a couple of sets of bookends she had found. She put the entire outfit on one hanger and poked a plastic, zip-type sandwich bag containing the jewelry over the tip of the hanger.

She hung the rest of the vintage clothes on the pole with entire outfits on one hanger. She added a flat board along the top of the gap in the bookcases too, creating a shelf. She tagged each of the vintage outfits with a number, so that she could label shoes, hats, parasols or other accessories with the same number, keeping the whole thing together. She guessed that the value of the outfit would increase if the parts were all available.

Most of the rest of the trunks contained men's clothes, but there were two others that contained women's. One trunk had clothes in the *Gone with the Wind* style of the Civil War and the other looked like something out of the Revolutionary War film, *The Patriot*. She held up a beautiful red and pink striped dress that looked like it would fit, but she didn't want to damage it or take the time to try it on. A few trunks must have actually belonged to the Last Tain, they contained blankets and other linens.

By the time Kayla was done with the trunks upstairs, Quinn had made progress on the boxes from the basement. The remaining bookshelves in the ballroom were now partly covered with an organized mess of things. There were old baseball cards, balls from all sorts of sports and eras, jerseys, helmets and other sports related items. One whole shelf was covered in clocks ranging from fairly recent models to old-looking pocket watches.

Three shelves were filled with boxes of books. Quinn had not taken the time to pull them all out, so he had no idea what kinds of books they were. Another shelf held all the ledger books for the Tain, dating back to 1890 with one book from 1737 thrown in the bunch. He expected to find others. The boxes appeared to have been packed up with no thought to organization. It seemed that whatever "junk" was lying around got tossed into a box or wooden crate and they were deposited downstairs, never to be opened again.

He had come across five boxes that had been labeled 'lost and found' or 'found items' or something like that.

They had random things from all different eras. There were sunglasses, eight track tapes from the 1970's, lots of keys, wallets belonging to men and women, books - both novels and journals, maps, and all kinds of other random things. Quinn sorted them out on the shelves. The other interesting thing Quinn found was money, quite a bit of it. The old wallets had some money in them, with no identification or other way to find the previous owner. He found at least five pounds worth of coins.

"At least we have something positive to tell Mr. Keltsea today," Quinn mentioned as they dusted themselves off and met in the courtyard. He closed the basement hatchway back up and snapped the ancient lock shut. "Some of those baseball cards could be worth some real money."

"Same thing with some of those old clothes I found. There must be at least a thousand dollars worth of vintage shoes, alone." Kayla stood still for a few minutes, stretching. "I was thinking that we could offer s'mores as a snack tonight. Also, we need to create a price list and run that by Mr. K."

"How could we sell s'mores?" Quinn asked gesturing Kayla back into the hostel common room.

"The fixin's are in the pantry. We could arrange a nice plate of supplies and put a couple of small candles on the plate to use to toast your marshmallows. Make it enough for two, maybe charge eight dollars or something. What do you think?"

"That's kind of fun. And s'mores are perfect date food."

Kayla was about to knock on Mr. Keltsea's door when she processed what he'd said. "How are s'mores a good date food? They're kinda messy. Ooh! We could include a couple of those moist towelettes I found a truckload of!"

"Of course they're good date food," Quinn replied, dismissing the excitement over the towelettes. "They're yummy and you get to see what kind of person you're really with. Will they eat the sticky, messy goodness or complain about the calories? Will they complain about calories and eat it anyway? 'I really shouldn't; one bite.' They're great conversation starters, too. Where were you when you had your first s'more?" Quinn wiggled his eyebrows and knocked sharply on Mr. K's door while Kayla shook her head.

While they waited for him to emerge from his sitting room, Quinn continued on about snacks. "What about milk and cookies? We could pair flavored milks with a sampling of cookies: plain and chocolate chip, of course, peanut butter cookies and chocolate milk, and what else? You definitely need a third one, right? What other flavor of milk can we make?"

"How about coffee flavored? There's some coffee syrup in the pantry right next to the maple syrup, I think. What kind of cookie goes with coffee?"

"I made molasses cookie dough. That'll go." He knocked again, a bit louder.

"How did you know how to make molasses cookies?"

"We made them in school."

"I've never baked cookies in school."

"I did that in fourth grade. Lorelei and I were living in New York State then."

THE CORDOVAN VAULT

"Oh." Sometimes it was hard to remember that Quinn had lived places other than Granby, Maine. He almost never talked about it and when he did, it was like this. Something small that could be passed over quickly. "Where else did you live?"

"We moved around a lot. I don't remember all the towns," he said dismissively. "It looks like he isn't here. Let's work out a menu and price list and we can leave it on the bar for him, with a note about the basement." The common room TV droned in the background while they discussed the menu.

Just as they were finishing up, Kayla noticed that Quinn was staring into space over her shoulder. "Hello! Are you paying attention?" She waved the menu in his face like a fan, her lip curled in annoyance.

Quinn batted her hand away with a disgusted sigh. "Shh. There's a cop talking on the news about a bunch of people who've been mugged." Kayla turned her attention to the report.

"This is a big city folks, and as such we have our share of random violence, but what I want to warn people about today is that it seems these particular muggers are attacking similar looking couples. Young people in their late teens and early twenties, traveling in groups of two, one tall, brunette male and one blond female of average height, should be especially cautious. The muggers appear to be working their way across the city for reasons unknown to us. To date, the injuries sustained by the victims have not been life threatening, but couples fitting this description, especially west of 17th Street, should be aware of their surroundings and try to avoid isolated, darkened alleys."

Kayla and Quinn listened to the questions being fired at the Police Chief with half an ear.

"Do you thinks that's us? That we're the intended victims?" Kayla asked, looking a little sick to her stomach with fear.

Quinn nodded his head with a sigh. "Probably. I mean we know people are after us and we fit the description. I guess we'll have to be more careful."

"Great, just what we need, something else to be worried about." Just as Kayla was finishing the note about the day's work in the basement and their proposed menu, Mr. Keltsea came in the door pushing a cart with a cappuccino machine on it.

Quinn rushed over to take the cart from the elderly man, although once he got there he felt kind of foolish. Mr. K didn't seem to be having any trouble pushing it. "This is great! I hope you didn't go to too much trouble, though." Quinn said.

"No, no. Billy Weeds over't the Appliance Emporium and I go way back. He offered ta loan it to me, free of charge. I don' want ta take charity though, so we struck a bargain. If we take in more than our $750 goal, I'll give him ten percent of the rest." Mr. Keltsea slowly made his way over to the nearest table and collapsed into a chair. "Twas such a nice day, I thought I'd take a walk over to see 'im. He's jus' over on Second St. Guess I ain't walked that far in a while, though." He wiped his brow with an old handkerchief and carefully placed it back in his pocket. "Ken youse pour me a glass o' water, there girly?"

Kayla quickly brought the drink over and sat opposite him, with the menu and price list they had drawn up. "We figured we could offer these refreshments. What do you think?" Mr. Keltsea tapped various pockets for his glasses and finally found them on his forehead. He put them on and took a look at the price list. They talked about the menu for a while and he approved all of their selections. He argued that the prices seemed a bit high, but Kayla and Quinn assured him that they were reasonable.

"Youse have a good plan so far, but how're youse gonna get people to come down 'ere?" he asked, sitting up with a bit more energy than he'd shown when he'd arrived with the cart.

"We're going to go over to the rally at Independence Park and spread the word. Can I borrow your address stamp and pad? We'll park ourselves under a tree over there and Quinn will play guitar to attract some attention. While folks are listening to him, I'm going to wander around the crowd and tell people about the event here tonight.

"I'll stress that it's the last weekend to hang out in a three hundred year old tavern. I'll also mention that it's free to come in and hear the music. This rally's wrapping up after a week of non-stop events. These folks are probably all out of money by now – well money to go out to a club. I bet they can still afford a cup of coffee and a muffin, though. So, I'll chat it up and stamp people's hands with the name and address."

"And we have two of the guys staying here telling everyone they meet," Quinn chimed in. "I bet we get a good crowd."

J MONKEYS

"How's yer search for yer kin comin'? When I said youse could work for yer keep, I didn't mean youse should neglect the reason for comin 'ere."

"Well, we're a bit low on clues right now, and frankly, we'll need the money to keep up the search. This is a good opportunity for us to add to our pocket. And it's only a couple of days. We're going over to another museum late this afternoon anyway."

"Have youse been to the Betsy Ross house?" Mr. Keltsea asked. Kayla and Quinn shook their heads. "No? Youse should definitely see it. It's 'round the corner. Maybe tomorrow. Well, youse be careful over at that meetin'. I heard tell of a couple of kids getting' held up yesterday." Mr. Keltsea rose from the chair slowly, like he could feel every joint and bone rubbing on each other.

Their trip to the rally was a huge success. Quinn was surrounded by a large crowd immediately upon their arrival. Apparently, even though these folks were passionate about their cause, they were starting to feel the effects of eating, sleeping and drinking righteous indignation for a week. They were desperate for some fun and quite light in the pockets as Kayla and Quinn had suspected.

Quinn played for about fifteen minutes in one location while Kayla wandered among the crowd spreading the word of the coffee house. After whetting their appetites, they moved to the other end of the big open grassy mall. Again, Quinn played a couple of songs while Kayla told everyone about the free show starting at seven o'clock that night in a three hundred year old tavern.

THE CORDOVAN VAULT

After advertising, they headed back to the Last Tain. They had a few hours to get everything ready by the time they opened the doors that night. After all the refreshments were ready, Kayla stacked plates, napkins and utensils, then prepared the common room for the guests.

Quinn worked on his play list for the evening. He figured that crusaders for social change would probably like 60's and 70's folk music, but he added a bunch of popular hits from the 1980's and a few of his favorites from today as well. The evening would last about four hours, so he needed four forty-minute sets and then a short encore. He hoped that twenty-minute breaks would be enough to get down a couple cups of tea with honey and take requests.

Quinn did a quick sound check on the equipment they had borrowed from a guy Mr. Keltsea knew. In addition to his guitar and the old, out-of-tune piano in the common room, he had a borrowed microphone, mic stand, amplifier and speaker.

Because he had hoped to play in public back in Granby, he had loaded his iPod with the drum track of hundreds of songs. He created an On-The-Go Playlist on the iPod to match his set list. They opened the doors at six forty-five, surprised to see that a line had formed already. Kayla was immediately swamped with orders for smoothies, coffees and sweets.

Quinn had picked the first songs of his first set strategically. He wanted songs that the mostly thirty-something audience would consider sing-along classics. Bob Dylan might be a brilliant songwriter with an iconic sound that defined a generation, but most people would agree that he wasn't a great singer, with his out-of-tune, scratchy voice. Bruce Springsteen's voice wasn't as bad, but could be pretty rough, too. Quinn figured that any off-key note he sang in "The Times They Are A-Changin'" or "Thunder Road" might be mistaken for a Dylan-esque intentional thing. By the time he moved into "Cecelia" by Simon and Garfunkel, he was feeling right at home on the makeshift stage.

After the first couple of sets, Quinn spent his next break collecting requests and chatting with folks. He brought a few dishes out to tables for Kayla. Happily, she was busy at the bar trying to take orders and get them out. She was so busy, that he guessed they were making good money. Most of the orders she was able to hand over to the customer right away, but some things took more time and backed up the line.

The break went by in an instant and Quinn headed back on stage for his third set. Before he knew it, he was wrapping up the final set with "Free Fallin'" by Tom Petty. He put down his guitar, and stood up. "You've been a great audience. Thank you," he said before he turned off the mic. He stepped off the stage area and took a bow.

The applause was fierce and so very gratifying that Quinn feared his smile would become etched into his face. With a twinkle in his eye, he looked at the audience after the cheering kept up for nearly a minute, and said, "Would you like an encore? I've got a couple more." Hard as it was to imagine, the cheers increased. Kayla gestured to Quinn as he sat back down. He turned the mic on again and said with a grin, "All right, everybody. Last call over at the coffee bar. Now sing along folks, cause I'm sure you know these."

Forty-five minutes later, Quinn was still grinning. Everybody had left fairly quickly after he finished playing the two encore songs. They started cleaning up as people were heading out and by the time only a couple of people were finishing their drinks, Kayla and Quinn had the room mostly cleaned up.

Mr. Keltsea emerged from his room when the sound of chairs being flipped onto tables was all that could be heard. He paid the bouncer their agreed upon wage of forty dollars and took possession of the cash register, counting the till while Quinn and Kayla counted out their tip jars.

Quinn had subtly emptied some of the tip jars on the tables at every break so that they wouldn't be too full. He had heard from other musicians that you wanted to have enough seed money in the jars to give people the idea of tipping, but not so much that they thought it was unnecessary. All together he had $243.15.

Kayla had placed a tip bowl at the counter with a note on it that read "Help me see the world!" She'd seen lots of people dumping the change from their purchase into the bowl, thanking them as they went along. As it filled, she had emptied the bowl into a pitcher under the counter. When she ran out of change at the register, she bought some back out of her pitcher so it had a pretty big wad of bills in it as well as the change. It took her a bit longer to count it all out than it had Quinn, but in the end she had made $87.65 in tips.

Mr. Keltsea looked to be the happiest of the bunch. After paying the bouncer, he set aside $750 for the Last Tain's bank account, which was really an old safe bolted to the frame of the closet in his bedroom, and began counting out the rest to figure the ten percent he owed to Billy Weeds for the cappuccino machine rental. He was shocked to find that there was an additional $657.90 in the till. He set aside $66 for Billy and added the rest to his pile headed for the safe. "I cain't believe how well youse done," he said to the kids as they all sat on bar stools with steaming cups of something. "Think youse can do it again Sunday?"

Quinn looked at Kayla and nodded with a shrug. His voice felt fine and he thought he could easily tweak the set list to keep it fresh. Kayla thought for a minute about what was left in the pantry. "We'll need to whip up a few new cakes and muffins. A few batches of cookies, too. But there's plenty of coffee and everything else."

Quinn chimed in, "Since we know what we're makin', we can probably bang most of this stuff out during breakfast Sunday."

"Did they eat me out of house and home or do we have som'em left for breakfast?" Mr. K asked, nodding.

Kayla put her mug down, and rubbed her aching toes as she replied. "Believe it or not, we still have plenty of frozen fruit. I must have made seventy-five smoothies and I don't think I made a dent in the supply. I have some left that's mostly defrosted, so I made up a giant bowl of fruit salad for the morning."

"Speaking of morning," Quinn added, "it's not too far off, so we should probably turn in." He stood up, tucking his tips into a pocket and picking up his guitar case. All the borrowed sound equipment had been secured in the ballroom. Kayla also rose, flipped her chair up onto the bar with an expertise far beyond anything she demonstrated on their first day cleaning up and bade Mr. Keltsea a good night. Neither of them said anything until they had reached their room and closed the door behind them.

"Can you believe it? Three hundred and thirty bucks. That's huge!" Kayla was nearly bursting with excitement.

Quinn smiled as they pooled the money, then added it to the cash they had stashed among their bags. After a lifetime of watching cop shows on TV, they had decided that they shouldn't use a bank. They didn't want to leave any more record of their trail than they had to, but they worried about having too much cash around. It was vulnerable to theft. In the end, they had decided to do the best they could, trying to hide it. They dropped into their beds, each so tired they couldn't think, then quickly drifted off to sleep.

Chapter Fourteen:

Making the News

Breakfast came much too early Saturday morning, but Quinn and Kayla dragged themselves out of bed and down to the kitchen with barely enough time to prepare for the crowd. Once breakfast was over, they spent a few hours going through more boxes from the basement in a daze. A bit after noon, they went out to get lunch and some fresh air before heading over to the Rosenbach Museum and Library.

They passed through subtle metal detectors on their way in, then wandered through the collection of original manuscripts written by people like Charles Dickens and James Joyce, 18th and 19th century furniture, and the world's largest collection of portrait miniatures painted on metal. They walked around and admired the exhibits.

They didn't see anything that would tie this museum to Jim and Lorelei, but they did see several pieces of furniture that looked like things they had seen in the basement at the Last Tain.

Before heading back to Independence Park to drum up more business for tomorrow's coffee house, the stopped at the Atwater Kent Musuem As they entered, they were again struck by the level of security they had to go through to get in. The guards seemed to be unsure of their assigned duties and they were turning some people away. When Kayla and Quinn got to the front of the line, a blue uniformed man of at least sixty years, instructed Quinn to leave his guitar in the open cloakroom. "Sir, this is a nine hundred dollar guitar, I can't leave it in the cloak-room. I'll be very careful with it. Across my back this way, it's doesn't stick out or anything."

"Nope, not in here. You'll have to leave it outside. Can't have anything like that in here."

"Why?"

"After the break-in last week, we can't have any bags of any kind. Best to leave it home next time."

"Thank you sir, we'll do that. Come on Quinn, we'll see the exhibit another day." Kayla pulled on Quinn's sleeve to get his attention when he would have stood there and argued with the man for the rest of the afternoon. Once they were outside, she said, "Don't you see? That's it, that's the pattern!"

"What are you talking about?"

"The break-in! The art thieves. Remember, the guard at the Rodin said that they had installed the metal detectors because of the art thieves. We should check, but I bet you that all of these museums had break-ins."

"Yeah," Quinn said in agreement. "We heard about that on the news. Let's find out when they were broken into and compare that with the notes in Jim and Lorelei's guidebook. Do you think they might have been on the thieves trail?"

"Maybe, but I don't understand why. What was so important about these art thieves that they'd change their honeymoon destination to chase after them?"

"No idea. How are we going to find out about these guys? We don't even have a computer. God I miss my iPhone."

"Quinn, Quinn. Don't you remember where we are? We're in Philadelphia. The City of Brotherly Love. Home of the cheese steak, the Eagles, and Benjamin Franklin." Quinn looked at her, 'and' clearly written on his face. "The founder of the free library system in these United States! Where's the guidebook? Let's find a library."

They walked across town to the Library Company of Philadelphia. A quick Google search proved Kayla's theory. Jim and Lorelei had visited each of the museums that had been broken into. They finally had a clue as to what Jim and Lorelei were doing in Philadelphia.

Quinn sat back and asked the obvious question. "Why would a couple of newlyweds from Maine spend their honeymoon trailing after art thieves in Philadelphia? And how do people's lives depend on preventing art from being stolen? That's what Jim said on the disk – people's lives depend on our success. "

"No idea."

"You know what? We should go get that disk and bring it over to see what else is on it."

"Good thinking!" Kayla squealed, earning a shushing glare from the librarian. "Let's go." Kayla signed off the computer and they started walking out, heading back to the Last Tain to get the disk.

Forty minutes later, they were back at the library, disk in hand. They sat at a computer and inserted the disk, practically bubbling with the expectation of finding information on it that explained everything and kicking themselves for not having done this days ago. Unfortunately, the short message from Jim and Lorelei that they had watched in the pantry was the only file on the disk. Their shoulders slumped in disappointment.

"This doesn't make any sense," Quinn said. "Didn't Jim tell us to take the disk and get out of the house? If there is nothing else on the disk, why would he care if we took it?"

"You're right." Kayla sat back in her chair in thought. Jim and Lorelei had sent them out of the house in the middle of the night. They had no idea what kinds of things Kayla and Quinn would throw into the backpacks in the few minutes they had, but Jim wanted them to take the disk. Why? The only answer was that the disk was important. She popped it out of the computer and turned it over in her hands, looking for some indication, but found nothing. With a sigh, she placed it back in the purple plastic case so that it wouldn't get scratched.

The cover popped up a little when she set it aside. Quinn noticed and automatically placed his hand on the case to secure it. The cover wouldn't quite close as it was supposed to. Quinn nudged Kayla's arm as he slid the case across the table to take a closer look. He pulled the disk back out and was able to get a fingernail under the black plastic disk-bed and pry it away from the rest of the case. It swung open and underneath, they found two pieces of paper folded together. Even before they unfolded them,

148

they could see that the papers were covered with hand-written script, like a letter. "That looks like it could have come out of my mom's diary," Kayla whispered. She pulled the book out of her day pack. The paper was a match. The entries were from 1982. She placed them where they belonged in the book, closed it up and put the book and DVD back in her bag. She nodded toward the door.

Once they were out on the street, she said, "Let's go sit in a park and take a look at this." A few minutes later, they sat under a light in an old church park. Quietly, Kayla started to read the new pages aloud.

April 9, 1982

I'm twenty years old today. It's my first birthday without my parents or my sister around. I doubt they miss me. Victor and I are living in a small apartment in Blacksburg, Virginia. The apartment is really one floor of a three-family house owned by the couple on the first floor, Mr. and Mrs. Cocoman. We're going by the name of Fredricks ourselves. After our narrow escape from Arbervale, Victor worried that they would find us, but we've been here for six months without any trouble. Still, I keep emergency bags packed for us so that we could leave at a moment's notice.

We've decided to have no part in either Lur Babsel or Denortus. We can find no trace of Victor's parents. I believe that Daddy might have harmed them or at least knows what happened to them, but clearly he's not going to tell me. Victor wants to go back to Arbervale and force Daddy to tell him, but I believe his love for me is the only thing that is stopping him. I'm not sure that I shouldn't encourage him to get the information from Daddy, but of course, I hate to contemplate the means he would have to use to force the conversation.

June 1, 1982
We were married today by a justice of the peace. Victor had asked me to marry him soon after we escaped from Arbervale, but he wanted to wait until now. I didn't know why until today. Before the ceremony, he presented me with a beautiful bouquet of lilacs. He said that since I couldn't have the wedding he thought I deserved, with the big white dress and a hundred guests and a dinner, he wanted to be sure that I at least had my favorite flower to accompany me down the aisle.

Well, there wasn't really an aisle, but the thought was lovely and very romantic. The flowers smelled heavenly. I've pressed some and will place them here once they are dry.

Tied to the flowers was an old key in a strange purple metal. Victor said it was an heirloom from his father's side of the family, a talisman that would keep us safe and bring us friends. I hope it works.

We both have jobs. I'm working at the local library and Victor is working at a toy factory. We make enough money to meet our needs and put some aside for later. I did take five hundred dollars from Daddy before I left home and we've put that and some of Victor's savings from his time in the service into an emergency fund, in case we have to run again.

150

THE CORDOVAN VAULT

We're happy, for the moment, though I sense that there is trouble looming. It's the same fundamental knowledge that I had when Victor was away, so it's upsetting. We're trying to enjoy our time now and be prepared to run at the same time.

November 12, 1982
We've left Virginia and made our way to the big city of Washington, DC. Hopefully, here we can get lost in the busy city. Again, we're in a small apartment and we've gotten jobs off the books. I'm working in a restaurant as a waitress, Victor is working at a mechanic's shop. I'm taking an art class at the library. I paint, poorly, but it's fun. We've started going to see some of the many museums here and the monuments. It's quite exciting.

It looked like some of the middle pages were still missing. How did her mom and dad get from Washington to Philly? It didn't escape her notice that Philadelphia seemed to haunt her family. Her parents apparently 'escaped' in 1983; her brother and sister-in-law might not have escaped last week.

For the first time, she considered that the outcome of her own adventures here with Quinn might be uncertain. With the confidence of youth, she hadn't really considered that the 'bad guys' who blew up her house and knew she was here, might actually win the day. She pushed the frightening idea aside with a shake of her head.

"Let's head back," she said, finally. While they walked, they talked about the diary and what it might mean, and the strange purple key.

"I don't know why my mom's diary is in pieces, but I think we need to find the rest of it. Quinn...Quinn, what are you doing?" Kayla realized that she was talking to herself and turned around to see where he had gone. He was about four stores back, standing still, staring through a shop window with an odd look on his face. *Not horror, not shock, not disgust – but something combining all three*, Kayla thought, walking back to him. "What?!"

Quinn pointed at a collection of TVs that were facing the street, playing the evening news. As she read the sign above the shop identifying it as an electronics store, she heard a familiar voice and whipped her eyes back down to the biggest screen. There was her house, reduced to rubble, with a news crew on the street interviewing her next-door neighbor, Mrs. Nessman.

"The firemen found the bodies yesterday, you know," Mrs. Nessman said helpfully.

"What bodies!" Kayla spat at Quinn. "What is going on here?"

Quinn motioned for her to keep her voice down. "Apparently, we're dead now, too."

Chapter Fifteen:

Denortus and Lur Babsel

"Well, that's ridiculous! Clearly, we're not dead. What is she talking about?" Kayla yelled loudly enough that passers-by on the street turned to look at them.

"Shhhh! What is wrong with you? We've barely escaped Maine with our lives, our sister and brother may not have been so lucky and we know that people are looking for us here in Philly. Do you really think that yelling for the whole world to hear is a good idea?" Quinn hissed as he grabbed Kayla by the elbow and started to march her back along the way they had been traveling, away from the still playing news clip.

Kayla yanked her elbow out of his grip and snarled back, "This is too much! Are you telling me that after blowing up our house, someone went back and planted dead bodies to give the impression that we'd been killed? That's insane! Who would go to that much work?"

"I'm not telling you anything – CNN is! I knew you were going to freak out about this. Why are you yelling at me?" Quinn poked a crosswalk button vigorously and repeatedly to make his point.

Kayla stamped her foot and huffed. "I don't know why I'm mad at you, but I am. Somehow this must be your

fault. Give me a few minutes and I'll figure out how!"
Kayla stalked off as soon as the crosswalk gave her the go-ahead, nearly walking into a cab that lurched to a stop.

"Now who's being ridiculous? This is not my fault. If anything, adding the bodies to the house gives us a hint to the scale of this thing. How easy do you think it is to find bodies of two dead teenagers that no-one would miss in order to stage something like that? Probably pretty hard. So why don't we stop arguing about it and figure out what we should do."

"Don't use logic on me! Aren't you musicians supposed to be all touchy-feely? Why aren't you freaked out about this?"

"I can't talk to you when you are like this! I'll see you back at the Last Tain. Maybe the reasonable Kayla I've been traveling with will be there instead of the witch from back home." Quinn turned up the closest cross street, apparently so anxious to get away from Kayla that he'd rather walk a few extra blocks than remain in her vicinity.

"Why don't we figure it out," Kayla mumbled in a sing-song voice. "Oh, I'll figure it out all right. You can count on that. Who does he think he is..." Kayla continued muttering as she stalked down the street, not looking to see where Quinn had gone. After a few more minutes of muttering, mumbling and mocking, a little flag went up in the back of Kayla's brain.

She stopped walking so suddenly the man behind her danced around to avoid her, earning her a glare that should have singed her blond ponytail. Kayla pursed her lips, and glanced up at nothing. She had the thought that she had missed something, something important. She tapped her finger against her lower lip replaying the last ten minutes in her mind. There was something about the news clip. She needed to see it again. Kayla looked around to see where she was. The corner of Sansom and 7th Street. Hadn't they seen an internet café near here? Kayla started to jog.

Kayla arrived at the Down-the-Patch internet café, more out of breath than she had expected. She huffed and sat at an open computer, navigating to the CNN website. As she found the clip, a young woman in jeans and a black t-shirt sidled up next to her.

"It's ten dollars for the first fifteen minutes and thirty cents a minute after that or you get twenty minutes for free with the purchase of a large drink and a pastry," the woman said, flipping open a small notebook. "What'll it be?"

Kayla glanced up at the waitress. "How about a large ice tea and a cookie?" She checked the volume on the speakers to be sure it was low and was waiting for the video to finish buffering when her snack was delivered.

The video showed a local Maine newscaster, Michelle Chris, standing next to a short woman, about sixty-five years old, wearing a faded purple housecoat and threadbare velvet slippers. "I'm standing with Mrs. Nessman, a neighbor of the Livingston-Wexford family of Granby, Maine to follow up on a story we broke for you a few days ago about a tragedy in this sleepy little town. Mrs. Nessman what can you tell us about the family who lived here?" The camera moved off the pair and closed in on the older woman.

"Misfortune seems to follow them. The mother, Penny Livingston, such a lovely woman, was in a car accident some years ago, then Jim and his new wife died on their honeymoon last week. Now these two kids accidentally kill themselves with the stove. I wish someone had realized the state they were in. Honestly, I thought they were rather young to be left home alone for all this time, but I guess Jim felt differently. The firemen found the bodies yesterday, you know," Mrs. Nessman said helpfully.

The camera panned away from the conversation and moved across the rubble. Tears pooled in Kayla's eyes as she surveyed the damage to the only home she'd ever had. The old oak tree by the road looked singed and the backyard was blanketed with a carpet of blue hydrangea petals. The pillars of the big porch gleamed gray, toppled down on top of the pile of char.

The chimney stood crumbling, with the odd brick spewed here and there in the yard. The log fence was tumbled down in places around the yard and the garage door was a twisted wreck. Strangely enough the staircase remained standing, leading from nowhere to nothing. In the back yard, the land sloped away down a hill, made more obvious by the lack of a house to obscure the view.

The camera returned to Michelle for her wrap up. "The two victims of the explosion, Kayla Livingston and Quinn Wexford, were both fourteen years old. In fact, Quinn Wexford gained local notoriety last winter in a popular video posted to You-Tube, which purported to count down the worst school play performances of the year. Unfortunately, we'll never know which of these teenagers was responsible for this last performance. And so, in a bizarre series of events better suited to fiction than reality, from car wreck victim to honeymoon heartbreak to victims of their own neglect, this seems to be the tragic end of this accidental family. Back to you, Peter."

Kayla sat back and stared at the frozen picture of the roving reporter, wondering what it was about the video that bothered her. Other than the fact that it was telling the world that she was dead and that it was her own fault.

What kind of reporter was this Michelle Chris? It almost seemed like she was implying that she and Quinn has been too stupid to live and certainly should have been chaperoned like a couple of 'tweens. Like she'd leave the stove on! It had only been engrained in her since birth, practically, that there were two things you never did – leave the door to the freezer ajar and be careless with a gas stove.

As Kayla thought about the stove, it struck her that the stove was in the kitchen, in the back of the house. If the explosion had been caused by the stove, then how was it possible that blue hydrangea petals had been blown *into* the backyard? The hydrangeas were in the front, by the road. For them to land in the back, they would have had to have flown over the flaming house which would have burnt them up. And certainly, when she had been prying Quinn off the ground after the explosion, it wasn't amid a blizzard of flower petals!

Kayla played the video again and paused the picture to look at the blue backyard more closely. The flowers looked as if they had been ripped off the plant like confetti and thrown on the ground, not through a fire. It was late-July. Hydrangea was a summer plant. Those flowers were blooming. What could have caused the petals to blanket the yard like that?

"When in doubt, Google," Kayla thought, typing her question in. She got 374,986 responses. The top responses didn't seem promising. She changed the search phrase to *flower petal storm* and got fewer responses, only 22,358. She flipped over to Google Images and after a few minutes, found some intriguing photos. Photos of flower-confetti strewn fields and lawns. Many of the photos linked to a website called TheOtherAmongUs.com. Kayla clicked on the site. Up popped a black page broken into three sections.

The left side of the page had a column two inches wide with links to Aliens, Area 51, Bigfoot and the Yeti, Nessie and Monsters, Magick and Spells, Secret Societies, Super Colliders, Stonehenge, Time Travel, Vampires, Witches, and others. The right side of the screen seemed to be devoted to government cover-ups in general. The middle was taken up by a treatise on all things mystical. Kayla read a few lines of the rant, but quickly lost interest and scrolled to the bottom, to a bunch of thumbnail photos.

She clicked on the first one only to bring up a ghastly picture of a vampire having a snack. She shuddered and quickly closed the image. The next few photos were similarly gruesome pictures of aliens, Bigfoot and the like. She scrolled back up to look at the topics on the left again, clicking on Secret Societies. A page opened with links to the usual suspects, the Priory of Scion, Skull and Bones society, the Men In Black, the Knights Templar, the Freemasons, the Illuminati, and other less well know societies like the Coven of Seven, the Lillith, and Falcon Rock.

THE CORDOVAN VAULT

Kayla clicked the last link labeled "Other Societies". Up popped a list of several societies so secret that almost nothing was known about them. Kayla wondered if nothing was known about them because they didn't really exist, but as her eye scanned the page, it tripped on the fifth set of words on the list: Lur Babsel and Denortus. The hair on the back of her neck rode the crest of a shiver to stand firmly at attention.

She glanced around the café, to be sure nobody was paying any attention to what she was doing. She even looked behind her, ignoring the little voice in her head laughing at her paranoia. Turning her attention back to the computer, she read the page that summed up everything the authors knew about these two societies.

Denortus and Lur Babsel almost certainly exist as evidenced by the complete lack of information available. We believe they are warring factions of the same original heritage, but no one knows what that heritage might be. Some of history's most famous writers mention them, but very infrequently. Eratosthenes, the third librarian at Alexandria noted them in his letter to Ariston, saying that they seem to be a cut above the rest of the human race, sometimes stronger, sometimes faster.

Eratosthenes called their abilities "advantages". He implied that he had undertaken a complete study of them and had written a history that was maintained in the Library. Presumably, it was destroyed along with everything else when Julius Caesar fired the building.

Orosius noted Denortus in his Seven Books of History Against the Pagans *at the time of the fall of the Roman Empire, saying that Denortus had conspired with Honorius*

159

and that Alaric the Visigoth was a Gezon of Lur Babsel. He claimed that the Visigoth settlement of what is now south/central Spain was prompted by their need to mine Cordovan, a purple metal the Gezon used in their sacred rituals. Cordovan has never been seen in modern times, but ancient texts claim that it was extremely rare, found only near the Strait of Gibraltar.

The 1200's seem to have been a high point for Lur Babsel at least, as they are mentioned in several texts dating to that time. Marco Polo mentions Lur Babsel in his book Travels in the Land of Kublai Khan, *stating that he strongly suspected that one of Kublai Khan's closest advisers was of Lur Babsel.*

And the old Irish epic poem called The Cattle Raid of Cooley, *mentions that the protectors of Lur Babsel guarded Queen Medb.*

They weren't mentioned again in known literature or historical sources until SS creepy guy Hesse, mentioned Denortus one time, stating in a letter to Ava Braun that some of his experiments were to discover the true work of Denortus.

Charlie Birdle, the zaniest of modern conspiracy theorists, suggested on his blog that the members of Lur Babsel could even travel by riding a strong wind called a zephyr. Some crop circles have been thought to have been made by the zephyrs.

Whoever they are and whatever they do is one of the world's best kept secrets, but it's clear that they've been 'the other among us' for a long, long time."

Kayla sat back in the chair frozen in horror, eyes wide, her mind a blank page. It was only when she noticed her

THE CORDOVAN VAULT

gape-mouthed expression reflected back at her, that she realized so much time had passed that the computer screen had gone to black. She quickly checked her watch, gathered her things and signed off the computer. She rushed out the door, and jogged down the street to leave the thought-halting information behind.

One of Philadelphia's many inviting green parks called to her, enticing her into its soothing peace. Kayla sat on a night-cooled stone bench and let the chirping birds and chittering crickets smother the panic she was feeling.

Her mother's diary, written years before the birth of the internet, stated quite plainly that she and Jim were decendents of both Denortus and Lur Babsel. Societies so secret that most people had never heard of them. Two factions, warring through the ages, but leaving no clue as to what they were warring about.

And it seemed "someone" had already gotten to Jim and Lorelei and that "someone" had tried to get to her. Thus far, she had assumed they were one and the same "someone"; now suddenly, they might not be. Maybe both sides were after her. She shivered in the stillness of the evening, glancing around, feeling like someone was watching her.

Maybe not someone, but "Someone".

Though she didn't see anyone who might be taking note of her, she didn't know what else to do. She got up from the bench and ran home to the Last Tain.

Chapter Sixteen:
Reading Emotions

A few minutes after their argument on the street, Quinn arrived back at the Last Tain wondering why Kayla had reacted the way she did. What was it about hearing that they were dead that made her so angry? Obviously, they weren't dead! He'd thought it over the whole way home and it really bothered him that he couldn't come up with an answer. Usually, he had no trouble reading people. Most people, but rarely Kayla.

Quinn walked through the courtyard of gardens, running his left hand along the purple-flowered oregano ringing the dead-looking tree in the center of the garden bed to the left of the building's door. His touch released the herb's scent into the air, reminding him of pizza. His stomach grumbled as he fumbled in his pocket for a key to the old oak door.

Once inside the gloomy entryway, Quinn turned right toward the common room to look for a menu for a nearby pizza place. Before he made it all the way into the room, he heard a strange noise, like a sniffle-cough-choke combo.

Mild concern grew to alarm as he realized that the noise was coming from Mr. Keltsea, sitting by the window farthest from the counter. His head was down; he appeared to be studying something in his hands. He hadn't noticed Quinn yet. Quinn scuffed his shoe and looked down at the floor as if trying to find the phantom that had tripped him. He wanted to give Mr. Keltsea a chance to compose himself in privacy.

Quinn walked through the room quickly, calling, "Mr. Keltsea, what happened?"

Mr. Keltsea wiped his eyes on the cuff of a sleeve, and fussed with a handkerchief that had seen fresher times. He waved the rag dismissively and shook his head as if the problem was no more than a trifle saying, "I was remembering the missus." He held an old photo in his hand, the object of his study.

Quinn reached out for the photo, "May I?" He pulled the old picture close, angling it toward a window clouded with dirt when Mr. Keltsea had handed it over.

"She was lovely. Was this taken at a special occasion?" The photo had the orangey tinge of one taken in the 1970's. The woman at its center was past middle age, but with a face that hinted at a youthfulness younger than her years.

She had chalkboard black hair, dark at its core, but with a gray fuzziness like years of white chalk dust pushed to the edges. It gave her a soft kind of glow. Her wide-mouthed smile reached the corners of her eyes and the lines carved there told Quinn that she smiled often. She was leaning against the counter of the common room – the ancient pitted mirror hanging behind her on the wall. She wore a red dress in a shimmery looking fabric and held a fancy glass of something like a milkshake in her hand.

THE CORDOVAN VAULT

Mr. Keltsea gently retrieved the photo from Quinn, nodding in agreement. "Christmastime 1973. Our little girl was seven years old. Every year, the missus would say to me, 'Barris, it's time for a party. Get the good glasses and linens out of storage.' She ran this place like a captain runs a ship." Mr. Keltsea ran his hand over the face in the photo. He gestured around the dingy room, "She'd be so disappointed now." There was another sniffle-cough-choke.

Quinn gestured to Mr. K's chair, leading the now sobbing man to his seat. After a few minutes of sitting with him in silence, Quinn asked, "Is there anything I can do Mr. K? What brought this on?"

"She knew she was sick long 'afore she let on to me, but when she finally told me she would be leaving me for her Heavenly Reward, she said that the Tain had to stay in the family. That was her only wish, that we keep open and family run. She always loved this place. And now, I cain't even do that much for her."

"What do you mean? Have you finalized your plans to sell?" Quinn asked.

"Nobody wants the place. No family, anyway. I've got the offer from that contractor, but he's going to demolish the place and replace it with apartments. He's pushin' for a decision and I don't know what to do. I thought Maggie would help me decide, but now, I cain't bear to be a disappointment to her." Mr. Keltsea waved the photo with one hand, pinching the bridge of his nose with the other, as if that could stop the tears leaking from his eyes.

"Is your daughter still coming next week to help you finish closing the place?" Quinn watched Mr. Keltsea nod before adding, "Maybe there's another solution...maybe a compromise?"

Mr. Keltsea looked up at Quinn blankly, not following Quinn's thoughts. "A compromise?"

"Yes. Mrs. Keltsea wanted you to keep the Last Tain operating as an inn and to keep it in the family. We can't do anything about the family if no one wants to take the place, but rather than see it destroyed, maybe we can help you find someone to keep it open."

"Keep it open? Who?" Mr. Keltsea asked, bewildered.

"Well, I don't know yet, but let me think about it. You've got a great location, you're not far from the river and this is a fantastic old building on the coolest street I've ever seen. With the right marketing, why wouldn't this place make a ton of money? We should be able to find a buyer. How long can you stall the contractor on his offer?"

Mr. Keltsea looked at Quinn and mumbled an answer, wondering if he'd ever been that excited, that energetic. He watched as Quinn started to pace along the windowed wall, rattling off all the reasons why the Last Tain would be a great investment for someone. Quinn's long-legged stride ate up the distance in five steps compared with his own nine-step shuffle from corner to corner.

A picture began to form in the old man's mind of the two of them side by side. Quinn tall and strong; while he was shrunken, stooped and feeble. Quinn full of energy, practically vibrating with zest; himself weak and clinging to life like a loose vine hanging from a tree in a hurricane. What wouldn't he give to be young again? To have the energy and strength to do things again. To take care of himself, to follow his dreams. To *have* dreams again. He could think of no price too high to get that back.

George Bernard Shaw couldn't have been more right when he said that youth was wasted on the young. Mr. Keltsea shook his head, rejoining the conversation. "Boy, don't you have enough to do? Why do you want to help an old man when youse got plenty of troubles of yer own?"

Quinn stopped in mid-stride. It hadn't occurred to him that he could choose *not* to help Mr. K. Quinn looked at the old man in surprise, temporarily speechless. He thought about the question and realized that he felt very strongly about the need to respect Mrs. Keltsea's wishes.

He took a deep breath and closed his eyes, to think about the emotions that were driving him and why. He felt upset about Mr. K's situation, torn between not knowing what to do and feeling that some action was required. He felt helpless, sad, angry and little bit jealous. Why was that? He opened his eyes turned his head to speak, although he didn't know what he might say. As soon as his gaze locked with the old man's watery gray eyes, a new shock rippled through him.

"What's wrong?" Mr. Keltsea asked worriedly, watching the boy's face register shock, then turn to something akin to horrified amusement.

"Mr. K, I've gotta run. I remembered something I have to do, but I don't want you to worry. I'll come up with something for you by tomorrow morning and we'll talk about it after the breakfast rush." Quinn tossed the words over his shoulder as he ran out of the room, wanting to be alone with his thoughts. He didn't know how it had happened, or what it meant, but he thought he had been feeling Mr. Keltsea's emotions!

Chapter Seventeen:

Advantages

Quinn hurried out of the hostel, through the deserted courtyard, out the gate, and down the secluded street, tripping on uneven cobblestones in his rush to find a place to be alone. Unlike Kayla who had really never left Maine before last week, Quinn had lived in enough different places in his short life to realize that there was no solitude like that of crowded city streets. He could never truly be alone in a place like Granby, Maine or on a street like Elfryth's Alley.

Small towns or neighborhoods like this one didn't have the social insulation of a city. There was no such thing as a stranger back home in Granby. If you lived in the area, you knew everybody. If you saw someone sitting off by himself, you would walk up to him to see how he was. You might offer advice or a shoulder to cry on, but you would never let him cry alone. The Elfryth's Alley neighborhood was like Granby that way.

Quinn didn't know if it was the closeness of the buildings to each other or their age that connected the neighbors, but even in the few days that he'd been here, he'd met enough people to recognize them on the street and nod a greeting when passing.

Though it was the City of Brotherly Love, Philadelphia was a major US city, with millions of residents and worth billions in business. *Everybody* was a stranger, and a stranger sitting quietly in public would be offered more space than a criminal in Granby. A stranger who seemed upset, or heaven forbid emotional, would find himself in a great wide open where mothers whisked children away from the crazy man and men paused to sniff the air before turning tail and running in the opposite direction.

If Quinn really wanted to be alone, surrounded by people on the crowded city streets was the best place. He left the quaint neighborhood behind and fell into a crowd of pedestrians headed toward the docks.

Safely encapsulated by anonymous people, Quinn pushed his hands deep into his pockets and faced the truth: he was a freak. There was no other explanation. It wasn't possible to feel someone else's emotions. He could sympathize; he could empathize. But neither empathy nor sympathy would make him feel jealous. He didn't even know what the source of the jealousy might have been. So, he was a freak.

What did this mean? Why could he feel Mr. K's emotions. Was it just Mr. K? Could he feel other people's emotions? Lorelei always said he was good at reading people, swaying them to his side of an argument.

Now that he thought about it, with the answer slapping him in the face, he realized that *of course* he had always been able to do this. He tapped into people's emotions, understood what they were feeling, and used that knowledge to predict how they would react to various situations or information. He had never really connected with someone's feelings like he did just now, not to this extent. But other people's emotions had always been part of his awareness, like the sight of dust motes glinting in sunlight or the taste of herbs in the air when you brushed past them in the Last Tain courtyard. There, but in the background, out of direct view.

How was this possible? Quinn asked himself. A hundred answers flitted through his mind building on each other, each more improbable than the last. What else could he do? Maybe he had super powers. Could he fly too? Maybe his parents hadn't really been his parents, but he'd been sent to them from another planet. Maybe he wasn't really human at all! Clearly he would need more information before trying to unravel the how or the why. But he could focus on the what. What could he really do? Now that he knew about it.

Quinn sat on a cement pylon with his back to the river and closed his eyes. He tried to clear his mind, which was a very difficult thing to do when part of him was wondering if he might actually be Superman. Hey, could he see through walls? Quinn shook his head quickly and flapped his hands as if erasing a bad drawing. *No, no. Focus.*

With his eyes still closed, he rolled his head back on his neck and took a deep breath in through his nose. He blew the air out through his mouth and repeated the process several times. His Vibram clad toes rested against the base of the cement cylinder he was sitting on, bracing him from the wind. He could feel the sun on his face, smell the tang of freshly caught fish in the air, hear the passer's by. He took another breath and felt a bit frantic. His brow furrowed in confusion and he took another breath. The frenzy faded and was replaced by nervousness, then glee, then profound sorrow.

He pulled his head down to its regular stance and opened his eyes. Without looking directly at them, he realized that he was picking up the emotions of the people walking past. A car blew its horn off to his right and he glanced in that direction as a reflex. The sense of emotion faded into the background. He turned back to the pedestrians and realized that he couldn't immediately pick up the 'scent' of their feelings. He closed his eyes again, took a few deep breaths and let the sounds of the street and smells of the river fade away. Happiness, excitement, sadness and fear walked by. Quinn smiled without opening his eyes.

Could he feel farther than the people right in front of him? He tried to reach out to the road. After a few moments, he could feel something rushing past him, but it went by so quickly that he couldn't identify it before the next emotion raced past. He opened his eyes, and realized that he was tapping into the people in the cars but they were moving so fast that he couldn't connect. It felt like watching a merry-go-round race along its course. If you watched for one person, you could see him or her fine, but if you watched the carousel, all you saw was a blur of light and color.

Quinn tipped his head to the side and wondered, like the carousel, could he watch one person? He looked down the stretch of road off to his left and picked the farthest car he could see, watching it draw closer. It had one person in it, a woman with long black hair. He felt something that he couldn't immediately identify: anger, sadness, fear, and jealousy all mixed together. After a few seconds, he realized that it was bitterness that she was feeling. Quinn had never felt this way before. A sense of naïveté crept through the haze of bitterness and Quinn recognized his own emotion rising to the top. He pushed it away to be examined later and tried to stay with the bitter woman. He watched the car drive across the bridge and fade into the distance.

As she drove away, Quinn's sense of her emotion faded too. Perhaps he needed to be able to see people to connect. He dismissed that idea right away since the first thing he had done was close his eyes. Clearly he didn't need to see. Maybe that was it, he didn't need to see the people, but he needed to be *able* to see them. Perhaps he had to be within a certain proximity of the person.

Quinn sat on the pier testing the boundaries of his abilities. Although he found that practice was making the connections come faster, he didn't learn anything else of consequence. At the end of half an hour, he had a headache and felt like he'd held so many emotions in that he might cry if his shoes came unvelcro'd. He took a few more cleansing breaths and shook himself off the pylon like a dog shaking off the rain. He headed back to the Tain, wondering if Kayla was back and if she was still mad.

****

"Everything OK in here?" Quinn asked cautiously, poking his head through the door.

Kayla jumped with a start, whipping her head up to look at him and kicking a stack of paper off the bed. "I was just making some notes," she replied. "I'm sorry I blew up at you earlier," Kayla stammered.

Of all the greetings that Quinn had considered on the walk back from the pier, somehow an apology had not made it to the list. He turned to look at Kayla, sitting on her bunk the way he imagined sorority girls did in college. Perfectly neat and tidy, not a wrinkle, spot or hair out of place. The covers on the bed weren't wrinkled even though she was sitting on them.

Here was an interesting test subject, he thought, watching her cornflower blue eyes blink at him. He had taken it all in at a glance and tried to clear his mind to sense her emotions. He caught a waft of nervousness before he was distracted by her voice, harping on him. Again.

"Quinn?" Pause. "Quinn. Quinn!"

"What?" he shouted back, annoyed that she'd broken his concentration.

"I offered you an apology, don't you have anything to say in return?"

Quinn didn't need to be able to read people's emotions to realize that she had slid from possible nervousness straight into definite irritation. He was sure anyone who could hear or see could tell that. "What were you so mad about anyway? There's no way you could blame me for that CNN clip."

Kayla unfolded herself from the bed, careful not to whack her head on the underside of Quinn's bunk. She bent to collect her summary pages and sat on the wobbly desk where her view of Quinn was un-obscured by the bunk beds. She ducked her head and inspected the fingernails on her left hand. "I don't know. I got freaked out that all these things have been happening to us and it's all *so* out of our control. I guess I was mad that you seemed to be unaffected by the idea that someone powerful enough to conjure up dead bodies was after us. I mean, who are we?" Kayla finished attending to her cuticles and glanced up at Quinn.

Suddenly, Quinn's mind brought back a picture of Jim saying, "We're not who you think we are." Kayla's innocent question of "who are *we*?" became a question of "who *are* we?" In the hour since he'd realized that he could feel other people's emotions, he had not considered telling anyone about this freakish ability. Now, he thought, maybe he should tell Kayla. He decided to see how she might react to freakishness. "I think I know who I am, but I don't know what I am." She looked at him, her nose scrunched and her brow slightly furrowed. "I mean, do you ever get the sense that you can do things that other people can't do?"

Quinn hadn't been this uncomfortable since his sister sat him down for "the talk" two years ago. His relationship with Kayla was tentative at best. He didn't want to completely alienate her, but he wondered now if she might just be as freaky as he was. Maybe this is what Jim meant.

"What do you mean, like archery?"

"Not really. That's something you probably worked at, right?" Kayla nodded and he continued. "Is there anything that you naturally do that you don't think other people do?"

After a long pause, Kayla spoke but it wasn't what Quinn had expected to hear. "Why? What can you do that other people can't do?"

Quinn had overplayed his hand, nothing to do now but throw his cards on the table and see what happened. He adopted a casual, confident pose, mirroring Kayla by leaning his shoulders against the wall behind him. "Well, I can feel the emotions of people around me."

The perplexed expression was back on Kayla's face. "What do you mean by *feel*?"

Quinn closed his eyes and concentrated for a second. "For example, you are feeling skeptical."

"Well genius, I doubt you need to be a psychic to guess that one," she laughed. Kayla stood up and asked, "What on earth are you talking about?"

Quinn also stepped away from the wall, rubbed his face with his hand and decided to tell her the truth instead of hinting around, hoping she'd guess. "After our fight earlier, I found Mr. K in the common room, really upset. He was staring at a picture of the late Mrs. K and crying."

"Noticing that someone is sad doesn't mean that you can feel their emotions. I'm sure you'd feel sympathy for him, sorry that was grieving, but most people would feel that way."

"Yeah, I know that. I'm not talking about sympathy. I talked with him for a while to figure out what he was really upset about. I mean, Mrs. K died a while back, so I would have thought he'd have gotten past his grief by now, at least to some extent."

"OK, so we come back to my question. What are you talking about?"

Quinn paused to shoot Kayla an exasperated glare. "Stop interrupting me and I'll tell you!" He softened the glare with a smile, sat on the floor and gestured for her to sit down on the remaining piece of carpet.

"Like I was saying, I talked with him for a while and finally realized that he was upset about having to sell the Last Tain. Apparently he had promised Mrs. Keltsea that he would keep it an inn-type-thing and that he would keep it in the family, but nobody wants it. And now he's ready to sell the place to a developer."

Kayla started to ask where Quinn was going with this, but he waived her off, shaking his hand dismissively and continued his story. "I starting thinking that this place has a great history and it's in a fun location. I was talking about trying to find a buyer when he asked me why I wanted to help him. I didn't have an answer and while I was thinking about it, I started to feel hopeful and a little bit jealous. That struck me as really weird. What could I have to feel jealous about?"

Kayla was watching Quinn intently. "So, what did you do?" she asked.

Quinn laughed, "I did what any self respecting man would do when confronted by overwhelming emotions. I ran away."

"Nice!" Kayla smiled, wondering at the easy comradery after the earlier fight.

"Anyway, I realized that the jealousy I was feeling, had to be coming from Mr. K. I went for a walk and wondered what this meant. How was it possible that I could feel other people's emotions?"

"Did you come up with any ideas?"

"No, and I stopped worrying about that for the moment since I have no clue. You'll be happy to know that I

quickly dismissed the idea of being Superman, though."
Quinn noticed Kayla's wide, toothy smile, and wondered if
her mind had gone to the same place his had. "I started
testing the theory on the people passing by and I was able
to feel their emotions."

"How do you know that you felt their emotions? I
mean, isn't it more likely that you were imagining various
emotions and assigning them randomly to people or maybe
guessing based on how the people looked or carried
themselves or something like that?"

Quinn thought about this for a minute. "I suppose
that's possible, but really it was more than my imagination.
I actually felt a variety of emotions that there was no reason
for me to be feeling. In fact, I felt one that I don't think
I've felt before." He proceeded to tell Kayla the story
about the bitter woman.

"OK, let's try this out. What am I feeling right now?"
Kayla asked.

"How's that going to work, as you said earlier, it
wouldn't take a psychic to know that you are skeptical."

"Good point, let me feel something else. Close your
eyes so you can't tell if my posture changes or something."

Quinn closed his eyes and they sat in silence for a few
minutes, facing each other. Slowly, he blocked out the
sounds of the Last Tain creaking with age, people in the
courtyard, traffic in the distance. He could smell Kayla
across from him. Her shampoo was fruity and her skin
smelled like rain. Odd. "Still skeptical." He paused,
tilting his head slightly to one side. "Extreme skepticism?
Not much of a change in emotion, Kayla. Come on, be
serious. Annoyance? No, wait that's gone now too. Pick

178

something and hold onto it for a minute, would you?"
Pause. "Ahh, there's full fledged irritation now. But wait,
you've slid into silliness." Quinn opened his eyes and
turned his hands up and outwards. "What are you doing?"

Kayla giggled. "Apparently, I can't change my
emotions on demand, but can by accident. You seemed to
keep up with me though. So do you have to concentrate or
can you do it on the fly?"

"I guess a little bit of both. I think that I have been
doing this my whole life. I just didn't realize what I was
doing. So I can definitely do it on the fly, but I don't know
how to control it yet unless I concentrate."

"Assuming you really do have this ability, what good
is it? How will it help us find Jim and Lorelei?"

"It's how I convince people to do what I want them to
do. I've always been very persuasive and I'm pretty sure
this is the secret to my success. I figure out how people
feel about something, then I tailor my argument to mirror
their wants."

"Example?"

It took Quinn ten seconds to think of an example that
would make sense to Kayla. Ten seconds of silence while
someone is waiting for you to prove yourself can feel like a
lifetime. "Remember when we first arrived at the Last
Tain? Mr. K didn't want to let us in because he only had
one room and didn't want to contribute to the delinquency
of minors or something like that, remember? I told him
that we weren't really brother and sister, but that we were
like family and you were not thrilled that I was airing the
laundry."

Kayla nodded and Quinn continued, "Well, I knew that if I told him the truth, he would want to help us out. We might have been able to convince him that we were brother and sister, but I think that was what he was expecting and I had the idea that if we gave him that line, he would dismiss us. As it turned out, he let us in and this has been the perfect place for us. We've got Lorelei and Jim's stuff. We haven't had to spend any of our money on accommodations in a week and we've even made more money at the coffee house. I think it has all worked out really well."

"I'm still not convinced that you can really read people's emotions, but things have worked out nicely for us here at the Last Tain, so maybe that was your voodoo working on Mr. K. Anyway, why don't we test it out? I give you permission to tap into my psyche over the next couple of days and tell me what you think I'm feeling at any point. I'll confirm or deny and we'll see where we end up."

"You have to be honest, though. You can't deny because you're embarrassed that I'm right," Quinn cautioned.

"Fair enough. While we've been talking about your freaky abilities, I've been thinking about my answer to your question."

"What question?"

"Your question. I think I do have a talent that most other people don't have. Or maybe it's a combination of abilities. I have really good memory. Better than that. It's not really a photographic memory, but sort of like that."

"How so?"

THE CORDOVAN VAULT

"Once I write something down, I can remember it. It's like the piece of paper I wrote on is filed away and I can pull it out to read it later on. I might remember what color I wrote it in or if I drew a box around it or something like that. Then I can imagine the piece of paper and see what I wrote. I'm pretty good at remembering something someone said word for word. I can play it back in my mind like a movie. But I don't remember everything I hear on the news or conversations in the hall at school. Just important stuff."

"But how do you know if something is important enough to bother remembering it?"

"I don't know, but I do. And there is one other thing." Kayla ducked her head in embarrassment.

"What? Come on, I told you about my freakiness..."

"Well, I think I can sorta see the future," she mumbled.

"What?!"

"Not all the time, but occasionally. And I only get about two seconds of warning!"

"Back up. What are you talking about? How?"

"It started happening about six months ago. And it's only happened four times. Sometimes, I get this sense of déjà vu. And I figured out that it comes from dreams. It seems that I occasionally dream the future. I had been keeping a dream journal and I confirmed that at least one of the déjà vus came from a dream. Then I had another one last week. When Lorelei called and the phone woke me, I had been dreaming of you flying while I was trapped in Jim's car at night. Then I remembered the dream before the explosion. That's what I was trying to tell you from the car, to get down. But I only had a couple of seconds and I was stuck in the car. I couldn't get the seatbelt off."

Quinn sat still though this announcement. Seconds passed before he thought of anything to say. Finally, he commented. "And you thought to mention the good memory first? I'd think that being able to see the future qualifies as a nice freaky ability. So what do you think all this means?" Quinn shifted his legs from crossed under him to stretched out and crossed at the ankles.

Kayla shifted too, and turned her head toward the risen moon glowing through the window. The curtains blew in the breeze and in a quiet voice, she dropped a new bomb on him.

"I think these are Advantages, extra abilities that give us an edge on other people. I think we have Advantages, and I'm afraid that means we are both part of Lur Babsel. By birth. I think that's what Jim and Lorelei meant when they said we aren't who we think we are. Lorelei did say we should use our advantages. This must be what she meant. And unfortunately, from the little I've read about Lur Babsel, I think that when you are born to Lur Babsel, the only way you get out is when you die at the hands of Denortus."

Chapter Eighteen:

A Family History

Kayla folded her lips into her mouth in a grim line and waited for Quinn's response. It wasn't long in coming. "What do you mean? You said you thought your mom had made them up. Now you think we're marked for death by some shadowy underworld secret society?"

Kayla told him about her trip to Down the Patch and her internet search. "Mom definitely didn't make them up. There was no internet when Mom wrote her journal so she must have heard about them from some source. Why couldn't it have been her parents?"

"This is huge. This is bad! What are we going to do?"

Kayla brought out the stack of notes she had been working on when he came in. "I was just thinking about that. I think everything is connected. Hear me out on this. Jim and Lorelei said that we were in a race to find information and protect it from the bad guys. So if "they" are the bad guys, we must be the good guys, right? If we're the good guys and of Lur Babsel, then the bad guys must be Denortus. Now, we've thought that the bad guys were these art thieves that are hitting the museums, so if our logic is true, then Denortus must be stealing art to find information that's maybe buried in the art somehow. Jim said we've got to find the information. If we find the information, we'll probably find Denortus. And if we find Denortus, we might find Jim and Lorelei."

Quinn blinked at Kayla a few times, giving the impression that he was trying to follow along and struggling. His stomach grumbled loudly, reminding them that it had been a long time since lunch. "Wanna get a pizza? We can talk about this on the way over."

Kayla agreed. They headed off to the Pizzeria Italiana. They had discovered the tiny place days earlier and had eaten there several times. The restaurant could best be described as a hole in the wall with little ambiance. There was a counter all the way at the back where they ordered their food. The chef/owner/waiter/bus boy worked behind the counter, in front of a giant brick oven. The menu was written on a chalkboard above the counter. It was simple: You can have any kind of Italian delicacy you'd like as long as it's pizza.

After ordering a large pie with extra cheese, hamburger and bacon on half, veggies on the other half, they settled into a booth. Kayla sipped a glass of water, Quinn a large Coke. As they waited for their name to be bellowed by the chef, their conversation resumed.

"I think we've got too many irons in the fire," Quinn said, slurping his soda.

"What do you mean?" Kayla asked.

"Well, we've got another coffee house tomorrow, and we need the money. We've committed to organizing Mr. Keltsea's basement and running breakfast for him. We told him that we'd set the stuff up so that he could try and sell it, right? I told him earlier today that I'd help him find a buyer for the place who'd keep it open. We've got to continue to elude the Train Twins who seem to be mugging half the city to get to us. We owe it to ourselves to figure out what is going on, who's after us and why. I can't abandon my search for Lorelei and I'm sure you feel the same way about Jim. Now add to that, a search for art thieves? I think we're in over our heads already. What do we know about solving crime?"

"Don't forget, we need to find out whatever we can about Denortus and Lur Babsel. I think that might be the key to staying alive."

"OK, add that to the list. That's what I'm talking about. It's too much."

"But I'm saying that I think most of this is connected. I don't think we have that many separate things going on. Wait a minute – you said the Train Twins are mugging half the city to find us. Why didn't I think of this before?!" Kayla stared at the wall over Quinn's shoulder, her eyes wide and her brain furiously making connections.

"Think of what?"

"If Denortus "got" to Jim and Lorelei and the Train Twins are trying to get to us, then the Train Twins must be part of Denortus! Maybe they are the art thieves! Or at least know them."

"Well that's great, but can we do about it? I still think we've bitten off way more than we can chew. I think we need to prioritize."

Kayla nodded absently, still trying to connect all the pieces. Together, they determined that since the coffee house was tomorrow, that should be their most immediate priority. Quinn's head whipped around at the sound of his name. "Ooooh our pie's ready." He scooted out of the booth and reached the counter in three of his long strides.

They ate in silence for a while, each thinking about the road ahead of them and enjoying the simple pleasure of a superior pizza. During a digestion break about halfway through the pie, Quinn offered up a concern. "Kay, what makes you think we can solve this art thing? The police have got to be all over it."

Kayla carefully wiped the corners of her mouth with her napkin before returning it to her lap. She took a sip of water, wetting her hands in the condensation on the side of the cup before rubbing them with the napkin. "I don't know why I think we can do this, but I do. And I don't think we should just try, I think we must succeed. I feel like we have to solve this if we want any hope of seeing Jim and Lorelei again. This is the path we have to follow."

"Well, I can't argue with that. It's instinct, huh? Let's go back to the Last Tain and get things ready for tomorrow night," Quinn said around a mouthful of pizza.

Suddenly, Quinn shivered violently, twitching his shoulders and torso. His brows pulled together and he glanced around the small open room as he scooted out of his booth seat and tossed the empty pizza tray on the counter. "Something doesn't feel right. I think we should go. Now."

They rushed back to the Last Tain and once they were safely inside, Kayla asked, "What was that all about?"

"I don't know, but I got really freaked out, like someone walked over my grave. Have you ever had that feeling?"

"OK, was this an Advantage type of feeling? Or a general creeped-out-ness?"

"I'm not sure. Advantage, I think."

"Well, good. That's useful, then. Well, you kind of stick out in a crowd, or above a crowd anyway, so why don't you stay here and finish prepping for tomorrow? I'm going to run down to that internet cafe and see what I can find out about these thieves. I'll be back in an hour and a half."

Quinn argued that he didn't think it was safe for her to be running around town by herself at night with the Train Twins or whoever was out mugging people who looked like them, but he realized that he'd lost the argument when the door slammed shut as she left. Luckily nothing happened and by eleven o' clock, they were both settled in their beds with everything ready for tomorrow.

****

The alarm on Kayla's watch woke her from a sound sleep. Morning had come earlier than either of them had ever noticed before, but after forgoing a shower to doze a bit longer, Kayla finally had to get up. She stretched and yawned, then shook Quinn awake before heading to the bathroom. When she came back to the room barely two minutes later, Quinn seemed to be asleep sitting up. She whacked his foot playfully saying, "Hey sleepyhead, wake up. Do you want to go start the coffee or head to the pastry shop?"

"I'll go downstairs and start both the coffee and the cookies if you don't mind making the pastry run," Quinn said hopping down from the top bunk.

"Sure, but you aren't going to fall asleep again, are you?"

Quinn rubbed his eyes and talked through a yawn. "Nope, I'm awake." Kayla watched Quinn drag himself out of the room ahead of her, before she bounced her way down the stairs.

Kayla stepped into the courtyard ready to jog to the pastry shop. The door closed behind her with a bang that made her wince. *Should have caught that*, she thought. With nothing to do for it now, she headed out the gate and up the street. She figured that she had an extra ten minutes this morning since Quinn was undoubtedly a bit behind her getting downstairs. She decided to go right and run a couple of extra blocks before heading down to get the pastries.

The streets were mostly empty this time of day. When she turned right, away from the pastry shop, she noticed a man standing in the shadowed alcove made by the corner of a porch two doors down. It seemed that as soon as he saw her, he turned to face the corner and crouched down to tie a shoe. Kayla glanced his way as she ran past and was so surprised to see that his shoes were lace-less loafers that she nearly missed a step in her stride. She added a bit more speed to her pace and decided to head directly to the pastry shop after all. She took her next left and backtracked running parallel to the street she had been on. She glanced over her shoulder several times and didn't see anyone following her.

She tried to picture the man in her mind so that she could describe him to Quinn and realized that she didn't have a good image of him. Just a man, in a dark jacket and hat, dark pants – maybe dress pants, and definitely shoes with no laces. She could picture his hands fumbling over his shoes, but couldn't see if they were pink, brown or tan. Maybe he had gloves on, but that would be odd for summer.

After a few additional blocks, she turned left on a side street, then left again onto the road with the pastry shop. Her heart raced as she ran up the hill, and she wasn't sure if it was due to the exertion or the anticipation of seeing the man again. After all, she was nearly back where she had started. She reached the pastry shop a minute before it opened and rested, pacing back and forth in front of the door to cool down. The house where the man had been hiding was a few doors up the road but some trees blocked Kayla's view. Still, she didn't think there was anyone loitering up there.

Once her breathing slowed, she stood with her back to the pastry shop wall and really looked at her surroundings. A few cars were driving up and down the street and a couple of shop owners seemed to be preparing to open. In addition to the pastry shop, there was a newsstand and a diner that catered to the on-their-way-to-work crowd. Most of the buildings on the street showed signs of life, people moving around, lights going on or off, shades and curtains changing position. Birds chirped, a train whistled and she heard typical city clunks, grinds, and screeches in the distance.

Everything seemed so normal, she wondered if she had imagined the man. She supposed that if he had been there, he could have disappeared into any of the buildings, and in fact, maybe he was just a guy out getting his morning paper to read over breakfast. Who knew? The pastry shop door opened with a jingle and Kayla dismissed the man as an overreaction and went in to choose this morning's order.

Back in the Last Tain's kitchen, with the coffee and pastries feeding grumbly guests, they got Friday's menu out and Kayla walked through the 'fridge, freezer and pantry to verify that they still had all the ingredients for their offerings. Quinn started making cookie dough for all the flavors of cookies. They had sold out of all the cookies last time and he wanted to have a few extra batches on hand for tonight.

Kayla settled into a chair she'd pulled up to the counter that ran parallel to the pantry door and announced, "It looks like we won't be able to make blueberry muffins, we only have a few pounds of frozen ones left and they work so well in the smoothies. Not too big to be properly pulverized. We have plenty of canned pineapple, so let's think of something else we can make with that. Any ideas?"

Quinn looked up from the dough he was dropping onto cookie sheets. "Lorelei makes really good cream puffs for parties. She mixes super stiff whip cream with crushed pineapple, cream cheese and fluff, then spoons it between the top and bottom of some kind of pastry thing. We could make those."

Kayla made notes on the old menu. "Good idea, I'll look in the cookbook and find something that could work. And we can use the juice in the smoothies." They continued cooking, organizing and planning until the last tray of cookies was out of the oven and cooled.

THE CORDOVAN VAULT

After they finished the breakfast clean up, they spent a couple of hours in the basement shifting furniture around. Though the damp basement wasn't the best environment for the old pieces, they had been there so long that another couple of days wouldn't matter. And there was one sure fire way to identify antiques from reproductions: the antiques were astonishingly heavy. Several of the pieces looked similar to those they had seen at the Rosenbach Museum, but they didn't know if they were valuable. They continued to bring up small things like boxes to be emptied or old paintings they had found to display them in the ballroom.

After a quick lunch, they spent an hour wandering around the rally grounds, stamping hands with the address for the Last Tain and sampling Quinn's music before going back to finish getting ready.

It was still early afternoon so Kayla suggested that they review the information she'd found on internet about the art thieves. Quinn thought it was a good idea, but suggested that they do it at a laundromat. He was wearing his last clean t-shirt.

"Do you know how those work? I've never been," Kayla said up in their room as they tossed their clothes into a two garbage bags. One for whites and one for colors.

"What do you mean?" Quinn asked, looking puzzled.

"The washers and stuff. They're not like the ones at home, are they? I mean, you have to put money in them right?"

Quinn stared at her, his mouth agape, his green eyes huge. "You've never been to a laundromat?"

"Of course not. I've always lived in the house in Granby and we had a washer and dryer."

"Oh, right. Well don't worry, I've been to lots of laundromats and they are all basically the same. Where did you put all that change from the tip jars?" Kayla pulled the pitcher of coins out from under the bed. They sifted through and pulled out eighteen dollars in quarters. Kayla grabbed her notes from Down the Patch and they started off.

There was a laundromat nearby. Once the machines were running, they sat on a bench and reviewed the activities of the art thieves, beginning with the first break-in about six weeks ago. Quinn drew a timeline of activity. "It looks like they hit the smaller museums first," Quinn noted.

"Maybe they thought the security would be lighter. Did you notice that they only took a couple of paintings from each museum and that they were all really old. They didn't take anything too famous either."

"I guess they figured they'd never be able to sell a stolen Monet, huh. Maybe they look better in real life, but none of these paintings seems very nice in the pictures you found online. They're crowded with images and it says here that most of them are painted on wood not canvas."

"It looks like they took some sculptures too – the first museum and the fourth each had relief disks stolen. There's no picture of them in the newspaper, so who knows what they were of." Kayla shuffled the notes, looking for her page of ideas on what to do next. "Which of these have we already been to?" They spent some time looking through the list of museums that had been hit, and determined that they should start with the most recently struck institution. Since the crime happened so recently, they figured that the staff would be more likely to remember anything of consequence.

"The Betsy Ross museum is around the corner from the Last Tain. Let's bring our stuff back and head over there. We've got everything ready for tonight and a few hours before we open," Quinn said.

The Betsy Ross House was situated on a fairly normal looking city street. The style of the house was certainly colonial, but that was nothing unusual in this city. The house was laid out for tourists, starting in the gift shop and then following through the small house. Before the first room, Quinn pointed out a huge family tree hanging on the wall, filled with embroidered names. "I guess she was something of an accomplished needle woman," he joked.

The family tree was the size of a square kitchen table for four people. It was under glass, but it looked like white silk with the skeleton of a tree sewn as a background. There were several main branches with many smaller limbs and dozens of little twigs coming off the limbs. Each stick was a line with a name stitched above it. The names were tiny and each one had a tiny birth and death date. Kayla couldn't imagine the number of hours that must have gone into creating the wall hanging. "Wow, look at all those relatives."

They spent some time looking at the thing in wonder and determined that it went back five generations, or about one hundred and twenty five years. There was no easy way to count the number of names, but there had to be a few hundred.

"Families must have been bigger back then." Quinn said as they entered the main part of the house tour.

"Did you see all the children who died? Everywhere you looked there were twigs with birth and death dates only a couple of years apart, if that long. It must have been hard on the parents." Kayla said, a little sad.

They talked and wandered through the house, from exhibit to exhibit. On the second floor, a woman sat inside one of the displays, wearing colonial style clothes and sewing something stretched out on a giant hoop standing on the floor. They lingered at the displayed linens until the room was empty of other tourists, then approached the woman. She had a name-tag pinned to her dress that read 'Peggy'.

Kayla asked Peggy what she was working on. "I'm working on a quilt." She turned the hoop so that they could see the front. The frame stretched a piece of a quilt taunt, about the size of a stop sign. The rest of the heavy blanket pooled on the floor. They could see that she was sewing in a design.

"Is that decorative stitching?" Kayla asked.

"It's quilting. A quilt is really a bunch of layers of blanket that has been sewn together. Today's quilts have a decorative top, then a layer of batting and a bottom. In Betsy's day, they didn't have fancy batting like we do. They would re-use something old that was worn out, like old blankets or canvas feed bags. Really, whatever they had lying around. The colonials were the ultimate recyclers."

Peggy showed Kayla how the sandwich of fabrics was sewn together so that nothing would slide around making it too lumpy. Since the colonial people didn't have the ready access to buy new things like modern day people, the art of quilting developed out of necessity. A heavy blanket that was well stitched would stand up to generations of wear. And the many layers were necessary in the days before central heat and insulation.

Quinn turned the conversation from the art of quilting to the art thieves. "I heard that you guys got hit by those thieves that are breaking into the museums. I hope nobody was hurt."

The woman turned to face Quinn. Short curls peaked out from beneath her mob cap and old style wire rimmed glasses perched on her nose. "Wasn't that terrible?" Peggy agreed. "No, nobody was hurt, thank God, but I was here that day! I couldn't believe it when I heard. I mean, we have some very nice pieces, but our collection is really nothing compared to some of the other local museums."

"Was anything stolen?" Quinn asked.

The woman nodded her head, her curls bobbing. "Yes, unfortunately. We lost two old paintings that were done by Betsy's son. They weren't terribly valuable, except that her son painted them. They were Revolutionary War scenes, local battles, that sort of thing."

"How did they get in? I haven't heard anything about how these thieves are doing it. I imagine that all the museums have alarm systems." Kayla perched on one hip, tilting her head in a somewhat ditzy, I'm-too-stupid-to-be-threatening-so-you-should-tell-me-everything-you-know sort of way.

Peggy looked at them skeptically and must have determined that two kids couldn't possibly be savvy

195

enough to be asking what kind of alarm the museum had. She leaned a little closer and nodded. "Our security is quite straightforward, but these thieves are very clever. They didn't leave any clue to how they got in. Every door was locked; the alarm was on. Not a window was unlocked or open or broken. We have no idea how they did it. In fact, if they had taken some small things from the room displays we might not have noticed right away. But the only things they took were the two big paintings that hung on the main staircase. It's hard not to notice that those were gone. I understand that the police found some fingerprints that they believe belong to the thieves, but they don't have them on file. Once they catch them though, they'll be able to match the prints up. Like on those crime dramas on TV."

Another group of tourists entered the room, talking amongst themselves about the hardships of colonial life. Kayla thanked Peggy and they continued on with the tour, heading down to the basement.

"Well, this looks familiar," Quinn said as they entered the cellar. It was one long room that ran the length of the house. They entered through a staircase inside, but at the opposite end of the room was a steep, dark exterior hatchway. Compared to the basement at the Last Tain, this one was empty. There was a display in the middle of the room depicting a kitchen. One wall had an enormous brick fireplace built in, big enough to roast an animal on a spit, which is likely what they did originally.

Around the fireplace there were a series of missing bricks that they thought was a design. But one of the plaques stated that those missing bricks were very common to houses from that time. They represented small ovens where things like potatoes could be baked. They held the heat from the fireplace, but not the flames.

There was also a hidey-hole in the back of the fireplace. This was common because in colonial times, a kitchen fireplace had a fire in it all year, even in the summer. There were no gas or electric ovens then, so cooking required fire. Whatever was put in that hiding place was well protected. If someone wanted it, they had to reach through fire to get it. And the hidey-hole wasn't obvious. It had to be well insulated from the fire.

Usually, there was a latch or a combination of hidden levers that would have to be used to release the door. The hidey-hole at the Betsy Ross house was opened by pushing down a series of five bricks in the enormous fireplace. They would slide down an inch, releasing a metal plate at the back of the fire. The plate would drop open like a modern day oven door, revealing a space behind it that was insulated from the heat of the fire.

When the Betsy Ross house foundation had restored the building in the late 1940's, one architect had figured out the code in the bricks, revealing a small stack of letters written in 1779 from Ben Franklin to Betsy Ross's niece Elizabeth.

Fireplaces weren't the only place for hidey-holes. The colonial people were very clever at that sort of thing. They had to be because while there were banks available for use, the most common way to store money in colonial times was to make useful household items out of it. Money was silver and gold. If someone wanted to, they could eat their breakfast with a silver spoon, then use it to buy something later in the day. The spoon could be melted down into coins, if people didn't want to carry silverware around in their pocket. The coins could be clipped to make change. If you had a silver dollar and something cost a quarter, the shopkeeper could clip a pie shaped piece out of the dollar coin and take that, leaving the rest. That's why coins eventually developed ridged edges, so that people could tell if they had been shaved down or were otherwise worth less than the expected value.

Kayla and Quinn exited the museum and walked back over to the Last Tain in silence. Quinn broke the silence by asking, "What are you thinking about? I can practically see the little hamster running in his wheel up there." He tapped her head softly.

Kayla flicked his hand away, ducking and turning to look at him with a slightly curled lip. "A genius hamster, maybe," she said. "I was imagining that family tree. I don't really know very much about my family. It might help to know some stuff in order to find my Dad later."

"I'm not sure we have time for extensive genealogy right now. In case you've forgotten, we're a bit busy, solving crime, avoiding death, uncovering basement treasures and conducting real estate transactions. You know, normal fourteen-year-old things."

Kayla nodded, knowing he was right. There wasn't time now for any sort of extensive search, but she thought that she might take a few minutes tonight and write down what she knew. It wasn't much, so it shouldn't take too long. Wasn't there something about not being able to know where you were going if you didn't know where you'd come from? She was sure she had read something like that somewhere. If she thought about it she could probably pin point exactly where, but that really wasn't the point.

"You know, my mom's diary mentions that she had a sister. I didn't know I had an aunt. Maybe she could help us out."

When Quinn didn't respond to her comment about finding her aunt, Kayla looked over at him with a snide remark ready to launch off her tongue. Quinn had been walking quietly along the sidewalk kicking a stone in front of him as people often do. Right when Kayla glanced over at him, he kicked the rock hard enough that it hit the leg of a person walking ahead of him. The woman turned around to see what had happened, took one look at Quinn's face and rushed away, crossing the street. The expression on his face was astonishing.

He was grinning, like he had wanted to hurt that woman, or at least frighten her. And he would enjoy doing it. It was a look of evil. Kayla put her arm out to grab him, to stop him. He batted her hand away and turned on her with a ferocious growl. She caught her breath and stepped back.

In the three years that she had known him, Quinn had made her frustrated and angry, he'd made her laugh, silently so that he didn't realize it and aloud when she couldn't help it, and he'd made her think, sometimes differently than she would have on her own. But in all that time, she'd never been afraid of him, until now.

"Quinn," she said sharply, "what is wrong with you?"

Quinn stopped in his tracks, his expression melting from nasty glee to wide-eyed fright. "I'm so sorry!" he gasped. "Somebody around here is feeling some really terrible emotions and I must have been feeling them too. We've got to get out of here, I think they've found us." He grabbed her hand and started to run.

Chapter Nineteen:

A Crash Course in Art History

"We've gotta lose 'em before we go home," he tossed over his shoulder. She silently agreed.

Quinn stopped running five minutes later, dropped her hand and rested against a tree in a park. He hunched over, his hands propping him up against his knees. He sucked in air by the lungful, trying to catch his breath. Kayla stood in front of him, pacing a few steps then spinning and covering her tracks in the other direction. He was happy to see that she was huffing and puffing too, but not to the extent that he was. "I think we might have lost him," he gasped between puffs.

She stopped pacing and stood right in front of him, closer than usual, looking up, right into his eyes. "What happened back there?" she asked.

"I really don't know. One minute we were walking along and I was kicking a rock, ahead of me. Then I started looking for the rock so that I could kick it. That was the difference, at first I was knocking it along ahead of us, then I didn't want to lose sight of it so I could kick that particular rock. I started kicking it harder and harder. When that woman turned to look at me, I was thinking that if she didn't get out of my way, I'd find a bigger rock and hit her with that one. I was a little disappointed when she ran away, but then you were there. It was horrible." He rubbed his face with his hand, as if trying to wipe away a picture.

"Why? You didn't look happy to see me," she added.

"No, that's it. I was very happy to see you. Thoughts flashed through my mind, terrible thoughts. Images from a bad slasher movie. And I was the slasher." Quinn shuddered, remembering the violent and gory ideas that had flipped through his head. "I don't ever want to feel like that again. If that's what this Advantage is about, I don't want it."

"Let's take a minute to calm down and think about this." They stood in silence for a few minutes, until Quinn finally caught his breath. "I think this truly is an advantage for us," she said to him.

"How? I may want to kill ya sometimes, but I don't want to *kill* you, you know what I'm saying?"

"No, no," she laughed lightly. "Do your thing now and try to see if he's still nearby."

Quinn wasn't too excited about 'doing his thing', but he could see the merit in the idea. He closed his eyes and concentrated on saying the alphabet backwards to block out distractions. Z, Y, X, W. What was that smell? No, block it out. V, U, T, S, R, Q – like for Quinn. He sighed and took a deep breath. Focus. P, O, N, M, L. Nothing, maybe a little anticipation, maybe a little residual fear. "OK, I think I'm getting you, anticipation and a little fear?" He opened his eyes and looked at her, still feeling the same emotions. She nodded. He looked around the park. They seemed to be alone, and he wasn't feeling anything else. "I think we're alone. I don't feel anything, I don't see anybody. But I barely know how to work this thing."

"I'd say you don't know how to work it reliably yet, at all," Kayla leaned back against a tree, too.

Quinn wanted to argue, but he worried she might be right. "Yeah. I think we're alone though."

"Don't worry about it. Let's get out of public and back to the Last Tain as quick as we can. You feel up to another jog?" The run back to their room was uneventful, but they did get back to the Last Tain a little bit earlier than they had expected. They rested for an hour then headed down to the common to get ready for the seven o'clock start of their second coffee house. It was even more successful than the first one had been.

Mr. Keltsea was beside himself with joy. In the two events, he had made enough money to cover half of the outstanding taxes on the hostel. Quinn and Kayla had added another $423 to their savings which was great, but even better than the money and the pride at having helped Mr. K, Quinn was most excited about how the crowd had reacted to him this time around. He had definitely seen some familiar faces tonight, and while the cookies and other snacks were good, he hoped he wasn't being conceited to think that they had some repeat business due to his skills with the guitar, the horribly-out-of-tune piano and his tricked out iPod.

The next morning, while they were working in the ballroom, they talked about what had happened as they left the Betsy Ross House. "I think we need to find time to practice our Advantages. Maybe I could have figured out which person on the street was following us. Maybe there's a way to direct their emotions back to them, to identify the source," Quinn said.

"Yeah, how do you practice something like that though? Do you even know how you do it?" Kayla asked.

"I think it happens in two different ways. One is kind of like reaching out to take something that's in front of you. When I was practicing at the pier, that's what I was doing. As long as I could see somebody, as long as they were within that type of distance, I could reach out for their emotions. The other way is more subconscious. That's what happened yesterday and to a lesser extent, that's what happened with Mr. Keltsea. It was more like the other person's emotions reached out for me."

"Practice sounds like a good idea, but I don't think I can. It's not like I can force a dream to come true. We need to learn a bit more about Advantages overall. And I thought I could start a family tree. The one at the Betsy Ross house got me thinking, maybe Advantages run in families. Membership in Lur Babsel, is supposed to run in families. I'll give some thought to the people in my family, and what their advantages might have been. It might help us to learn a bit about them, and maybe help us learn about ours."

"Also a good idea." Quinn decided to work on a family tree of his own. After an hour of scratching names and things down when they thought of them, they both came to the pitiful conclusion that neither one knew much about his or her family. Siblings, parents and a tiny bit of information about aunts, uncles and grandparents was all they could muster. They dragged out the list of wedding invitees that Quinn had found in the glove box of Jim's car as a reference source and that coughed up a couple of additional distant relatives.

A short time later, they finally cleared out enough basement to arrive at an actual basement wall, revealing the old fireplace. "I wonder if the Last Tain has one of those hidey-holes," Kayla asked. They spent some time looking at the bricks around the fireplace. Even though they were looking, they were both surprised to find that there was a secret hiding place.

It wasn't the bricks that moved, but when Quinn accidentally kicked the andirons they discovered that if both of them were tipped up toward the back of the fireplace, a hidden door on the opposite side of the room popped open. They cleared a path to the door and found a small space behind the paneling. Eleven framed paintings had been hidden away from the clutter of the room. They carried the paintings upstairs to get a better look at them.

In the midday sun of the courtyard, they leaned the paintings against the stone walls of the four raised flower beds so that they could see each piece of art clearly. No two paintings were the same size. There were three still life paintings of fruit, four pastoral scenes of women in white flowing dresses with parasols and big floppy hats having picnics in different locations.

Three of the paintings depicted street scenes of buildings with courtyards, horse traffic and pedestrians, and there was one portrait. Kayla squatted down in front of a particularly pretty picnic painting to look closely and see if she could make out the artist's signature. Quinn had gone inside to find out if Mr. Keltsea wanted to get a good look at the paintings before they joined their basement brethren in the ballroom.

Mr. Keltsea's shuffling waddle surprised Kayla out of her study of the signature on a painting of Independence Hall in the early 1800's. She had guessed the date of the subject based on the style of clothing the ladies in the picture wore. Mostly empire-waist dresses, where the "waistband" was high up on the ribs. "I can't make any of these signatures out. Do you think they are worth anything?" she asked.

"Huh. The missus always said there was treasure hidden here. Where'd youse find these?"

"In a space hidden behind the paneling. I'm guessing they've been there a long time since they were so hard to get to." Quinn handed Kayla a glass of water as he spoke.

"Well sir, I think youse found the art from the Last Tain's walls. The missus' father took them down during the Great Depression. Youse ken still see the marks on the walls where they used to hang."

"Really?" Kayla drew the word out like stretching a piece of bubble gum from her teeth with her fingers. "Maybe we should hang them back up to give the place a little pizzazz for potential buyers."

"Buyers?" Mr. K asked, turning to look at Kayla with a raised eyebrow.

Kayla chuckled. "Hey, on top of everything else, Quinn did say he hoped to find a miracle for you."

"Yeah. Good idea. We should spruce the place up a bit. And speaking of buyers, when do you want to have the tag sale, Mr. K?" Quinn asked.

THE CORDOVAN VAULT

"My daughter will be here the day after tomorrow, so maybe we should do it the next day, Thursday." Mr. Keltsea's voice trailed upward when he spoke, as if he wasn't sure of himself. "Before youse spruce the place up, I'll talk with Kathleen about sellin'. I think destiny had a hand in sending you kids to me, youse been that big a help. Raisin' the tax money and the fixin' the basement. But youse got yer own problems and I don't wanna take youse away from 'em. I had some ideas about how to get the word out about the tag sale. Mayhap youse could help me make some calls, as a last favor."

Kayla and Quinn's eyes met. She shrugged; he smiled. They turned to Mr. K and said "Sure," at the same time.

Back in the common room, Mr. Keltsea unveiled his plan. They called all of the local museums notifying them of the impending sale and contacted a couple of professors at UPenn to help them appraise some things. A professor from the art history department and the chancellor of the student-run Daily Life History Museum came over to begin reviewing the items. Mr. K offered the university dibs on things that they wanted to buy as an incentive to get a free appraisal. Kayla and Quinn spent the afternoon trailing along after them, jotting notes about things, their backgrounds and worth.

As Mr. Keltsea had suspected, most of the stuff had little value, but they found a bunch of items that were worth quite a lot of money. There was a chest of drawers just like one in the Rosenbach Museum which was worth $35,000. The oldest dresses they had found looked to be from the late 1700's. Together that collection, including the trunk, was estimated to be worth $25,000 dollars.

J MONKEYS

There was a shoebox full of old baseball cards. Kayla had done a bit of a Google search on them and found that two of them were worth several thousand dollars and that many of them were worth a couple of hundred dollars. Given how many there were, that could lead to some significant money.

They had found a copy of *Gone With the Wind*, which was confirmed to be a first edition. It appeared to be signed by Margaret Mitchell, but they would need to have that verified. A Google search showed a similarly signed copy for sale for nearly $10,000. They also found some confederate money, which was interesting since Philadelphia had never left the union, but they had no idea what it was worth.

All in all, Mr. Keltsea was quite happy. With the other antique furniture, the professor had estimated that they likely had about two hundred thousand dollars worth of stuff, if it went to the right buyers. It was late afternoon by the time the appraisers had left. They historian from UPenn had asked that several items be reserved for the university to have the opportunity to purchase them for the museum. After he left, the three of them sat at the counter discussing what they'd learned.

"It's too bad there's no Antiques Roadshow in town," Quinn said. "It would be great to bring a couple of things over."

"What would we pick, though? If we're going to dream, let's dream big and have a couple of Antiques Roadshow guys come here."

"Hey, that's a good idea! Do you think we could?" Quinn asked, getting excited and jumping off his stool.

THE CORDOVAN VAULT

"Oh, I don't see how. I was just talking," Kayla backtracked.

"We should try that…it would be a great way to get the word out about the Last Tain and drum up business for the sale. Is there a local version of the show? Maybe we could tap into that," Quinn looked at Mr. Keltsea. The old man was propped up on a stool, one leg resting on the floor with his hip perched on the seat of the stool. He leaned on the counter of the bar.

"I know some folks, lemme talk to a few of 'em and see. How're youse doin' searchin' fer yer kin? I don't want youse spending all yer time on the Last Tain." They caught him up on their progress. They had visited nearly all of the museums that had been broken into. They still had very little information to go on. There were two museums left: the Philadelphia Museum of Art and Carpenters' Hall.

Of course, they hadn't told Mr. K about their other practice and searches. They were making regular forays into libraries and internet cafes to search for information about Lur Babsel, Denortus and people with Advantages. They had been making little progress on that front too, as there really seemed to be very little reliable information on the subjects.

Surprisingly, they had found nuggets of information that lead them to books written long ago. Unfortunately, they couldn't be sure that the current translation of the books accurately captured the original meaning. For example, they had been lead to a particular saying in the Bible, but had no way of knowing what the original said since they didn't read ancient Greek.

Interestingly, Kayla had learned that the quote in her mother's letter that she had said was from Plato was actually said by Albert Einstein. She didn't know what that meant, but found it odd that her mother had gotten it wrong.

"That's good, that youse have plans. I don't want youse to neglect the real reason you're here jest to help an old man." He fumbled in his shirt pocket and pulled out a couple pieces of paper. "A friend had extra tickets to a ghost walk tonight. I thought I'd offer 'em to youse, to say thanks for all youse done fer me." His pushed the tickets over toward the kids.

"Thank you!" Quinn said, looking at the ticket. They were to meet at the park next door to Independence Hall at eight o'clock.

"Yeah, that's very nice of you Mr. K," Kayla said examining her ticket. "The tour starts in a little more than an hour. Do you want to head over there now?" she asked Quinn. "We can get some dinner on the way."

Chapter Twenty:
Doors Full of Meaning

They cleaned up and started the ten-minute walk to Independence Hall and stopped for dinner along the way. "Do you think we're safe?" Kayla asked, carefully pouring ketchup in a circle over her cheeseburger.

Quinn paused with his fork halfway to his mouth, as Kayla added mustard eyes, nose and smile to her ketchup circle. "Nice artwork," he chuckled softly.

Kayla looked up at him, and said completely seriously, "I like a specific mustard to ketchup ratio. The smiley face always gets it right." She put the bun cover back on her burger and smooshed it around to mix up the condiments. "Distribution method," she said, taking a bite. "Fafdy?" she mumbled through burger, gesturing for Quinn to get on with it.

"Safety, right." Quinn looked around the diner. Kayla glanced around as well, but nobody seemed to be paying them any attention and no one seemed to be specifically or suspiciously not paying them any attention either. She didn't see anyone who looked like the Train Twins. "Bear in mind that my…abilities…for lack of another, generic word, aren't perfect." Kayla nodded in agreement and he continued. "I'm not aware of any reason to fear for our safety at this moment."

Kayla swallowed her mouthful, gave him the hang-on-a-minute-there-fella finger and took a large gulp of her water. "Burger ball," she said thumping her chest with a fist. She burped delicately into her napkin. "That's a lot of caveats. Do you think we're in danger, being out and about like this, or not?"

Quinn stared back at her intently, meeting and holding her gaze. "I don't think so, but I wouldn't be shocked to be proven wrong," he said with a huff. "I'm not the Oracle at Delphi. How on earth am I supposed to know if we're safe? The house blew up and Jim and Lore are missing. Are we safe? No way! Are we in imminent danger at this very moment? I don't think so."

"Fair enough. I'm not asking you to predict the future," she scoffed. They finished their meals without further discord and headed out to the park. They waited on a cement circle with sidewalks that branched out like rays of the sun. There were several other people waiting. An older couple wearing matching light-weight royal blue jackets, khaki shorts and white sneakers with white socks stood hand in hand off to one side. Even their hair matched, seagull-butt gray.

Another small group stood near the center of the circle, three women and one man. They seemed to be in their mid to late twenties. Out of college, and probably working together at jobs they didn't like, considering the complaining they were doing. Kayla heard something about a witch of a boss with a nasty Napoleon complex. Another pair stood off to one side, two women, dressed

THE CORDOVAN VAULT

similarly. Kayla glanced at Quinn, then down at herself to see if they matched too. It seemed to be a theme of the evening.

Just as she was debating the merits of their similar style shorts, but in different colors, t-shirts that looked nothing alike and shoes that couldn't possibly be more different since his had individual toe sockets, a figure approached from a distance. He wore a long black cloak, the hood pulled up shading his face. In his hand he carried an old style, punched tin lantern. The light flickering within indicated that it was lit by an honest-to-god candle.

Quinn pulled on the back of Kayla's shirt, subtly telling her that they should be prepared to run. She turned to look at him, questioningly, only to see that his eyes were closed. He seemed to be trying to gauge the cloaked figure's intentions, but he didn't loosen his hold on her shirt, as if he needed to maintain the safety of that contact.

All this passed in a fraction of a second. Before the figure had even reached the edge of their block, Quinn must have determined that though this figure dressed somewhat menacingly, he meant them no harm.

"This must be the leader for the ghost walk," he whispered to Kayla.

They stepped closer to the middle of the circle as he approached. The man wasn't as old as they had suspected. He was probably twenty-two or so, bearded and mustachioed with bushy, dark-blond hair. He wore glasses that seemed to be the most prominent feature of his face, even more so than the shrubbery on his chin. The black cloak was fastened with wooden toggles down the front and seemed to be of a light-weight fabric that flowed as he walked. Up close he cut a much less frightening figure than he did at a distance. Of course, none of the other folks waiting in the circle seemed the least apprehensive of the man.

"Hi, I'm Mitch. I'll be your spirit guide this evening," the shrub said to a few quiet chuckles. "But seriously folks, we're going to take a stroll around the old part of town and talk about some of the vibrant history of the City of Brotherly Love and some of its other worldly residents. I'll keep a moderate pace, but try to keep up." Mitch collected everyone's tickets, and had them all go around and state their name, where they were from and what brought them to town.

Kayla looked at Quinn, wanting to say something but not wanting to be heard. On the spur of a moment, she decided to test his Advantage. She closed her eyes and thought of the scariest thing she could, needing to terrify herself, hoping to convey that to Quinn.

At first it seemed like nothing was happening. Then, when the old couple were introducing themselves as Melvin and Melissa Hooterstank from Glenville Missouri, Kayla felt a gentle tug on her elbow. She glanced up at Quinn, noting his concerned expression and smiled, flaring her eyes wide. He looked down at her, raising his left eyebrow in question, as if wondering why she would have tried to reach him that way. She gave him a play along kind of nod and the minute Mel and Mel Hooterstank stopped rambling on about the grandchildren they were visiting here in the city, Kayla jumped in to the conversation.

THE CORDOVAN VAULT

"I'm Sandra Vellum and this is my fiancé Bill Adley. We're from Indiana and we're here looking for a place to have our wedding. My family's from the north, Bill's is from the south and we wanted to meet in the middle," she said with a giggle. She looked up at 'Bill' adoringly and clung to his hand. Quinn's height certainly seemed to be helpful; everybody assumed that they were older than they were.

"Hey, ya'll," Quinn said with a nod to the group. He laced his fingers through Kayla's and peered down, returning her smile, then they turned to look at the last people to introduce themselves, a family from Michigan here on a college visit.

After everyone was introduced, Mitch started walking over to the brick courtyard behind Independence Hall. Quinn and Kayla hung toward the back of the group of walkers. Once they were fairly certain they were out of earshot, Quinn dropped her hand and asked, "What was that all about?"

"Oh, no, don't ruin our cover." She grabbed his hand and walked a bit closer so that their shoulders were practically rubbing together. Well, her shoulder was rubbing his elbow. Freakin' giant. "I didn't think we should give our real names. I figured we could pull off the fiancé thing since we spent months living with a pair. Some of their lovey-dovey-ness should have rubbed off on us. Where did you get that great southern accent?"

"We lived in South Carolina for a couple of years. So I'm pretending to be Jim and you're pretending to be Lorelei? I think a therapist would have a field day with that. No, no, it makes sense," he said waiving off her protests. "You're not so repugnant that I can't stand to flirt with you for a couple of hours."

"Thanks a lot!"

"I'm kidding," he said bumping her shoulder in a playful way. "I meant what was the bit of fright you threw my way? Were you actually scared or were you trying to get my attention?"

"You are getting good at this, honey." She batted her eyes at him in a 1920's melodrama way. "I was trying to get your attention and I figured I could scare myself pretty easily these days. We should work out some kind of code we could use."

"Well, let's not do it now, kitten," he replied, using the same so-over-the-top-it-has-to-be-real lovey-dovey voice. "Let's hear what Mitch has to say." They caught up with the rest of the group in time to hear Mitch launch into his monologue about a lady in a green dress said to haunt Independence Park. After a few minutes, they moved on.

"Before it gets fully dark, I wanted to walk up this street. The architecture you see on the front of the houses has a nifty history of its own. This was the colonial era's rich part of town. First let's talk about doors. If you look at these houses, you'll notice that the doors are different colors. That's not only decorative. The color of the door was an indicator of what the resident did for a living. Of course, that would be the male resident. The women who lived in this part of town were society ladies. They managed their homes, with the help of live in servants of course, and worked on various charities.

"But back to the men for a minute. A black door, meant that you were a minister. A red door meant that you were a butcher. A green door meant that you were a printer and a blue door meant that you didn't do anything, you were independently wealthy."

Mitch pointed to the structure of the door itself. "If your door had a cross down the front then you were a Christian. If the door was made up of a series of blocks that meant you were Jewish. If the door had a twice-crossed cross it meant your family was Quaker."

"Let's take a quick look at the windows too. In Colonial times, the tax collector would wander down the street and assess your house without ever stepping foot into it.

"One thing they taxed was window panes. Most windows had six panes to a window. Glass was expensive so it was much cheaper to repair small panes than big ones. If you had six window panes, you paid tax on all six. If you had one, you paid tax on one. Shutters were used for more than keeping out the light.

"Once the tax collector started working his way down the street, news of it spread like wildfire. Up and down the street, all the shutters would be closed. If your shutters were closed when he got there, the tax collector couldn't see your windows and therefore couldn't tell how many panes you had. He would have to assume there was one and would tax you accordingly."

"Finally, notice that this house has a small shield on the front. It is made of metal. This isn't decorative either. These shields were assigned by the local fire insurance company. If you had a shield on your house, and it caught fire, the fire department would put it out. If you didn't they didn't respond because the fire department worked for the insurance company, not the town."

Kayla tugged on Quinn's sleeve. "That is a pretty neat idea. To have messages built into simple things like a door. That way, if you were approaching a house, you would know something about it before you got there. Kinda like caller id."

Quinn agreed. "Cool. Everyday stuff had hidden meanings. We should take a closer look at the Last Tain. I wonder what it might tell us?"

As they completed the rest of the Ghost Tour (seeing no ghosts along the way) Kayla continued to think about things being hidden in plain sight. How much information about their current quest might be available if she knew what to look for?

****

Kayla was walking, but her feet didn't seem to touch the ground. She felt air blowing along her skin, but wasn't cold. A glance down showed that she was wearing a long tunic of all white. Her hair was hidden behind some sort of tight wimple, a nun's headdress. Surprisingly, it didn't bother her much. She walked along a well-defined dirt pathway. The building on her left was made of rough-hewn stone, as was the low wall along the right side. Outside the wall, there was a long field, then forest for as far as the eye could see. And from this elevation, the eye could see very far.

After a time, Kayla turned left when the walkway turned left. At the end of that walkway, she turned left again. Halfway down the length of the building on this side, a wide gray stone archway opened up. She turned left yet again, walking under the arch. Here, there were small fruit trees laden with ripening red apples and green pears along the left side. There were large pots of flowers and low herb gardens. Benches were placed at various angles and distances, a respite from the walk.

This alley followed along for a minute or two, then turned right, then after another few minutes, right again. She had walked into the inner courtyard sanctuary, completely hidden from the outside. Along the walls, orange tiled roofs collected rain into barrels. In this heart of the abbey, for that is what Kayla knew these buildings to be, sat a well.

Around the well there was a low wooden bench. A woman sat on the bench, restfully dragging her hand through the water she had drawn up in a bucket. Her back was to Kayla, but she too wore a long white flowing gown and was barefoot. Her hair was covered in a wimple identical to Kayla's but Kayla knew that it would be long, straight and a luxurious brown. Her small pointy ears were likewise hidden from view.

Lorelei turned her head toward Kayla, having heard her silent approach. Her hand continued to drag through the water. "I've been waiting for you," she said.

Kayla opened her mouth to ask…something. She wasn't sure if it was how or why, but before she got the chance, a loud growling roar split the air. Like a dinosaur or a dragon. Something big and probably lizardy.

Lorelei's head whipped around to see what was coming behind her. Kayla could see nothing but the surrounding buildings and the very tops of trees in the distance. Lorelei's yell reached her as Lorelei disappeared, "Go!"

Kayla's eyes snapped open. She sprung upright, forgetting for a minute that she was in a bunk bed in Philadelphia, not in her beautiful canopy bed in Maine. She banged her head on the bar that hung under Quinn's bed. Quinn flipped over in his sleep, mildly disturbed by the noise. Kayla shook off the fear of the dream and checked the clock. It was almost three o'clock. The middle of the night. She laid her head back on her pillow and closed her eyes, quickly falling back to sleep, the dream forgotten.

Chapter Twenty-One:

The Cloister

The next day brought more of the same routine they'd developed over the last week. Prep breakfast, eat, clean up, work in the basement, lunch, then decide where to spend the afternoon. There were only two museums left that had been broken into by the art thieves, Carpenters' Hall and the Philadelphia Museum of Art. Carpenters' Hall was closer, so they decided to go there first.

Carpenters' Hall was an old building. In fact it was so old that the first continental congress was held there. The second congress was held in Independence Hall. Of course, it wasn't called Independence Hall until many years after the Declaration of Independence was signed there.

But Carpenters' Hall was really an old Masonic Temple. The Masons, or Freemasons as they were sometimes called, were an ancient secret society. Some said that they were formed back in the 1100's after King Philip of France ordered the murder of the Knights Templar on Friday, the 13th of October. Hundreds of the monk-like knights were killed all across Europe on that one day, forever after marking it as an unlucky day.

Whether or not they had any connection to the Knights Templar and their famed treasure, the Masons were a medieval guild of free men who were stone workers. They built roads, bridges and buildings, all kinds of masonry work. No puzzle there in how they got the name.

Being a mason was like belonging to an elite club at a time when all the political and military power was held by the noble families.

The majority of people in Medieval Europe were peasants. Peasants were tied to the land. In a way, they were similar to slaves in that they weren't free to pick up and leave. They worked for a particular noble family. They had no rights in the absolute power of the nobility. If the lord wanted to steal a peasant family's goods, he could do it. Not that they were likely to have anything he'd want. If the lord wanted to roast peasant children over a spit in his kitchen and have them for dinner, there really wasn't anything the peasants could do to stop him.

This was a world where people were not created equal. There were very strict laws determining your place in society. That society was like a ladder, if you were born on the top rung, you stayed on the top rung. If you were born on the bottom rung, you stayed there too, and there wasn't any way you could move up the ladder.

In that stratified world, the Masons were free men. They were not tied to the land, they didn't belong to any particular estate or lord. They might travel the world, an uncomfortable prospect in a world without cars, trains or planes, but if he wanted to, a free man could do so. And, the Masons were learned men. They understood math, geometry and physics in a time when most people, even the nobility couldn't read.

THE CORDOVAN VAULT

To be a learned free man, subject to no one, able to hire out their skills to the highest payer was a rare and treasured bit of freedom in an unfree world. Of course, if the Mason's secrets became public knowledge, then their bit of freedom would be gone, either from a lack of mystery or from an attack like the one that wiped out the Templars. So, the society was a secret one. They passed their knowledge to each other and the next generation using a language of symbols and hidden messages that nobody unaffiliated with the society would be able to understand.

Carpenters' Hall was big but not much of the building was open to the public, just the main room which had a variety of displays laid out for visitors. Quinn and Kayla wandered around the hall, looking at the displays, surreptitiously seeking someone to pester with their questions. There were several old men who seemed to run the place lurking in corners.

Kayla indicated to Quinn that she would head over to one of the gentlemen and try to persuade some information out of him. Quinn stayed where he was, looking at a table of information related to the signing of the Declaration of Independence and the signers themselves.

"Do you work here?" she asked, thinking what a dull opening that was.

"Yes, miss. How can I help you?" the man replied in a wheezing voice that had seen too much smoke, whiskey and time.

"I had heard that the Hall had been a victim of those art thieves recently. Is that true?"

"Oh, true enough, miss. T'were a terrible thing. Never had a theft before, not in over two hundred years."

The man coughed into a handkerchief and reached for a cup of water resting on a coaster on the windowsill.

"That is terrible. It seems like you have such a nice collection here, did you lose anything of value?" Kayla looked around the room wondering where the valuable stuff might be. Most of what she saw were books and ledgers, photos and things.

"I don't know for sure, but I did read in the paper that we lost a journal written by one of the signers of the Declaration of Independence and a couple of old paintings. One of the paintings was of the same man." He rested back on his perch.

Our second to last stop and we're still getting nowhere, Kayla thought in disgust. "Which signer was it? Ben Franklin, John Hancock, maybe Jefferson?"

The old man smiled a pompous little grin. "Youse kids only learn about a handful of the framers. No, no. It weren't any of them famous fellas. 'Twere the journal and portrait of a man from New Hampshire. Peter Livingston were his name."

Kayla felt her jaw drop open, but wasn't able to think what she should do about it. Out of the corner of her eye, she saw Quinn's head snap up and turn toward her, then he crossed the room quite purposefully, walking straight over to her. He arrived in time to hear the old man say, "What's the matter, miss. You look like you seen a ghost."

Without thinking, she replied, "That's my last name, Livingston."

"Huh, what a coincidence, honey," Quinn said with a laugh, reverting to his 'Bill' accent and role. "Did you see the garden out front? I think I saw that flower you wanted for your bouquet. Did you want to come take a look?" He waved to the tour guide and grasped her elbow, steered her out the door and down the steps. "What was that all about? I thought you might have been stabbed or something. I felt that shock like a cattle prod to the butt," he ground out in his normally accented voice, in a gruff whisper thinking she had been practicing using his Advantage to her advantage again.

Kayla looked at him, her eyes huge Mediterranean blue spots in the middle of her head. She spoke in a raspy whisper, as if she didn't have enough wind in her lungs for regular speech.

"The art thieves broke into Carpenters' Hall, committing the first robbery in its two hundred year history. They stole an old portrait and a journal of a signer of the Declaration of Independence. A guy from New Hampshire named Peter Livingston. Presumably, these are the same art thieves that Jim and Lorelei were chasing. Jim and Lorelei *Livingston*. What a coincidence, huh?" Kayla's voice had started the recitation at a fairly level pitch, but by the time she was through, she was somehow managing to yell in a whisper.

"None of the other museums had books stolen right?"

"Nope, just old paintings. Mostly daily life scenes, with a couple of disaster types thrown in the mix."

"So do you think they were hiding what they really were after by stealing a bunch of stuff that isn't connected."

"I don't know, that seems like an awful lot of work to throw people off their track. Let's get over to the last museum that was robbed and see if we learn anything there." They rushed back over to Independence Park, but

225

tried to do it in a casual way. There was no sense in attracting the wrong attention, especially when so much of it seemed to find them anyway.

As they walked through the park, they were saddened to see that all of the vendors and people from the Environmental Rally were leaving. They stopped at a tent to say goodbye to some people they had met. A man they didn't know was working at the next tent over. He introduced himself, saying he had noticed Quinn, not hard given his height.

"Phillipe Kendall," he said, offering his hand to Quinn. "I saw you playing the other night at that old hostel, right? You were great," he continued at Quinn's nod.

"Thanks a lot. I had a good time."

"Do you have a CD out, or a website? I'd love to download some of your music."

"No, nothing like that. I'm only starting out," Quinn said, both pleased and slightly embarrassed at the same time. After the disaster of the Sound of Music, the Last Tain coffee houses were really his first success. Phillipe looked to be his first fan. Well, first fan who wasn't a sibling. Lorelei would be mad if he didn't count her as a fan.

"That's too bad, man. Well, here's my card. Drop me an email if you get something together." He handed Quinn a small rectangle of heavy paper. Phillipe Kendall, CEO HydroLion Coffee was embossed across the front. Phillipe was quite a bit shorter than Quinn, maybe only five foot nine, but he was broad. He moved like a guy used to lifting heavy things, either weights in a gym or perhaps he was Chief Executive Officer of a very small company where he was also Chief Lifter-of-Heavy-Things. He was dressed in old jeans and a dingy old concert t-shirt with a rip on the shirt tail. He definitely looked more like the Chief Lifter-of-Heavy-Things, than the CEO.

"You run a coffee company?" Quinn asked, gesturing toward Phillipe with the card.

"Yeah, we grow and sell a specialty coffee made from hydroponic dandelion root. You really can't tell the difference and it's much easier on the environment. Did you know that the coffee plant is grown for the seeds? An incredible amount of the world's forests have been cleared to grow coffee. It's one of the world's biggest commodity crops. Coffee beans are actually the seeds of a cherry-like fruit. There are two seeds in each fruit and in ninety-nine percent of the cases the fruits are discarded.

"Each cup of coffee requires forty gallons of water to grow and produce. A lot of the areas of the world that produce coffee have water shortages, meaning that water is diverted from people and other crops to produce coffee. Our product uses only one gallon per cup."

"Wow, I had no idea." Quinn looked over at Phillipe's tent filled with crates of things. "Hydroponic dandelion coffee, huh. That's neat."

"You wanna try some? I've got a ton of samples left over," Phillipe gestured to his tent.

Quinn thought for half a second about their tight budget and instantly decided that he should not be too snooty to drink free coffee. Or at least he should be willing to try free hydroponic dandelion coffee. "That'd be great, thanks." Quinn took the three steps over to Phillipe's tent, where the blond man was tossing things into a canvas bag with a picture of a lion swimming on it.

"Here's a bunch of stuff, you'll save me from having to bring it back. Plus if you like it, you can give me a call when you are rich and famous. You can be my spokesperson."

Quinn laughed, "It's a little early to be thinking about endorsement deals, but I appreciate the stuff. I'm sure we'll like it. Good luck." He accepted the bag and stepped back over to Kayla. She seemed to be receiving a similar bag of goodies.

They said goodbye to their acquaintances and continued walking through the park. Every few feet they were stopped by another group of folks hoping to get rid of some overstock. By the time they got to the Phlash bus stop, they were loaded down with freebies. They condensed their bags down to one full bag apiece, offering a bunch of extra items to a homeless man begging for a meal.

After an uneventful ride, they arrived at the Philadelphia Museum of Art. The museum was a huge stone monolith perched at the top of what seemed like a hundred steps. From the ground, the museum couldn't really be seen, but once they had climbed the long flight of steep stairs, the building appeared at the end of a brick patio that would look at home in front of a castle. They passed fountains and giant statues of people on horseback as they walked closer to the building.

The main entrance was up still more steps at the center of the building. Both the left and right wings were covered in enormous hanging banners depicting different exhibits that were inside. As Kayla pushed the heavy metal and glass revolving door, she noticed the breathtaking view reflected in the door. She spun the full way around through the door, not actually entering the building. She took a step out of the doorway and stood, back where she had started, at the top of the world looking out at the city below her.

It was a perfect day, blue sky with a few small puffy white clouds. The sun shone down, but not directly on them. There was a hint of a breeze, keeping them comfortable. Like most eastern US cities, there was little smog to obstruct the view. Straight ahead they could see a pointy tower, with a major traffic rotary between them and the tower. Cars whizzed by, heedless of the part they played in the scene.

And the cars were important. The view was startling in its contrast of old world charm and modern business hub. It was a planned landscape with carefully drawn parkland and a chaotic, traffic-filled hive of activity. And flanking the view were the huge statues of some kind of thing standing at the wings of the entrance to the museum. It was quite a sight to behold.

Through body language, Quinn and Kayla agreed in their "wow" assessment. Quinn gestured with his head back toward the museum entrance and Kayla nodded, leading back through the revolving door. Once inside, there was a trip up a few more steps, then the admittance counter. They fished their Granby High School student IDs out of their wallets and paid the discounted student price.

"The article in the news said that the theft occurred in the Medieval European wing," Kayla standing in a cavernous four-story high atrium, turning a map until she could orient herself into the picture. "We want to go this way." She pointed her arm out toward the left without looking up from the map. When she did glance up after she spoke, she noticed that there were huge signs labeling the different wings. Quinn stood with his shoulder propped up against the wall plaque that announced the direction of the Medieval European wing, waiting for her. "Smarty pants," she said with an exasperated smile.

The wing was set up as a series of rooms. One room lead to another, and each room had a couple of exits to some other rooms. Every room was set up with a variety of items around the periphery. Some were large like an ancient fireplace, some were tall like a four foot, cast iron candle holder. Some were small, like the 1000 year old nails used to hold ancient buildings together. And some items were gigantic.

There were imposing doors from castles and churches, and a portcullis - the giant iron castle gate - that would crash down like a two ton garage door dropping free from its mechanical system. The spiked ends of the portcullis ensured that nobody wanted to be standing underneath it when it closed.

As they wandered from room to room, getting more and more turned around, they noticed that there was a blue uniformed guard in every third room. The guards were almost exclusively old men. Definitely senior citizens. It seemed that their presence was more to offer directional assistance, a sense of dignity and quiet reverence to the galleries than to truly protect the treasures.

Quinn and Kayla wandered through the armory display, looking at the plate metal suits that would have been worn by knights on horseback. Quinn caught up with Kayla to offer an observation. "I guess it must be true that people then were really smaller than we are today. Look at these suits. There's only one or two that I'd fit into and not because of my height. Check out the waists on these things. They're tiny! And these guys would have been wearing clothes, leather and padding underneath the armor."

Kayla nodded, looking around the room. "Well, you'd definitely fit in that one," she said, pointing across the room to a suit that was clearly the largest in the room. It was both tall enough and broad enough for Quinn. Compared to the others, it was monstrously huge.

"Ooooh, yeah, now that's what I'm talking about!" Quinn rushed over to the display with a boyish energy and excitement that Kayla hadn't seen before. She smiled to herself as she walked to join him.

By the time she got over there, Quinn was walking around the display, looking under the skirts of the hauberk, probably trying to imagine what wearing the suit would be like. She half imagined him putting his foot up next to the armor's shoe to check the size. "Maybe this is where the myths about giants came from," Quinn said. "Just look at this guy – can you imagine how imposing he would have been at the head of an army? His horse was huge too, look." Quinn pointed to the horse armor set up behind the man's suit. The horse headpiece was easily the size of Kayla's rib cage.

"Yeah, I guess. If he had brothers or cousins who were of similar size, that would have seemed like an undefeatable force. Pretty cool. Look at his sword, it's almost as tall as I am." True enough, the sword standing next to the giant armor came up to Kayla's shoulder, with the point on the ground.

They moved on through the gallery to the inner sanctum of the wing walking from room to room, glancing at the items on display and looking for a guard who seemed chatty. They got lucky after ten minutes of wandering. A man in a blue uniform stood in the center of a large room with his head tilted back, staring at the ceiling. He was turned so that they could see his back and a slice of his profile. From the doorway, Quinn and Kayla glanced up, wondering what he was seeing. He turned his head toward them and chuckled, "That's two more."

Kayla smiled. "Are you trying to see how many people will look up to see what you are staring at?"

The man grinned, a dimple forming in his left cheek. His skin was a smooth rich brown, like peanut-buttery fudge and his tuft of short white hair looked like cotton. He shuffled his feet a few times, taking a few steps to look around the room, presumably to ensure that they were unobserved. It was his posture and his walk that conveyed his years, more than the hair. He turned back to the kids, seeming to take their measure. "Not much to do in this job, so I have to entertain myself somehow. Hope you don't mind."

Quinn laughed, a boisterous sound in the echo-y room. "Do what you gotta do, man. I'd get bored too."

Sensing an opening for the conversation they wanted to have, Kayla tugged Quinn further into the room so that they could speak quietly, avoiding the echo that carried sound to the other rooms. "Not much excitement in this job, huh?"

"No, miss. Perfect for an old man. Chat with some folks, give 'em directions. That sort of thing." He continued to gaze through the doorways into the two other rooms that this one opened into, perfectly capable of talking and watching at the same time.

"Wasn't there a break-in here not long ago? That must have been exciting," Kayla said leading him to the topic of the thieves.

"Shore 'nuf, miss. Over a week ago." He tsk'd, shaking his head in disgust. "More security now."

"Did they steal much?" Quinn asked.

"No sur. Twere the strangest thin'. They stole a couple of plaster disks from a room ahead and several old paintings from the American History room. Sure seemed like they knew what they wanted. No easy way to get over to that wing from here."

"Right through there?" Kayla asked pointing to a door at the end of the room, away from the door they had walked in.

"Sure, I'll show you." He walked them through the door, then through two others making the deft turns of a man who had walked these floors hundreds of times. His pace was slow and they had plenty of time to glance at each room's treasures as they passed by. He stepped into one last room and pointed to a giant gray stone archway that was the central focus of the room. "Through there."

They thanked him as he turned away and walked through the arch in awe. Kayla ran her hands over the stone as she passed under the twenty-five foot arch. She had a fleeting sense of expectation and perhaps recognition but then her focus turned from the arch to the room behind it.

She stopped inside the room. "Oh. My. God." she whispered.

"What?" The single word carried with it, horror, terror, a need to know the source of the shock and dread at the thought of knowing. Quinn's voice was so deep it was nearly inaudible. But Kayla heard it.

"This is a cloister. I've been here before. In a dream. Yesterday."

Chapter Twenty-Two:

An Unlikely Warning

Quinn stood in stunned silence. He had walked through the arch at her side and turned his head to stare at her. Emotions had raced through his heart so quickly he couldn't name one before three others passed. But he felt them all. And the last was an abiding sense of familiarity combined with shock. It was a shock so profound that it made every other shock he'd experienced mellow to mild surprise.

For a half a second, his mind wandered, thinking he was doing that a lot nowadays – standing still, shocked into silence. He wondered if that would continue, or if at some point, the life they were now leading would stop surprising him, and perhaps even become normal. He shuddered at the thought and tugged his brain back to the shock d' jour.

"What do you mean you dreamed it?" his whispered demand echoing in cavernous room.

"I had a dream last night that I was walking through here, although it was different. It was peaceful."

"How could it be the same if it was different?" Quinn's sandy eyebrows knit together in confusion.

Kayla gestured for him to follow and they walked the short, straight, distance to the fountain in the middle of the display. They sat on the stone bench and Kayla continued after checking to be sure there wasn't anyone else in the room. "I dreamt that I was at a building at the top of a hill, I think.

The beginning of the dream is really fuzzy. I was walking along a path that seemed to wind through a building somehow but was still always outside. Maybe it was between buildings or something. But you couldn't see the path from outside the buildings; it wasn't obvious that there was a path, I mean. So anyway, I was following the path, kind of floating along, wearing some weird dress and when I got to the center of the path, there was a well, not a fountain."

Quinn had sat quietly through the description of the dream, but didn't understand. "But how do you know it was this cloister? How do you know it wasn't some other old building?"

"The red curvy tiled roofs were the same, with the same perimeter thing," Kayla pointed at the museum ceiling, toward the square that circled the inner courtyard. It looked like it could have held open tubes that collected rainwater or perhaps the infrastructure for a pergola. Inside the museum, it was an open square that hinted at some other purpose lost to time. "But I haven't gotten to the most important part of the dream yet," Kayla paused, remembering now how frightened she was when she awoke. "When I got to the center, there was a woman sitting here."

She pointed to the bench to her left, alongside the fountain. "She seemed at peace, like maybe she had been waiting for me, but knew I was on my way, you know?

Anyway, she was sort of running her hand through the water, humming or something. She must have heard me, although I didn't make any sounds. My feet didn't crunch the grass or anything. You ever do that in dreams?"

Quinn shook his head, not really sure what she was talking about and wishing she'd get on with it. "Anyway," she continued, "the woman turned around to smile at me, and it was Lorelei. When she started to talk, there was a roar of some kind. She shouted 'Go!' and I woke up terrified, but went back to sleep and forgot all about it until we walked in here."

"How could you have dreamed of this place? Have you ever been here before?" At Kayla's negative head shake, Quinn ran his hands through is hair, nearly tugging on the ends in frustration. "That doesn't make any sense. Are you sure it doesn't seem similar to the dream? Similar in a completely-different-I've-never-been-here-before kind of way?" he asked desperately.

Kayla looked up at him almost apologetically. "You see, this is the type of freak out I had the other day. You know, when we saw that CNN video clip that had me yelling on the street and you didn't seem to be bothered by it. Our roles are reversed here. I'll be over there when you're ready to talk. Enjoy." She patted him on the knee and got up to walk around, brushing off the seat of her jean shorts as she went.

Quinn hid his face in his hands and closed his eyes for a minute, taking a deep breath through his nose and holding it as long as possible. When that didn't fully re-center his mind, he blew the breath out and took another one. After a few minutes, he felt himself come back together. So,

J MONKEYS

Kayla'd had a dream about a place she'd never seen before. Or was it a place she didn't remember seeing before? Maybe she'd seen it on a commercial or in a movie or something like that. He got excited for a minute thinking about rational explanations for the dream.

Then he remembered that dreams of the future seemed to be her Advantage. Hey, it turned out that he could feel the emotions of others. And it seemed that their families were somehow in a society so secret that he'd never heard of it until a few days ago. And that new, surprising things seemed to happen to them nearly every day.

Given all that, why did it seem far-fetched that Kayla could have a dream about a place they hadn't yet visited? And Lorelei was there. He sighed. He looked around the room, quickly finding Kayla in a corner looking at a column. He walked over to her, much calmer than he'd been a few minutes ago.

"So. What do you think it means? Your dream about Lorelei in this place?" He was really quite pleased with the normal tone of voice that he'd managed to use.

"I don't know. It was definitely this place, like I said, but it didn't seem like this time. I think it was the original cloister, not this giant display in a museum. I looked at the sign over there, but it says that these are pieces from a couple of different places in France. Mostly thirteenth century." She spoke casually, as if she wasn't really paying attention to the conversation.

Kayla was looking closely at a square on one side of a column. Near the top of the column, there were four squares, one on each side. The squares were carved so that different shapes protruded out of the surface. They were similar to the Rodin disks. The square Kayla was studying had a carving of a winged lion.

"What's with the lion?" Quinn nodded toward the top of the column.

"I don't know, seems familiar though. A griffin, I think." Kayla wandered off to look at the other squares on the column. Two were faded, rubbed off by time. One was hard to distinguish, some sort of circle. A planet or star maybe.

They wandered around the room, looking at all of the columns. Most of the pictures were indistinguishable, but some had survived including the griffin, a falconish kind of bird, a sea serpent, a sunburst or star, and a bull. After the second time around the room, looking closely at each side of each column, Quinn asked, "What are you looking for? It's been half an hour."

"I know. There's something here I'm not seeing. All of the surviving squares have the same five pictures on them. And they are exactly the same color. Do you see how some of the squares are more gray than the rich white granite of the griffin? Why are the existing squares so similar and the others so varied. The squares with no definite pictures go from light gray to relatively dark, almost tan."

"Huh. You said all the pieces in this room didn't come from the same place, right? Maybe these with the pictures on them are all from the same place, different from the others in the room." Quinn looked around the room as if to see if anything disproved his theory.

"Maybe, maybe." Kayla shrugged with a deep sigh.

Quinn turned around the room and quietly sniffed the air. "Do you smell that?"

Kayla sniffed, too. "Apple. Do you want to go get a proper dinner? We can eat these freebies tomorrow. I'm craving salad."

Quinn looked at Kayla with a concerned look on his face. "You're craving salad? I've never heard of someone craving salad. A rabbit, maybe. Or a goat. But not a human! That's barely food."

She raised an eyebrow at him and smirked. "Very funny. Let's go. I'm sure we can find someplace around here that serves both salad and fried things."

****

After dinner, Kayla still couldn't identify whatever was bothering her. While Quinn showered, Kayla wandered down to the ballroom. She meandered through the room, checking on the set up, thinking about what they would want to tell Mr. K's daughter when she arrived tomorrow. Mr. Keltsea seemed to think that his Kathleen would be able to settle everything, so Kayla wanted to be able to tell her what they'd done and found so far. She dragged her hand along the rack of clothes, her fingers barely touching the fabrics. She straightened this and moved that.

She walked past the wall of paintings that Mr. K had asked Quinn to hang in no particular order, just to display them. Her eye fell on one of the street life paintings. It was a building with a guy leading a horse off to a barn. There was a tangle of winter trees along the left and right of the top of the painting, making a kind of painted-in mat. At the very top of the center of the painting, in a small square space left blank by the wandering tree branches, flew a griffin with a snake clutched in his paw and a tear in his eye in front of a sunburst. Kayla turned to look at the small winged lion more closely. It certainly looked an awful lot like the one in the Cloister.

Kayla stood in front of the painting for at least fifteen minutes, staring at the images, trying to discern their meaning, but came up empty. Finally, she gave up and yawning, trudged up the stairs to their room. She tripped over Quinn's sloppy wet towel, lying on the floor of the dark room and barely missed cracking her head on the corner of the bunk bed. "Quinn!" she whispered furiously into the dark.

"Sorry," he grumbled quietly.

Just as he settled back to sleep, Kayla whispered again. "I think it's all connected," she whispered

"What is?" Quinn rasped, pulled from the edge of sleep by her voice.

"I think all these things are connected. My mom's death, Jim and Lorelei, the secret room at the house, the people after us. Maybe my mom's letter. Even this thing with the art thieves."

"What makes you think that?"

"Well, the thieves stole a couple of discs from the cloister room. I had that dream of Lorelei in the cloister. And, one of the paintings we found in the hidden part of the basement has the griffin on it, right in the middle. "

"OK, but that still doesn't help us figure out what it is we're looking for. We're stumbling around in the dark hoping to bump into something that it turns out we want.

Wouldn't we be better off trying to achieve a concrete goal?"

"Like what? Trying to help Mr. Keltsea sell this place? That doesn't get us any closer to the most important goal of all – finding Jim and Lorelei!" Kayla's voice had gotten louder with every word so that by the end she was shouting in a loud whisper.

"We've already had this argument." Quinn's bed creaked as he flipped over onto his side, facing the wall. He was frustrated enough that he pounded some life into his pillow, wrapped his arm around Puffin and pulled the covers up over his shoulder. "I don't know. I don't want to argue about it any more. Go to sleep, we have an early day tomorrow."

Kayla shook her head, angry that Quinn refused to see her point. She flopped over onto her back, threw her right arm up over her head and blew her hair out of her eyes. She knew he could feel her frustration, which actually made her angrier. He knew how strongly she felt about this but still wouldn't budge or even discuss it. She glared up at the springs of his bunk for a long time before finally giving herself over to sleep.

The next day, Kayla mulled the situation over in her mind as she washed the breakfast dishes. It seemed quite clear that there was nothing else to do, but figure out the riddle of the art thieves. Unfortunately, based on the way Quinn was storming around this morning, she assumed his thoughts on the matter hadn't changed over night.

Even when breakfast was over and they were heading down to the basement, Quinn grumbled something about working in the back corner, the one they hadn't tackled yet, and the one the was the furthest from where Kayla had been working. She tossed her head, her long yellow hair flipping over her shoulder and bounced off to finish yesterday's trunk. Two could play at this game.

****

Quinn continued to focus his energy on the task before him. A dedicated focus seemed to be the only way to block the rage that Kayla was directing toward him. This ability to feel other people's emotions was very unsettling when the emotions were so heated and directed at him. Last night he had laid on his bunk for what felt like hours, silently fuming, until he realized that the anger he felt wasn't even his own frustration at the situation they were in. He was absolutely furious and when he realized that he was channeling Kayla's anger toward him, it really threw him.

Generally speaking, he was a pleasant individual. He tried to be kind to others, tried to be open to other points of view. All the traits that he'd been taught were virtuous. Sure, it seemed that things generally went his way. Was that his fault? Was he supposed to feel some sort of guilt for this ability to massage a situation? It wasn't really manipulation, it was just an ability to nudge things in the direction he wanted them to go.

He really wasn't comfortable feeling so much anger and resentment that it was akin to hatred. Not true hatred, but that spur-of-the-moment, crime-of-passion kind of hatred. He didn't like it at all. If the only way to keep these emotions at bay was to stay away from the source, then so be it. He'd stay as far away from Kayla as their situation would allow.

He moved a bunch of art up to the ballroom. A box of books had been stacked under the table. He flipped through it, disappointed to find nothing but guest ledgers and other hotel books in it. He almost missed a slim volume tucked under a box flap. It had no name on it and he flipped through it to see where it should go. It appeared to be a hand written volume about a pirate. He tossed it in the box and brought the whole thing up to the ballroom, thinking that it would make interesting reading.

Once that corner had been organized, he wondered if they had been approaching the basement job from the wrong angle, too. Instead of pushing their way through the swamp of stuff and organizing one area at a time, he wondered if they might be better off flitting around the room, taking care of the items in plain sight.

With that in mind, he looked around the room and spotted several other groups of artwork leaning on various objects. He climbed over to them and carried them upstairs. He continued moving like items up to the ballroom and after half an hour, had made noticeable progress. There's always more than one way to skin a cat, his sister had said. Although why anyone would want to skin a cat, he had no idea.

Of course, Kayla was so single minded, she'd never find a new way to do anything! Everything had to be done her way. If someone had any other ideas of how to do stuff, she wouldn't consider that they *might* have a point. It didn't matter if the idea related to anything important or not. The other morning, while they were working, they had talked about movies that they liked. Kayla liked the movie version of *Percy Jackson and the Lightening Thief,* but he liked the book better.

"The movie was faster paced and had fewer characters in it. I couldn't get into the book," she'd said.

"But the book included so many more of the Greek gods and told many of their stories. The Greek Gods were cool! There was so much fighting and backstabbing and just general craziness going on with them. The movie barely covered any of that."

"Yeah, but the movie skipped over all that boring drama and cut straight to the action. Now that's a story." She wouldn't let it go. Even on inconsequential things, it had to be her way. It was enough to make him crazy!

All day he'd been struggling to balance his own emotions and the fire that Kayla was constantly sending him. It was very tiring to be absolutely furious all the time. Avoiding Kayla seemed to be the only thing he could do, but their present circumstances made that difficult. And avoiding her seemed to make her angrier. Which made him angrier, which made him avoid her more, which fanned the flames even higher. He sighed and stretched his back, thinking that they were nearly done with the basement and that it was a good time to quit for the day.

Apparently Kayla had the same idea. He brushed past her heading up the stairs, having truly not seen her standing there. She huffed at him, again. "What?! What is your problem?" he'd yelled back.

Kayla took a step back, away from the force of his anger, but then immediately stepped up to her original space. "What is *my* problem? I didn't say anything as you shoved past me. Go, if you're in such a hurry." She shooed him up the hatchway with her hands.

"You don't have to be so condescending. It's rude," he muttered. Hadn't he read somewhere that if you find yourself in an indefensible position, the only thing left to do was to attack? Not sure it was meant to apply to this kind of situation but…

"Are you kidding me?! You pushed past *me*! You are unbelievable. The same pompous, know-it-all-jerk that I always knew you were in school. I can't wait until we find Jim and Lorelei. In addition to being rid of you, I'm going to give her a piece of my mind about how she raised you!" Kayla tossed her hair over her shoulders.

Quinn's emotional cauldron boiled over at the suggestion that his beloved, missing, possibly dead sister was anything less than perfect. He had started to climb the stairs before she spoke, but rounded on her at her words. "Don't you say a WORD about my sister! She's a kind and generous soul, unlike some blond harpies I could mention. You aren't fit to lick her boot!"

In the face of a hundred and ninety pounds of six-foot-tall-five-inch raving insanity (Quinn seemed to actually have a little bubble of spit in the corner of his mouth that resembled foam) Kayla thought, for the first time in her life, that her temper might actually have put her in danger. He loomed over her, his hands held tightly in fists at his side. And the glare! It was trite to say that if looks could kill, his would, but if they could have, they would have. His eyebrows were knit together in a single line with an actual point like a "v" in the middle.

THE CORDOVAN VAULT

His face was flushed brick red and he was enunciating so that his word ending consonants launched spit straight into her face. She did the only thing she could do. She ducked under his arm and ran.

Quinn chased after her for a few seconds, not sure if he was going to apologize, try to explain or yell some more. But by the time he reached Elfryth's Alley, she was nowhere to be seen. He gave up and walked up the street aimlessly. He really couldn't believe how he'd shouted at her. He didn't think he'd ever spoken to anyone like that in his life. He reached a park and sat on an empty bench, trying calm down. He didn't know what to do.

Maybe he needed to trust Kayla more. He knew that she was very good at solving puzzles. How many times in their various classes together had he heard the teacher say that she had arrived at a correct answer, even though she hadn't approached the problem the way the teacher would have? Maybe that was what was happening here. She was solving the puzzle in her own way.

Quinn shoved his hair out of his eyes, pushing it back by running a hand through it the way he always did. Unbeknownst to him, that action created a wind blown look that models spent hours and hundreds of dollars trying to achieve. He sighed, leaning forward to prop his elbows on his knees and study a small colony of ants working in the grass between his feet. Each one followed the one before it, working together to push pieces of food into the hill for the good of the colony. Maybe he and Kayla should try to be more like ants, working together in harmony.

Quinn sat on the bench without realizing how much time had passed. He had been so focused on working out his own problems that he had effectively blocked out everything around him, including the emotions of the other people nearby. He was still new to using his Advantage, and certainly had not figured out all the particulars about it yet. That was why he had no warning of the two men who had been watching him from the other side of the small park. A tall guy and a short guy.

A black van pulled up along the sidewalk in front of him and blocked the late afternoon sun. He glanced up from the ant line in time to see the side door open. The two men who'd walked across the park behind him, grabbed him by the arms and tossed him into the van, pulling a knit cap down over his head. The door of the van slid shut with a bang and the van drove unhurriedly down the street.

Quinn fought his captors, kicking and yelling, trying to pull his arms free. He shook his head trying to dislodge the smelly cap while keeping up the fight. He felt a crunch when his knee hit something fleshy, and hoped it was a nose. He guessed from the howl of pain that it was. Soon after that, he found that he couldn't continue to fight, that his limbs and head felt heavy. He tried to yell, but only managed a soft growl. The hat had been doused in chloroform, hence the smell. As Quinn blacked out, he smacked his head on the floor of the van, but didn't feel it.

****

Quinn woke to inescapable hot, blinding light. It was so bright, he could see its red hue through his closed eyelids, as if he was laying on the beach with his face to the sun. But this was no day at the beach. He pulled his hand up to shade his eyes, only to have it jerked back down by some unseen rope. He tried the other hand with the same result. He turned his head to the left and peeked through his eyelashes with his left eye hoping that his nose would offer a hint of shade. His cheek and ear burned gently against the hot surface behind him, but he was able to catch an unsettling glimpse of his surroundings. He moved his head again, instantly cooling his skin. He turned his head to the right and glanced in the other direction, pushing the pain out of his mind.

Quinn took stock of the situation. The surface he lay on was hard, and seemed to be only a bit wider than his body. His hands were tied, but there was some slack to the tether. He rapped his knuckles on the surface to guess what it was made of. Metal. That explained the heat. It was being reflected by the light. He moved his head again and wiggled, testing to see what bounds he might have. His legs and chest were tied down, but the bindings didn't cut in.

Not rope, he thought, *maybe a strap of some kind, like a seatbelt.* He thought about what he had seen of the room. A hint of tile floor, light walls and a door with darkly tinted glass. Quinn wondered, idly, if it was an interior door or an exterior door. Neither answer seemed to bode well for him. Who would tint a door that was inside? But then again, what did it mean if he was being held hostage by people who were so confident that they bound him to a table in view of anyone who happened to walk by. That couldn't be good.

He listened carefully, holding his breath so that he heard even nearly silent sounds. A distant voice, the words unintelligible, a door slammed closer by, the low hum of a power tool, the buzz of the light. He sniffed deeply, but could smell only the caustic bite of chemicals. Suddenly, the light went dark, soaking the room in blackness so thick Quinn could feel it penetrating his pores. Then there was a new sound, a single sweep, like a door against a tile floor.

"Hello. Who's there?" he demanded sharply. No reply. Then three slow clicking steps, like a man's dress shoe. He detected a new smell, human. Not body odor, not foul breath, not hair product, not soap or maybe a combination of all four, but the unmistakable smell that tells you there is another person nearby. The absence of light brought a coolness that Quinn hadn't realized he was craving, until the chill itself added to his terror. In the cooler air, he could feel the comparative warmth of expelled breath against his face. Whoever was in the room with him, was very close, nearly nose to nose.

Images from every horror movie he had ever seen flashed behind his eyes. Visions from every scary book or ghost story raced through his mind. Predator? Zombie? Crazed killer? He stifled a whimper and spat in the direction of the breath. Whatever was happening, Quinn wasn't going to lay here waiting for it.

He thrashed his body, his hands, his head, making as much sudden noise as possible, and even managed to crack his forehead against the breath's nose. He felt a prick on his right shoulder and his last thought before fading into a druggy haze was that the scariest thing wasn't the guy you knew was there, but the third person you had never suspected was in the room.

****

THE CORDOVAN VAULT

Kayla flipped over in her bunk with an angry bounce. She beat the lumpy pillow with her hand hoping to move the lumps into something resembling a cushion. She was too hot to sleep, too angry. Too scared, too, if the truth be told. After their fight, she had gone for a run, but came back to the Last Tain after a few minutes. The hair on the back of her neck was standing up as she ran and she kept having chills. She went straight to their room and locked Quinn out.

That had been twelve hours ago and since he never tried to get in, or shouted through the door or indicated in any way that he was back at the Last Tain, she hadn't had a chance to yell at him and release the anger. Her emotions were like a steam valve, the pressure building and building. If there was no release, the valve exploded. And she was more than a little nervous about Quinn. They both knew that people were after them, bad people. And they had been getting closer in the last couple of days. How dare Quinn not let her know he was back?

She flipped again, kicking off the covers in the steamy room. She blew her hair off her forehead, forcefully closed her eyes and began to imagine sheep jumping over a small fence in the middle of a green meadow. One, two, three. Along came a tall, brown sheep wearing a guitar case saddle. She shook her head like an etch-a-sketch to erase the Quinn-sheep and started again. One, two, three, four. How dare he not even come to apologize!

She tucked her leg back under the covers, wondering how she could be chilled and sweating at the same time. Come to think of it, the air in the room did seem a bit nippy. The gauzy, used-to-be-white curtains floated on a breeze like ghosts dancing in the room. But inexplicably, she felt hot, as if she had a bad sunburn. She finally drifted off to sleep rubbing at a sharp pain in her shoulder.

When the dreams came, they were disjointed as dreams often are. She floated from one scene to another like a summer leaf on a rushing river, pushed by one seemingly random thought to another. She dreamt of sandwiches and shushing librarians. She dreamt of baking cookies for Cookie Monster and old-fashioned dresses that waltzed by themselves.

Finally, her dream settled in the cloister they had seen in the museum, but it was more real than in the museum. It was outside, part of a real building. She wandered through the sanctuary, searching for something or someone. This time, she could feel her feet crunch the dried leaves on the path and smell the crisp scent of grass and dew. In her dream, she knew her way around the place as if she had explored it many times. She was frustrated at not finding what she sought. She felt certain that if she knew what it was, it would be easy to find.

Around a corner, she stopped suddenly, her feet sliding in mud. The well stood out of place and a figure sat before it, her long brown hair hanging over her shoulder, her hand trailing through the water again. The woman turned to look at her, but her features were clouded and unclear. Even so, Kayla recognized Lorelei's serenity. "You have to help him," Lorelei said. "You're the only one."

"I'm looking but I can't find him. Who am I looking for?" Kayla asked, hoping to understand.

"My brother is calling to you, listen and follow his voice. They are coming for you, too. You can find him while they are away." Lorelei faded from view. Another familiar voice sounded behind her, so close she jumped.

Her eyes snapped open, the dream as clear in her mind as if she had been watching a TV show. Jim might as well have been sitting on her bed talking to her. "Kayla, you need to wake up. Now," he'd said.

Chapter Twenty-Three:

Improbable Rescues

Kayla lay still, frozen in fear and confusion for several long minutes. She didn't blink or move or even breathe. Her skin crawled with terror. Lorelei said she had to help Quinn, that she could find him if she listened. Was Quinn in trouble? She shook her head and rolled onto her side, sighing at the absurdity of it all. It was only a dream. A collection of images fueled by the events of the day and her own imagination. Jim and Lorelei were missing; they certainly weren't sitting in the Philadelphia Museum of Art sending her telepathic messages.

Of course, it was the clearest dream she could ever remember, especially Jim telling her to wake up. It wasn't like the other dreams she'd had that had come true. Jim and Lorelei were missing. She rubbed her shoulder again, wondering what she had done to it. "Needle" popped into her mind. Kayla sat up and frowned. She hadn't gotten any shots lately, why would she think that. She walked to the small mirror hanging on the wall, turning on the light along the way. She pushed the sleeve of her t-shirt up and looked at the reflection. Sure enough, there was a trace of a tiny puncture. "What is that?" she whispered.

J MONKEYS

They're coming for you, too, she heard. She whipped around, half expecting to see Lorelei sitting on the bed, but Kayla was alone. She looked back at her reflection in the age-speckled mirror and said, "I think I need to go." Her eyes searched the wall, the floor, looking anywhere for an answer. Kayla could practically feel the devil and the angel sitting on her shoulders arguing. You need to leave; don't be stupid – it was a dream. No you should really go – take this seriously; don't be ridiculous – where are you going to go?

She sat heavily in the desk chair, propped her elbows on her knees and hugged her head, trying to squeeze some sense into her brain. Reason warred with instinct. Stay or go? Stay or go? "Yeah, I'm going," she finally said aloud.

For the second time in as many weeks, Kayla frantically and silently packed up their most critical belongings, shoving them into her day-pack. Now that the decision had been made, she wanted to be out of the Last Tain immediately, certainly in less than five minutes. She threw on a sweatshirt, jammed her feet into sneakers without bothering to tie them, tossed money and the clues they'd collected into the bag.

She grabbed Puffin from under Quinn's covers (who did he think he was kidding?) and her mom's diary. In an instant, she decided that the rest could be replaced, including Quinn's guitar. It was too much for her to carry.

Kayla turned off the light and listened at the door before opening it. She could just make out a noise downstairs. *Probably Mr. Keltsea getting a drink or something,* she thought. She crept down the stairs, keeping to the edges which she knew creaked less, skipping the creaky second-to-the-bottom step altogether. At the bottom of the stairs, Kayla peeked around the corner toward the common room. Through the open door, she could make out the shadow of two figures in the room. They didn't appear to be getting drinks or anything else innocent. They moved too carefully, too stealthily.

She moved as silently as possible toward the back door of the Last Tain, avoiding brushing against walls and furniture. She opened the door carefully, catching the screen before it could slam or click. Once outside, she crouched below the window height and ran as fast as the crouching allowed to the far side of the property. She tossed her bag over the fence and climbed after it, then ran as if her life depended on it. Two blocks away, she paused for breath in the shadows of an old church and considered her next move.

Lorelei had said she could hear Quinn if she listened. *It's a puzzle, just a puzzle*, Kayla thought. *Unless I'm on a wild goose chase.* She thought she might have made the right decision to leave, after all. Those two figures sneaking around in the common room had seemed familiar, but she couldn't place them. Kayla was pretty sure that they weren't folks to whom she served breakfast every morning. Lorelei said she could find Quinn while they were away, presumably away from wherever they were holding Quinn. *So, how do I find Quinn?*

She laid her head back against the stone wall, her bag against her left leg and squatted down as if she was sitting, her back against the wall too. With her eyes closed, she worked to control her breathing, in through the nose, out through the mouth. She shut out the sounds of the night, cars on the road, the occasional beeping of a crosswalk, the birds in the trees and focused her thoughts on Quinn. She imagined their conversation back in Boston when they had been waiting for the train. After their initial awkwardness, it was the first time they had felt comfortable in each other's company.

She remembered their fight earlier today and felt badly about her reaction. She thought about all of the questions they still needed to answer and hoped, no wished, that they would get the chance to find the answers together. In through the nose, out through the mouth.

An image formed in her mind, of a bright room with a stainless steel table in the middle. Other than the table, it was an empty room, but the table itself appeared menacing. Six leather straps lay limp, but pulsed with the terror of past victims. A tinted door stood ajar in one wall. She peered into another room, larger than the first, then looked out another door, onto the street. A silver pole stood on the corner outside this door. A green sign at the top of the pole read 12th and Independence. Kayla's eyes blinked open, she hefted the bag onto her shoulders and started running.

Out of breath, Kayla stopped running, panting hard. It had been a twenty-minute run to 12th and Independence, but she recognized the street corner from the image in her mind. She pushed away the thought that she had never been there before and concentrated on the task ahead. She looked around, trying to picture exactly what she'd seen when she'd mentally looked out the door, hoping that would help identify the building where Quinn was being held.

THE CORDOVAN VAULT

A small whisper in her mind continued to say that she was on a fool's errand, fueled by her imagination. *In for a penny, in for a pound* Jim always said. Across the street, she saw an average looking blue glass building and though it didn't seem menacing, standing in the shadows across the street with her back to the front door showed her that it was the door from her...she wasn't sure what to call it. Vision, maybe.

From her place in the shadows, she looked carefully at the building to see where it might have security cameras or guards, but oddly neither seemed present. She back tracked two blocks, crossed the street and walked a block up, keeping to the darkness as she walked around the building looking at it. Still no guards or cameras. Very little traffic on the street. She continued on for an additional two blocks, and had to conclude that it looked as deserted as one might imagine an office building to be at nearly two in the morning. It was now or never.

She approached the door she'd seen in her vision, amazed to find it wasn't locked. She waited a moment once inside to allow her eyes to adjust to a darkness much more oppressive than night on the street. She crossed the room to the tinted inner door and opened it carefully. The table looked lumpier than it had in her mind, with a chandelier hanging over it.

She stood, frozen in the doorway. Frozen in fear and horror. In the three seconds it took for Kayla to realize that the lump on the table was slowly and rhythmically growing and receding, she was paralyzed in true terror for the first time in her life. Smells were crisper, sounds were louder, sights were clearer. The stench of bleach and sweat burned her nose. A furnace turned on in the distance. And a body strapped to a stainless steal table.

Breathing.

"Quinn" she gasped in relief. She didn't see or hear, or smell for that matter, anyone around. She rushed over to him, her vision shockingly clear in the dark, her fingers scrabbling on the wrist straps. "Quinn. Quinn!" she whispered frantically.

As she freed one hand, he started to come around, making soft, moaning, wake-up noises. She had moved her focus to the other wrist strap when a hand snapped onto her arm, instantly and out of nowhere.

She shrieked and jumped backwards, knocking down a table behind her. A tray of bizarre surgical instruments clattered to the floor. She ripped her gaze from the floor to Quinn's face, her heartbeat still racing as she realized that, of course it was Quinn's hand that had touched her.

He waved an apology and started to work the duct tape off his mouth. Kayla took a deep breath and released the buckles on the rest of the straps. In less than two minutes, she had him free. She helped him to stand and said, "We've got to get out of here before someone comes back."

****

Quinn stood for a few seconds, looking around the room. From this vantage point, it looked different than it had earlier. Normal. A room, not a cell. He forced himself to take a good long look, to wipe the crumbs of terror from his mind. It was a room, nothing more.

"Hurry," Kayla said, tugging on his hand.

"Wait," he croaked, his mouth and throat painfully dry. Quinn reached up and ripped the chandelier from the ceiling.

"What are you doing?" Kayla panted. "Leave the light; we've gotta go!"

"Not a light. Tools. Lur Babsel tools." Quinn grabbed his shoes from the floor where they'd been dropped before the interrogation began, shoved his feet into them and ran out the door with one of his hands clasping Kayla's hand, the other clutching the tools. In another three minutes, they were four blocks away and still running. A church nearby chimed two o'clock in the morning.

After another block, Quinn dropped Kayla's hand. "I gotta stop," he panted, leaning over with his arms propping him up from the knees.

"Sure. But don't stop, walk. There's a park down the road. We can rest there." As they walked, Kayla pulled a bottle of water out of her daypack and offered it to Quinn. He took a long drink, sucking the flimsy bottle in on itself, then wiped the mouth and handed it back to her.

"Thanks. Do you have anything to eat in there?" Kayla handed over two biodegradable bags of smoked nuts before he even finished the question.

"So. What happened?" Kayla asked heavily, as if unsure she wanted an answer.

Quinn had heard enough songs, read enough books, and seen enough TV shows and movies to know that bottling up his fears and emotions was unhealthy and would only lead to more trouble later on. Even so, reliving the nightmarish time spent on that table was a thought that his brain shied away from. Of course, she needed to know. He had to tell her. To prepare her.

They reached the park and sat down on the dew damp grass facing each other, close together but not touching. Quinn's fingers twiddled in the grass as he gathered his thoughts. He worried that Kayla's silence while she waited was the measure of her concern for him. If she was able to stifle her usual chatterbox and sit without fidgeting then she must be *very* concerned.

"After we fought yesterday afternoon, I ended up on a park bench thinking about this Advantage and what to do with it. I think that as much as I was getting on your nerves the last couple of days, it was doubly frustrating for me. On top of my own emotions, I was feeling your anger." Quinn looked up at Kayla and gently shook his head, "I don't know how to handle that."

He said nothing more for a half minute that seemed to drag to quadruple that time. Kayla reached out and gently placed her hand on his shin, maybe to remind him that he wasn't alone, but said nothing.

He took a deep breath and squared his shoulders. He blew the breath out his nose, then ran his hand over his face, pinched his nose with his thumb and forefinger then wiped his mouth. "I didn't even realize they were there until they grabbed me from behind. It happened so quickly. They dumped me in a van and pulled a cap over my face. It was doused with something, 'cause I passed out after a couple minutes of fighting them off.

"I woke up strapped to that table with a white hot light blaring down on me, which got turned off, leaving me blind. I heard someone come into the room, but didn't hear the second person. He jabbed me with a needle. Truth serum they said. God, it burned. I could feel it moving through my arm, into my chest. And it made my brain foggy. Then they started asking me questions. When I didn't know the answer or wouldn't tell them the answer they wanted, they got mean," he whispered.

As he spoke, his voice so quiet that Kayla had to strain to hear him, she reached over and took his hand in hers, wrapping both of her hands around his, as if to shield him. Still, she said nothing, letting him get it out.

Though she didn't know the particulars yet, what had happened to Quinn was bad. Very bad. She imagined that it was like having a piece of glass stuck in your arm. It hurt so much to pull it out, but the wound couldn't begin to heal until the glass was removed. He needed to tell this story and she needed to listen. "Mean how?"

Quinn continued to stare at the ground in the near dark. The park had a few lights and the street lights shone in, but it was always the darkest before dawn and dawn was still a few hours away.

"Well, I feel OK now, so I think they were trying to make me feel foolish or something. Maybe scare me. But the first thing they did was to take off my shoes and socks. When the light came back on, I had a blindfold on and couldn't see anything. One of 'em had a lighter. I could hear him flicking it on and off. He burned a bit of my leg hair, enough to stink. Then he'd put the lighter close to my foot, so I could feel the heat, then take it away. It got a little hotter each time and the smell of the burning hair and the foggy drug and being tied to the table…it made me want to tell them whatever they wanted to know."

Quinn dropped his head to his hands. "God, I'm such a coward." When Kayla saw his shoulders shake, she immediately moved closer to him and wrapped her arms around his arms and chest. She pulled him to lean on her and tentatively reached out a hand to gently stroke his hair.

"Stop that. You are NOT a coward. Of course you told them whatever they wanted to know. *Of course* you did! That's what they wanted. They weren't going to stop until you did what they wanted. You must have told them something to make them go away, so you did the right thing."

They sat in silence. Kayla kept her arms around Quinn until he eventually loosened his hold on her. After a while, they both started to feel a little uncomfortable being so close together. Quinn dropped his arms away from Kayla and reached up to wipe his eyes, surprised at the moisture he felt there. He had cried when he thought that Lorelei was dead, but before last week, he couldn't remember the last time he cried. He laughed, a derisive sound devoid of humor. "I must seem manly, now."

"Don't be ridiculous. You seem human." Kayla watched as Quinn continued to dodge her eyes. Time to change the subject. "Who do you think they were and what did they want to know?"

Quinn's head snapped up, finally meeting her gaze. "Oh, yeah. How could you know? I caught a glimpse of them when they dragged me into the van – it was the Train Twins. And, when I heard them talking while I was blindfolded, I recognized their voices. It was funny, I had thought there was something familiar about them on the train, but I couldn't place it. When I couldn't see, I realized who they were: Dax and Heywood."

"No!"

"Yup. When I could see them, they were clearly both men, so I think that was clouding my judgment. When I could only hear them, I realized that I recognized their voices and it all clicked. When they came to the house, they were in disguise."

"Wow – I can't believe it!"

"Yeah. I know." Quinn thought for a moment, happy to have turned the topic of conversation, even a little. "I don't think that there ever was a car accident. I doubt Dax and Heywood, if that's even their names, are police officers. The police here didn't have any record of a car accident on the bridge, and Lorelei called us after they had said she was dead. And they asked me if we'd had contact with Jim and Lorelei and where they were."

Kayla sat back, blown away. "Why on earth did they come to our house then?"

"I don't know, but they blew it up."

"Wow."

"Yeah. Well, when they were questioning me, they asked where we were staying, they asked about our Advantages. But mostly, they asked questions I didn't know the answer to. They asked what these things were," Quinn gestured toward the 'chandelier' laying on the grass.

There were two crossed bars, with objects dangling off the ends of each bar. One object looked like a rectangular piece of lace made out of a brassy metal. Another looked like a telescope. The others really didn't resemble anything Kayla could think of and would certainly need study later.

J MONKEYS

"Dax asked me again and again if we'd found it, if we'd found it, found the painting. He kept asking me for the Cordovan Vault, demanding to know where it was and how to open it. It was the same questions over and over. If I didn't answer fast enough, Heywood would pull about that damned lighter again and burn my leg," Quinn's voice trailed off.

"Huh. Did they ask anything else?"

Quinn frowned thoughtfully and shook his head. "No. Wait, I think they asked why we'd been following them, but that doesn't make any sense. They were following us."

They sat in silence for a few long minutes. Kayla rested her right shoulder against Quinn's left, happy to have his warmth in the crisp summer night air. Quinn picked at the grass, folding long blades in on themselves like a double helix. Suddenly, Kayla's head snapped up.

"I've got it!" she shouted in a whisper. "Yes, it all makes sense now." Quinn looked over at her, feeling her excitement like a poke in the kidney.

"What?" he asked.

"You said that you didn't understand how they could think we were following them when they were following us. Don't you see?! That's it!" Quinn's blank face glowed in the dim light of the street lamp. "They must be the art thieves!" Quinn continued to look skeptical, squinting his eyes, shaking his head and mouthing words like 'what'.

"OK it's like this: they asked you if we'd found it, right? You said they asked that over and over, did we find it, did we find the *painting*. You know what? I found it, yesterday! Darn, I was looking right at it, thinking that there was something that I should have been seeing, but

266

was missing. Ach! It was right in front of me. Oh, God!
They asked you where we were staying…and I know there
was someone in the ballroom when I crept out of the Last
Tain…and Lorelei said they were coming for me too…and
obviously they weren't with you at the time. Oh, crap!
We've gotta do something!"

Quinn blinked his eyes and gently shook his head as if
trying to catch up with the hurricane blowing out of
Kayla's brain. It took fifteen seconds to process everything
she had blurted out. "*Lorelei* told you they were coming!
When did you talk to Lorelei?" Quinn reached out and
grabbed Kayla's hand to pull her attention to him.

"I didn't actually talk with her; I had a dream about the
cloister again. But she told me that I was the only one who
could find you. And I did find you. She said they were
coming for me too, then I heard Jim tell me to wake up. I
grabbed the most essential stuff I could find in our bags and
left in a couple of minutes. But I'm positive that there were
two people in the common room when I left and I got the
feeling that they were familiar but I didn't give them much
thought at the time."

"OK. What can we do about it now? That was forty-
five minutes ago."

"Yeah, but there's a lot of stuff in that room. Maybe
they're still there. Let's get back there and see if we can
catch 'em." Kayla jumped up and slung the backpack over
her shoulders again. Quinn had stood with her, reaching
through the grass for the Lur Babsel tools. "We'll talk
about those later," Kayla said as she started to run.

Ten minutes later, panting for breath, the pair turned
onto Elfryth's Alley. They slowed to a fast walk, keeping

to the shadows and watching their steps on the cobblestones. At the turn to Skyler Path, they crept along silently, hiding in the shadows. They walked through the gate and hunched over, keeping their heads low and out of view until they reached the grimy ballroom windows.

As Quinn was ready to stick his head up and peek in, Kayla motioned for him to stay down. She rustled around in her bag and pulled out a small mirror. With her back against the wall, she raised the mirror to see through the window. She could barely make out two figures standing near the middle of the room, with their backs to the door.

The figure on the right was shining a flashlight onto something in front of them. Kayla turned the mirror to get a better look at something that had flitted in and out of view too fast to recognize, only to be blinded by the reflected glare of the flashlight. She whipped the mirror down, away from the window and swore.

"They saw us!" she gasped as she shrunk back into a shrub for cover, kicking the Lur Babsel tools into the bush opposite her and out of view.

Quinn grabbed Kayla's bag and ran back through the courtyard to the hostel door, pulling Kayla's key out of the special key spot. *Thank God she's a little OCD*, he thought. He threw open the door, catching the screen with his toe and the main door's knob with his hand before either could make a bang. He dashed through the common room on silent feet, and found the ballroom door ajar. He pushed it a titch wider to see what was happening in the room. In a second, he took it all in. The tall guy, who he instantly recognized as Dax, was trying to push open the window, while Heywood was wiping away the years of dirt with his shirttail and waving his light around, both of them anxious to see whatever was outside. Behind them, closer to Quinn, Mr. Keltsea stood with something in his hand, arm raised, about to cosh Heywood on the head!

Chapter Twenty-Four:

The Double Ancient Tain

In another second, the cosh was finished and Heywood went down, knocking into Dax on the way. Dax reacted immediately, turning and backhanding Mr. Keltsea with the side of his fist in one motion. Quinn watched as Mr. K fell backwards, crushing a table loaded with antique linens.

After the day and night he'd had, seeing frail, little old Mr. K get hit was the last straw. A rage like Quinn had never experienced before raced through him in an instant. He roared and raced across the room in a blur, swinging Kayla's bag at Dax's head with all his strength. He jumped the last couple of feet as the bag connected.

Quinn's arm lashed out and punched Dax in the face, breaking his nose for the second time that day, if his blackened eye was any indicator. Dax staggered, bent forward and slightly left, clutching his face with a yell of pain.

Without thinking, Quinn made a fist with his left hand and punched him in the right side of his abdomen with all of the anger, fear and frustration he had felt over the last thirty-six hours. Dax dropped to the ground and didn't move.

"Kayla get in here!" Quinn shouted, dashing to the table with old fishing gear on it. He grabbed a clothesline type rope and quickly tied Dax's hands behind his back, looping the other end of the rope around his ankles, effectively immobilizing him. Kayla came rushing into the room as Quinn moved over to secure Heywood in the same way.

"Mr. Keltsea! Are you all right," Kayla gasped reaching out for the old man as he struggled to stand.

"Call 911, Kay. I'll get to Mr. Keltsea in a second," Quinn directed. Kayla nodded and rushed back into the common room to get the phone.

"Call her back, son. I don' want youse involved with the police. I'll call 'em," Mr. Keltsea said, stumbling for the door.

He yelled the new plan for Kayla, and with the art thieves/kidnappers tied up, Quinn took the first easy breath in days and collapsed into a nearby chair to keep watch over the revolting pair. A minute later, both Kayla and Mr. Keltsea were back in the ballroom. "All right now, youse kids git up to yer room. I'll tell the police that I caught 'em tryin' to escape out the winder. No need fer youse to be involved. Who do youse think they are?"

Quinn glanced at Kayla and caught the tiny shake of her head. "I'm pretty sure they're the ones responsible for the rash of art thefts, and probably all the muggings around town, too."

Kayla chimed in, "From what we understand, the police have enough evidence to confirm that these are the guys. The police will be so excited to have caught them, that I doubt you'll get too much questioning."

THE CORDOVAN VAULT

Heywood came around in time to hear this last. "Stinking Neofytes! You'll never escape Denortus. Erus killed the Gezon, he will get you too." Showing more strength than they thought he possessed, Mr. Keltsea shocked Quinn by kicking Heywood in the stomach. Hard.

"Filth. Who are you ta taunt these people?" Mr. Keltsea asked the gasping man.

Another minute had gone by, so Kayla and Quinn headed to their room. When they drew even with the common room bar, Quinn remembered the mobile of tools still hidden in the bushes. He hurried out to retrieve them and could hear police sirens in the distance as he and Kayla made the final dash up the stairs to their room. They kicked off their shoes, Quinn pulled off his shirt and they both waved their hands through their hair to make it look slept on.

Less than ten minutes later, they stumbled out of their room with the other nine guests staying on their floor and tried to look confused walking down to the common room to talk with the police about what they hadn't heard.

An hour later, Dax and Heywood had been taken away, Mr. K had been seen by paramedics, and everyone had been interviewed with their statements recorded by the investigative team. Mr. Keltsea had introduced Kayla and Quinn to the detective as his niece and nephew, Stanley and Mary Jane Keltsea, visiting from Atlanta. The police officer didn't argue when Mr. K said that all their luggage had been lost and that was why they had no identification.

"I think that's everything we need. We'll contact you with any further questions. It seems like these two *are* the guys responsible for the muggings that have been going on around the city. And they match the surveillance video we have from one of the art robberies. I think you were very lucky, Mr. Keltsea. This could have turned out badly." The investigative team left the Last Tain and Mr. Keltsea shooed everyone back to their rooms.

"We can talk in the morning, but whadda youse think they were after?" Mr. Keltsea asked from the doorway between the common and the tag sale rooms.

"I don't know, sir," Quinn lied casually, while bending down to right the linens that had flown off the table when Mr. K. had fallen on it.

Mr. Keltsea shook his head and muttered something under his breath that sounded like something about "kids these days".

"We'll lock up," Kayla called to Mr. Keltsea's retreating back. He waved over his shoulder without turning around and shuffled off to his room. Once he was safely away, Kayla and Quinn went over to the place where they had seen Dax and Heywood standing with the flashlight.

Sure enough, the painting of the street scene with the griffin in the center had been pulled down from the wall and propped up in front of some books. "This is it," Kayla said pointing to the picture.

"You think *this* is the painting the thieves were after all along? That's a huge coincidence. What are the odds that it was in the basement of the Last Tain?" Quinn was amazed. It seemed unlikely, too much of a coincidence to be believed. He followed Kayla, carrying the painting into the common room to look at it in better light.

THE CORDOVAN VAULT

"Didn't Mr. K say something about destiny having a hand in things?" Kayla's question was rhetorical. Quinn guessed as much and didn't try to respond which was a good thing because she kept right on talking.

"Come on. Jim and Lorelei stayed here and they are missing. You were kidnapped and tortured. The kidnappers, who were also art thieves, were standing here looking at this painting after asking you where you were staying and if you'd found it. Lorelei and I met in that cloister twice. That's the cloister with the relief disks all over the place, the kind we had at home. And those disks had these same symbols on them."

Kayla pointed to the small symbols on the painting. "Jim and Lorelei probably chose to stay here on their honeymoon because they suspected the painting the thieves were after was here. They said we needed to find it first, and protect it."

What Kayla proposed made a lot of sense, but it still seemed incredible to Quinn. Who would have guessed that they found what they were looking for days ago, but didn't realize it?

"Hey," Quinn said so suddenly it surprised even him. "I thought of something. What we were looking for was right under our nose the whole time. What if other things we're looking for are hidden in plain sight, too."

Kayla nodded, making a thoughtful frown-y face that didn't seem unhappy. "Like Mitch was talking about during the ghost walk. With the doors having hidden meaning in their shapes."

"And the Masons, over at Carpenters' Hall. That was their thing too, hiding knowledge in plain sight. Their codes and symbology. Lorelei and Jim said that they were trying to protect information." Quinn was warming to the topic. "So how is this painting information? What else is hidden in plain sight?" Their gazes roamed across the common room, each starting on their side and meeting in the middle.

Right where the painting was resting, propped up on a table right in front of them. They moved the painting to a chair next to the bar and stood close together for a good look.

"Maybe that's not the question we should be asking ourselves. Maybe the question we should be asking is *why* was everyone after this painting?" Kayla took a step closer to the picture. They reached it at the same time, both moving in close to see the picture better.

It was an old painting, dingy with age, although it had been somewhat preserved by being in the basement hiding place. It was an everyday life domestic scene. There was a house in the center of the picture, the main focus. A barn or stable was off to one side. There was the hint of a road off the edge of the painting, with trees between the yard and the road.

A pasture seemed to take up the field at the top left side, between the house and stable. In the foreground, a man was turning the reins of a horse over to a small boy and there was another horse entering the stable, also being pulled along by a small boy. Both boys wore the same clothing but had different color hair. The rest of the front yard held a small kitchen garden with what looked like vegetables, flowers and maybe herbs growing inside small, organized beds.

THE CORDOVAN VAULT

The sun was setting off on the right side of the painting, casting shadows and a rainbow of pinks fading to blue sky. On the other side, the moon seemed to be coming up, starting to shine its glow onto the yard.

The house itself seemed fairly average. It was a couple of stories tall, maybe three including an attic, and it looked rather wide, but maybe the family was large. Through the windows of the house, the artist had carefully painted scenes happening in the various rooms that faced the front. The kitchen seemed to be busy with activity, everyone working. The other window on the ground floor looked into a room with a couple of tables, another window in it and a long table against one wall with two figures standing near it.

The upstairs rooms appeared to be bedrooms. Inside each upstairs window the same scene could be seen. A bed, a small table with a candle that provided the light in the room and a washstand with a pitcher.

The trees along the road gave way to a small forest behind the stable. It was clearly a scene of late autumn because the trees had dropped their leaves, forming a scroll of twisting vine-like naked branches. The very top left corner of the painting had three red oblong dots on it. They were painted one above the next. The top and bottom dots were oriented wide and the middle dot was standing tall between them, like a capital letter "I". Together, the dots were no bigger than Kayla's pinky fingernail. And, in the center of the trees at the top was the small griffin.

Kayla sat back for a moment wondering about the picture. "It seems like a normal, everyday scene, doesn't it?" She had turned to Quinn, hoping he had seen something she had missed.

"Maybe it's one of those 3-D things that you have to look at from a distance." Quinn backed up a couple of steps and cocked his head to the side.

"I think those are computer generated. This thing is old, much too old for a computer."

"How old do you think it is?"

"I don't know. Is there a signature or something?" They looked around the bottom and on the back of the painting, average places where one might sign one's work, didn't find anything. "OK, let's think for a minute." Kayla started pacing along the bar in the common room. She muttered to herself, not using words that Quinn could distinguish.

Someone wanted this particular painting for a reason, and they wanted it very badly. Why? Kayla tried to eliminate possible answers, hoping that whatever she was left with would be the right answer. Given everything else that was stolen, the thieves clearly weren't looking for something of huge monetary value, like a Monet, so it was fair to say they weren't stealing it for the money.

It was quite an average painting as far as artistic scenes went. It was dingy and somewhat dull in color, so she couldn't imagine anyone going to all this effort just to hang it on a wall in their house. So if it wasn't wanted for it's intrinsic value nor for it's artistic value, what was left? "Maybe there's a hidden message in the painting. Like the Masons, they put messages in everyday things all the time right? So let's assume it's a riddle. What is it telling us?"

Kayla walked back over to the painting, pulling Quinn along. They looked at it again. "What does this house look like to you?" Kayla asked him.

"I don't know, a house? Well, there are a lot of bedrooms. And it's near the road." Quinn pointed at the hint of roadway visible off to the left. "Could this be a hotel or an inn?"

"Yeah," Kayla said, drawing out the word as an idea started to unfurl. "It *is* an inn! Look at the boys taking the horses into the stable and the formal dress of the men walking away from the horses. They must be guests arriving. This one even has a bag. OK, it's an inn. But why? Why were so many people after this picture of this inn?"

Quinn stepped backward again, looking at the picture from a distance. Kayla shook her head, "It's not 3-D. You don't need to look from so far away,"

"No, it seems familiar somehow. But not really. Does that make any sense?" Quinn continued looking at the painting, turning his head one way then the other. Kayla walked back to join him, wondering what he was talking about. They stood side by side, like synchronized swimmers, bouncing their heads from shoulder to shoulder.

After a moment or two, Kayla stood bolt upright. Her posture was so straight and tall that Quinn was sure she had added four inches to her height. He whipped his head around, again feeling that unbelievably strong sense of shock. How was it possible that such a little person could contain such big emotions?

"Oh, God. What now?" The dread was back in his voice.

J MONKEYS

Kayla's eyes were chihuahua wide as she turned to him, silently mouthing her new favorite phrase: Oh. My. God!

"What? What?!"

She looked around the room, as if to ensure they were alone, then grabbed his shirt front to pull his head down. He felt himself being pulled closer, so that they were face to face and started to resist, horrified and worried, thinking that she was going to kiss him.

"What?" he asked, pulling back. The question now was completely different from the prior, even though the word was technically the same. His squeaky tone conveyed this horror, different from the fear and dread of probable death. And maybe there was a little something else in that squeak too.

Kayla gave him an exasperated look, took the time to roll her eyes and pulled his head down to her level. She left no room for resistance and forcefully, but not painfully, turned his head so that his ear was level with her mouth. "I think the inn on the painting is this one. The Last Tain." She whispered nearly inaudibly, but Quinn heard her. He turned matching chihuahua eyes to hers. She pursed her lips, tucking them between her teeth so that her mouth formed a dimpled straight line and nodded.

She pointed to the flower and herb beds in the courtyard, the little black line of fence-work around them. The positioning of the garden beds certainly seemed to match the orientation of the beds that they had rested on so many times over the last week. The multitude of small bedrooms upstairs. The window placement and the shape of the building matched. The layout of the building, the kitchen off to one side, the big dining room taking up the rest of the front of the ground floor.

She pulled Mr. K's magnifying glass out of a drawer and looked into the dining room window. The window that they had seen in the back of that room, was really a long mirror. Reflected in the mirror were two figures standing behind a table. A small one in a green shirt and one taller figure in blue. The faces were obscured, like an impressionist painting. Kayla gestured back and forth between them, pointing at their green and blue shirts.

"No! No way." "Quinn whispered harshly. "There's no way that could be us. This painting is a couple hundred years old. It would mean that the artist would have to be in the courtyard right now looking through that window." Quinn pointed to the window to the side of them, then took off trying to catch Kayla as she dashed outside.

The door to the Last Tain banged shut after him as he jumped down the three steps into the courtyard. He could barely make out Kayla's green shirt in the darkness and rain. She was running through the gate and heading down the alley to the street. He heard the sound of multiple pairs of feet hitting the pavement. She was chasing somebody.

Quinn ran after her, fairly sure that though Dax and Heywood had been apprehended, those two weren't the brains behind everything. And somebody was driving the van that pulled up for his abduction when Dax and Heywood had grabbed him from behind. That meant that whoever was after them was *still* after them. And Kayla shouldn't be running off into the night alone.

He caught up with her in a couple of seconds, at the end of the alley. She stood in the shadow of the old tree with her chest heaving, looking around. "Where'd he go?" Quinn panted. A strong wind gusted a bunch of leaves against his shirt, pushing him hard enough that he took a step backwards.

"I don't know. One minute he was here, then he was gone."

"We're not going to find him in the dark. There's too many places to hide. And this storm seems to be getting worse. Let's get back inside." Lightening flashed overhead and the wind continued to whip down the street.

"What did you do with the painting?" Kayla asked, turning back toward the Tain.

"I didn't do anything with it. I raced after you." They didn't say anything else, but a glance at each other showed that they had the same thought. The painting was sitting all alone on a table in plain sight. They walked quickly, breaking into a run as they reached the hostel. A glance through the window assured them that their luck might be changing. The painting was right where they'd left it. Kayla turned on the top step, before they walked inside.

"It really is the same place. Look at the gardens." She gestured to the raised flowerbeds situated across the courtyard. Taking in the sight of the grounds, they could see where the stable might have been. Behind that, other old houses stood clustered together. They could see where the field would have been.

"You know, there's something wrong here." Kayla turned back into the Last Tain, walking up to the painting. She pointed at the mess of skeletal trees along the top left side. "These trees couldn't have been there." She pointed down to the trees by the stable that ran alongside the road.

THE CORDOVAN VAULT

"These are fine. I imagine that a few of these might even still be out there. But these trees at the top couldn't have been there. The other houses out there are at least the same age as this building."

Quinn looked closely at the painting again, studying the top left. "You know, this letter I shaped thing reminds me of those stones in your mom's flower bed back home. Where we found the key."

"Yeah." Kayla peered closely at the trees on the left of the painting, pointing to a smudge. "Does this look like a pineapple to you? It's right where the gate is today. I have an idea." Kayla walked out of the common room, heading up to their room at the top of the stairs.

She returned less than a minute later, carrying the brass lace template that had been on the Lur Babsel tool set. "Look at this," she pointed at the top left corner of the lace template where there was an opening rimmed in red. The opening was the same shape as the one they found on the painting. She placed the template over the painting, so that the stacked stone shape showed through the red rimmed opening on the brass template. An arrow in the template lined up exactly with the pineapple smudge.

"Whoa, look at this!" Quinn said. The holes in the lace-like template revealed cursive letters hidden in the curving twirling branches of the trees, obscured from view without the template. He read the hidden message, "Behind the double ancient Tain, the Gezon are safely lain. A Cordovan Vault hides our reign."

Chapter Twenty-Five:

The Cordovan Vault

"Huh," Kayla yawned. A glance at the clock on the wall showed that it was almost 4:00 in the morning. Even though she had barely slept in the last twenty-four hours, and Quinn hadn't slept at all, she felt sure that this was the last clue, they were nearly there, wherever it was they were supposed to be.

"The Cordovan Vault. Well, now we know why they were looking for this painting. They already had the decoding template, they just needed the code to get the location of the vault. The painting is a map. That's probably why they came to the house too, to get the key." Kayla pulled the purple metal key out of her daypack. "I read something about Lur Babsel mining cordovan thousands of years ago. Cordovan is a rare purple metal. I bet this key opens the Cordovan Vault."

"So, where do you think it is? Behind the ancient tain? What does that mean?" The day had clearly taken a toll on Quinn. His frustration was showing.

Kayla waved at him to keep his voice down. "'Behind the ancient tain' has got to refer to here, this building. This is a three hundred year old Tain." Kayla was momentarily distracted by her reflection in the pitted old mirror behind the bar. She tilted her head and caught her tongue between her teeth, walking around the bar to stand in front of the mirror for a closer look. "You know, a few days ago, I was flipping through one of the old log books for this place, one of the early ones and I found an interesting anecdote. Do you know how a mirror is made? Or was, back in the day." Kayla glanced over her shoulder to see Quinn shrug.

She looked closely at the far left edge of the mirror, looking at the mirror and the wall carefully, working her way right. "Mirrors were hard to come by, major luxury items. In addition to being easily breakable, they were difficult to make. The maker would paint liquid silver onto the back of a piece of glass. Once that dried, they covered the silver with black paint. That created the reflective surface. The reason why old mirrors like this are pitted is because the silver on the back flaked away from the glass leaving the black visible."

"OK, interesting. It's four in the morning, Kay. What does all this have to do with anything?" Quinn asked from his place on the other side of the bar.

"Ya know what they called the silver lining?" Kayla met Quinn's gaze in the mirror. "They called it a 'tain'. Here we have an ancient tain, in a really old place named the Last Tain. A double ancient tain." She smiled as Quinn's jaw dropped. "You know what I think is behind this mirror?"

"The Cordovan Vault," they said together.

"Maybe that's why Mrs. Keltsea was so adamant that this building stay an operating inn. So, how do we get to it?" Quinn asked, walking around to bar to join her.

THE CORDOVAN VAULT

"I never noticed before, but the wall behind this has small decorations burned into it to look like a frame for the mirror. They're so subtle you'd never see 'em. Do the shapes look familiar?"

"Yeah, it's a bunch of animals, so what?"

"There are all kinds of animals around the mirror. I bet there's a snake, a winged lion, a fish and a bird – they same as the squares on the columns in the cloister. A lot like the Rodin relief disks." Kayla was happy to see Quinn nodding. "Grab the painting, will ya? If I'm right, we'll find these same animals in the picture."

Once he'd brought the painting over to the other side of the bar, they started to systematically look closely for animals hidden in the picture. "I think I found a snake," Kayla said pointing to a tree branch in the upper left corner. A branch with a head and forked tongue. "OK, there's the griffin in the center."

"These kids are fishing in a little pond here," Quinn said, pointing to a small detail on the right side.

"And there are chickens in the yard in the bottom left corner. OK, let's see if we have matches around the mirror." Kayla started at the left side, looking for a snake in the top left corner of the wood behind the mirror. "Hey you're tall. Is that a snake?"

Quinn peered closely at the wall, "Looks like it."

"Give it a push. Maybe this is like the hidey hole in the Betsy Ross house basement."

Quinn pushed the little snake square and even though he hoped it would move and really, almost expected it to move, he was still surprised when the snake pushed into the wall. They continued around the mirror, and found animal squares corresponding to the painting in all four locations. When Quinn pushed the bird square on the bottom left corner, a small part of the mirror opened up at the opposite end of the bar, like a medicine cabinet in a modern bathroom. Kayla and Quinn looked at each other, smiling the broadest smiles they'd had since the 'police' had arrived at their door in Maine.

Behind the little door was another piece of wall. Unlike the mirror, this wall was made of purple metal. "It looks like the same metal as the key. Cordovan, right?" Quinn said. "But there's no key hole."

"It's pretty." Kayla ran her left hand over the panel and felt a slight indentation. She traced the pattern with her finger a few times. "I think that's a big pineapple with a key in its center."

"Maybe it's a welcome. Let me try something."

Quinn took the purple key from Kayla's bag and held it up against the indentation on the wall. An audible click was heard from behind the wall and when Quinn pulled his hand away the purple door opened to the right, revealing a space carved into the wall. They looked at each other, then both turned their heads to look behind them and around the room, to be sure they were still alone. They turned back and faced the open safe.

The hole in the wall looked to be a foot wide by a foot tall by a foot deep. Most of the space was empty. Laying on the floor of the safe were three envelopes. Two were large plain envelopes that had once been white. The other envelope looked very old, was made of a brittle yellowy-brown paper and was addressed in a fancy calligraphy script.

THE CORDOVAN VAULT

To Mister Wexford and Mistress Livingston
July 2010

Chapter Twenty-Six:

The Impossible Happens

Kayla's hand trembled as she reached for the old envelope with their names on it. She pulled it out of the safe and paused before opening it. Quinn looked around the room again, over her head and said, "That is really creepy. First with the painting, now this? Clearly, someone knew we'd be here and when."

"Yeah," Kayla agreed. She broke the wax seal on the back, opening the envelope. They turned closer to the light to read the old handwritten script.

November 4, 1789

Dear Mister Wexford and Mistress Livingston:
I have tortured my Brain but have been unable to discover the best course to prove that this Message is legitimate, so I will have Faith that you will trust it is so until such time as proof is offered.

Your Destiny is extra ordinary. There is much that you need to know and it will be revealed to you in time. Presently, believe that Denortus exists and They are seeking you out. You have the Advantages needed to defeat them if you work together. Individually, I greatly fear it will be you defeated. And if you are defeated, we will all lose.

I know that you feel alone with strange happenings. But you are the first of the Neofytes of Lur Babsel. By your time, Denortus will have ravaged the Gezon, destroying nearly all of us. You, and others like you who were born to the fight but have not yet been initiated, will be all that is left. Find other Neofytes like yourselves, and open their eyes to who they really are. As I shall open yours.

Mister Wexford, you are an Emote, able to feel the emotions of all those around you, human and other, alike. Mistress Livingston, you are a Seer, able to see into other times. Use these abilities to stop Denortus, before it is too late and everyone perishes.

Yours in War,

B. Franklin

"B. Franklin. Is that who I think that is?" Quinn asked, his green eyes wide.

"It says July 1789. Was there more than one B. Franklin in Philly then? It's gotta be Ben Franklin, right? Didn't Mr. K say that he had been one of the Last Tain's famous patrons?" Kayla's voice shook with disbelief and amazement. They heard a creaky sound coming from Mr.

K's suite. Without a word to each other, Quinn grabbed the painting and quietly ran it back into the tag sale room, locking the door behind him once he was done. Kayla took the remaining two envelopes out of the Cordovan Vault and carefully closed the doors. She collected the cordovan key, the brass template and the envelopes, and they carried them up to their room, skipping the squeaky treads on the stairs.

Once back in the relative safety of their room, they put the Franklin letter aside and opened the other two envelopes. Quinn dumped the contents on Kayla's bed. Out dropped a pile of twenty or so photographs of people and some pieces of paper. They sifted through the photos. Quinn picked one picture from the pile and showed it to Kayla. "This my mom and dad." He peered closer at the photo. "And that looks like a black pineapple gate behind them."

Kayla pulled another photo from the pile. "And it looks like our parents knew each other. I'd guess this one was taken around 1986." Kayla's photo showed her parents and Mr. and Mrs. Wexford sitting together at a table in the Last Tain courtyard, laughing and eating. Two small children sat on the cobblestones, playing in the background.

"Ya think that's Jim and Lorelei?" Quinn asked.

"Yup, and this is too." Kayla waved a third photo at Quinn.

"Let me see that." Quinn looked at the picture. It was the newest of the bunch. At closer examination, Quinn noticed that something looked off about the photo. Jim's hair was longer than he ever remembered seeing it and Lorelei's was very short, cut in a style that she had worn five years ago. Long before they had moved to Granby, Maine. "I'm pretty sure this photo wasn't taken in the last couple of weeks. It's like five years old." He flipped the photo back around for Kayla to see.

"Yeah, you're right. This shirt of Jim's got ripped while he was on a camping trip. I remember 'cause it was my favorite shade of blue and I used to like to wear it."

"Well, I guess they've been keeping more secrets from us than we thought. Obviously, they didn't meet in the Granby High Principal's office nine months ago."

"No, I guess not." They flipped through the rest of the photos. The only other person they recognized was Mrs. Keltsea. She appeared much older than in the photo Quinn had seen Mr. K holding. Although there was no date stamp on it, the shape of the photo and the quality of the print suggested that it was not much more than ten years old.

Kayla picked up the pieces of paper that had been in the remaining envelope. "These look like a couple more pages of my mom's diary. And a list of names and dates." Kayla flipped the two pages with the dates to the earliest. "It goes from 1572 – Eneas de Malagon, through 2003 – Jim Livingston, Lorelei Wexford."

"Check 1776ish."

"Yup, looky here – 1742 – Benjamin Franklin, and 1757 – Phillip Livingston. No wonder the other side wanted this so badly, it names the Gezon of Lur Babsel. I guess that's what the official members of Lur Babsel are called. And if Lur Babsel membership runs in the family then this list is an indication of how to find the Neofytes as well." Kayla checked the time on her watch with a yawn. "We've got about an hour before we have to be back downstairs to get breakfast together. Let's get a quick nap in; we can sort through all this later."

Quinn agreed and it seemed that seconds later, they were awoken by Quinn's alarm. They staggered out of their beds at the last possible minute, and stumbled downstairs. Quinn lost a rock- paper-scissor battle and had to run out for the pastries. When he got back to the kitchen, he flipped on the morning news while they worked in silence to prepare the food.

"In a shocking twist that has state and local police completely baffled, the two men arrested early this morning in connection with both the recent spat of muggings and the rash of break-ins at Philadelphia's museums, were found in their jail cell dead thirty minutes after they were processed. The police have released the following video surveillance footage, in hopes that someone might recognize the alleged killer. I want to warn our viewers that the video is quite graphic. We will begin the video in three seconds, so that those of you who would like to do so have a chance to change the channel."

Kayla dropped the bag of frozen fruit that she was holding, while Quinn walked closer to the TV. They stood there in silence as they watched a grainy picture of Dax and Heywood apparently sharing a jail cell in the local police lock up.

From off screen, a cloaked dark figure swept into view and appeared to walk through the bars of the cells. It was unclear from the video, but Quinn and Kayla both assumed that the video was edited to hide the use of the door. The figure walked up to Dax and appeared to wave his hand, causing Dax to snap to attention with such force that it looked like his spine might have broken. Then he collapsed to the floor like a towel dropped after a shower.

Heywood's hands flew up in a position of terror, only to show the scene repeated. The cloaked figure spun around and disappeared, leaving the crumpled bodies on the floor.

"Oh. My. God." Kayla's blue eyes shimmered with tears of terror.

"We've gotta get out of here," Quinn muttered. He looked at Kayla and stated more clearly, "We've gotta get out of here. Today. This morning. Now."

Before they could take the thought any further, the doors to the kitchen flew open. Both Quinn and Kayla jumped with a start, spinning around to face the new threat, both expecting to see a cloaked figure sliding into the room.

"Here they are, Katey. Here's the pair that saved me. Saved the Tain, too." Mr. Keltsea shuffled into the kitchen with a much younger woman in tow. She appeared to be forty-ish, trim, with neatly groomed red hair.

"I've heard so much about you two, I feel like I already know you." She rushed over to shake their hands.

"I'm Kathleen Keltsea. Thank you so much for helping my father this last week. I'm convinced that it was your efforts that sparked the three offers I've had for the place since I got here yesterday. And all the work you've done for this tag sale. I don't know what to say. We've even been approached to have the place named an historic site, that can't be destroyed, while keeping it a running hostel. I can't thank you enough," she gushed.

THE CORDOVAN VAULT

Quinn and Kayla got over their surprise quickly and smiled widely. "Oh Mr. K! I'm so happy for you!" Kayla's eyes started to tear up – happy that he was going to get the resolution they had hoped for.

Quinn offered his hand in congratulations. "Mr. K, that's great! I knew it would work out."

"I don' see how I coulda done it without youse. Thank youse, both." Mr. K's eyes looked suspiciously damp, too.

"If there's ever anything I can do for you, please don't hesitate to ask," Kathleen said.

Quinn thought quickly, taking a few seconds to make a decision that he hoped Kayla would be okay with. "You know, there is something that you could help us with." He quickly relayed what they'd learned from the news program about last night's intruders.

"You see, I think the police are going to come back here hoping to find some answers to what has happened. It would be best if we weren't here when they arrive. I was thinking about those bicycles we found in the basement. Do you think we could buy two of the newest from you? We need to move on. Right away."

Mr. Keltsea pursed his lips and looked Quinn in the eye, much the way he had when the they'd first arrived at the Last Tain. "No sir. I won't sell 'em to youse." Before Quinn could finish deflating, Mr. Keltsea continued on. "I'll give 'em to you. Take yer pick."

Kathleen jumped in, "And anything else you need. Food, clothes, linens. Whatever. Why don't I finish getting breakfast out; you've already done most of the work. Go ahead and get packed up." Kathleen checked the clock on the wall. "It's six thirty now. I imagine the police

J MONKEYS

will be here by eight. Go." She made a shooing motion with her hands. Kayla and Quinn said thanks again and rushed upstairs to gather their things.

Chapter Twenty-Seven:

Tour de Virginia (Part 1)

Once back in their room, Quinn rushed off to take a quick shower, needing to start this next journey clean and not knowing when he'd have access to a shower again. Kayla got her shower things together and started packing up the backpack that she'd taken off the wall in the hidden room.

It was hard to believe that they'd discovered that room just ten days ago. She looked at the four bags stacked on the only open floor space, all identical. There was no way they could take them all.

She dumped the contents of Jim and Lorelei's bags onto the bed. Most of the stuff seemed unimportant to them now. Clothes, towels, shoes. Everyday things like that. She tossed those back into the bag and found a small, brightly wrapped package in the remaining heap. Attached to the tiny bow was a little heart shaped note-card that read, "For my Wife."

Tears burned at the back of Kayla's eyes as she wondered what gift Jim had for Lorelei that he didn't get the chance to give her. She sat down on her bed, holding the package and became lost in thought. Why didn't Jim give it to her? Was he planning it for a special moment?

J MONKEYS

They were on their honeymoon; every moment should be special.

Quinn came back to the room wearing a towel and carrying his shampoo. He had expected the room to be empty, the way it had been the last week of mornings, with Kayla getting dressed in a bathroom down the hall. As soon as he closed the door, his eyes began to sting so much that he was worried the she'd sprayed pepper-spray while he was out.

A glance at Kayla proved that in fact, he was reading her emotions. She sat on her bed crying over a little gift. He snatched his shirt off the end of the bed and pulled it over his head. "What's going on?" he asked.

Kayla mumbled something nearly unintelligible ending in an indelicate snort. Quinn glanced around the room, for a place to hide and don his pants discreetly, but came up empty. There was nothing else to do but pull his pants on, hopefully modestly, and figure out what the problem was now. A few seconds of fumbling later, he joined her on the bed and handed her a tissue. He asked again, more gently this time. "What's wrong?"

She snorted again, blew her nose and dried her eyes on her sleeve. "I found this little gift in Jim's bag. The card says it's for Lorelei and I got to thinking about how he never got a chance to give it to her. It's not fair. They were just starting their lives together."

"Whoa, hold on. They aren't dead, remember? Lorelei called us. We'll find them."

"How can you be so sure?" Kayla sniffled.

"After everything that's happened, how can you *not* be sure? Jim warned you about the bad guys being on their way here. Lorelei told you how to find me when I was kidnapped by Denortus. Benjamin freakin' Franklin left us a letter implying a quest of some kind and we found a two hundred year old painting of *us* in the basement!"

"But those things have nothing to do with them being alive." Kayla's eyes were glassy with tears.

"No, but I think it's like Mr. Keltsea said. It's all about destiny. I bet that if we follow Franklin's quest, we'll end up right where we need to be at just the right time."

Kayla chuckled. The idea of Ben Franklin's quest was silly. When she had read that letter, she didn't see 'quest', she saw 'run-for-your-lives-Denortus-is-out-to-get-you'.

"We can't take four backpacks with us when we leave. Wherever Jim and Lorelei are, they don't need this stuff. Let's go through two last bags and donate their clothes and non-valuables to charity. Hold on to the little gift. When we catch up with them, you can return it to Jim and he can give it to Lorelei."

Kayla took a deep breath, nodded and smiled. She'd keep the little box safe for Jim. Kayla stepped out of the room to take a quick shower herself, hoping that freshening up would help her wake up. She was bone tired but full of frantic energy at the same time. The clock was ticking, they wanted to be away from the Last Tain in less than an hour. By the time she got back to the room, clean and dressed in jean shorts and a t-shirt, she found Quinn dressed much the same way, closing the top of his pack.

"I went through Jim and Lorelei's bags. I left the clothes, but took their camera, money, maps, books and anything else that looked weird. I grabbed all the stuff we found in the safe last night, the set of tools and the canvas bag of free stuff we got from the rally."

Kayla nodded, reaching for her own bag. She replaced the shower things she'd taken out of it and swept her gaze around the room. She hefted her pack onto her shoulders, clipped her day-pack in front of her onto the shoulder straps of the big bag and held the door for Quinn. He carried his pack, his guitar case and the two other bags.

Downstairs in the common room, he found Mr. K and explained what they'd like to do with Jim and Lorelei's bags. He agreed to add them to the donation items. They placed the bags by the door and Kayla gave him back the key to the locked room with a smile. Mr. Keltsea gestured for them to follow him outside.

Kathleen stood in the courtyard with the two newest bicycles. They looked like mountain bikes, but with pannier style baskets on the back of each bike. "I know these look funny, but I saw them downstairs when I got the bikes and thought they'd help you. I added a couple bags of food and some basic tools. A hammer, a can opener, some rope, whatever I could find handy. And I saw some camping stuff downstairs too." She gestured to the larger bike. "I think this is an old tent and I grabbed a couple of tarps, too."

"Thank you so much! We really appreciate it." Quinn gently wedged his guitar case into the open basket with the tarps.

"You are so very welcome. It's really nothing compared to what you two have done for my Dad. Here's my card. If you ever need anything, *please* call me. No matter what it is." Kathleen reached out a hand to Quinn for a final farewell. Kayla hugged both Kathleen and Mr. K. The said their final goodbyes and left, walking their new bikes down the cobblestone alley.

Once they were off Elfryth's Alley and back onto pavement Kayla asked, "So, where to, quest partner?"

"This camping gear gave me an idea. What do you think about riding to North Carolina to see my Great Aunt Tally?"

"Isn't that like two hundred miles away?" Kayla asked with a choking cough.

"Yeah, but we aren't really in a rush and if we bike we won't leave a paper trail."

"What about finding Jim and Lorelei?"

"I don't think they're still in Philly, do you? Wouldn't we have found them by now, or they us? We had their stuff; we were staying in their place. I think we finished what they started. We saved the information in the Cordovan Vault from Denortus. If they were here, we would have bumped into them. Let's go see Aunt Tally and see if she can tell us more about Lur Babsel and Denortus. Maybe she knows what those tools we found are used for, or what this quest is all about."

"All right. It seems as good a plan as any. And if Jim and Lorelei have really been talking to me in my dreams, and it's not a stress induced hallucination, then I guess it doesn't really matter where I sleep."

They headed south out of the city, ready to leave Philadelphia behind and begin the next step in their adventure. For surely, they had too many unanswered questions to be finished yet.

Epilogue:

Another Piece of Hay

They had had failed him. He breathed in through his nose very deeply, closed his eyes and held his middle finger and thumb together in the ancient symbol of peace and harmony. He was feeling far from peaceful, but knew from long experience that his tempestuous emotions brought nothing but trouble. It was far better to force those emotions to submit to his will.

He sat on his throne and focused his roiling inner energies into a tight ball of fury, contained and compartmentalized. It was like setting that fury-ball on a shelf next to the last one and the one before that. There was space, he knew, for another.

Dax and Heywood had been dismissed from service. He remembered the moment with a crocodile smile on his plain features. Completing that task should have decreased his fury, like flattening a beach ball. Certainly he would use this situation as a teaching example for the other servants.

Even the Indigo Guild, his most trusted and high ranking lieutenants, had become fussy in recent centuries. Allowing the spectacle to be filmed should help. Erus considered hundreds of gruesome methods in which others could be dismissed, for death was the only way a Servant was dismissed from the service of Denortus.

Erus looked around his ancient throne room. It had changed very little in the thousands of years that it had served this purpose. There had been ten Erus before him. The time had come for their fortunes to change as prophesied so long ago. It would take less than two passes on the celestial path for Erus to see the resurrection of the ancients. They would surface again, and those who had labored for their return would be rewarded.

The Neofytes were becoming bothersome. They'd thwarted his men. He might have to re-think his plans for them. But either way, he had men traveling to encourage the next Neofyte to the proper path and would see him work for Denortus before he know what he was about.

Erus stopped at a mirror that hung on a wall. It was old, and elaborate with a gold frame, a peaked top and a clear reflection. It was small, one foot square. He glazed into the reflection and watched his features fade from view.

Slowly, almost imperceptibly, his eyes faded to an unremarkable color, his hair faded to a plain color and style. His chin, lips, nose and forehead all followed suit, melting into the background so that what was left was a view of Everyman. There was nothing special about his visage, and if anyone thought to glance his way, they wouldn't be able to describe him to a friend. This was one of Erus' greatest talents, to hide in plain sight, to be indistinguishable from everyone else. Truly, a human needle in the proverbial haystack.

Not even a needle, just another piece of hay.

About the Author

J Monkeys has always been a storyteller, although mostly just for self-entertainment. J was shocked to learn that everybody didn't spend their time with their head in a cloud imagining what they would do if some kind of adventure presented itself. After getting a degree in Creative Writing from the University of Connecticut (Go Huskies!) and spending WAY too long writing boring things for a regular paycheck, J is proud to offer this debut novel.

J lives in Connecticut with a menagerie of children and pets and is hard at work on the next book in the Livingston-Wexford series – The Peacock Tale. In The Peacock Tale, Kayla and Quinn will tackle a centuries old legend of pirate treasure as they continue their search for Jim and Lorelei and try to discover what it means to be Neofytes of Lur Babsel. Look for it in the fall of 2011.

For story extras, visit J's website at:
https://sites.google.com/site/booksbyjmonkeys/

Made in the USA
Charleston, SC
19 January 2014